THE SHADOW OF MALIGNIN

BOOK TWO
THE SEVERANCE TRILOGY

BY: DANIEL WIEBE

Copyright © 2020 Daniel Wiebe
All rights reserved.
ISBN: 8585811494
ISBN-13: 979-8585811494
First Printing: 2020

Follow the author, Daniel Wiebe, at:
https://www.facebook.com/bladesofthenight/
or
https://wiebewritingblogs.wordpress.com

Table of Contents:

To *Blades of the Night*, because without you, this one wouldn't be here. Also, of course, to all my friends and family who helped and supported me throughout.

PROLOGUE

The pair of horses grunted as air passed through their searing lungs, lather long since coated their fur. The reins taut against them as they pulled the wagon behind them as quick as they were ushered. It jostled dangerously across the uneven path, every bump threatened to tear it apart. The woman who urged the horses on seemed to not care, it had been five days since her friend Aroc had left, and she had not yet returned. Jasmine feared that no matter how fast she traveled, the worst had already come to pass.

She rode for what felt like a day along the same path, the very one that Aroc and Sainte had traveled a few days before. Any traces they may have left behind had been washed away by the almost constant rains, so Jasmine was nervous she may pass them up, if she had not already. Those troubled thoughts did not trouble her very much longer, however. A body was laying

1

across the middle of the path, she would have run it over had the horses not come to an abrupt halt.

Jasmine gingerly slid from her seat on the wagon, arse sore from the rough ride. She stepped through the mucky road and stood over the body. He was a naked man but quite unidentifiable as his head was smashed to nothing but meat. The man's torso had begun to bloat, this was not a fresh kill. The rain and mud he laid in did no wonders for him either. A cool breeze slid by rustling the trees on either side of the path.

She knelt down to get a closer look at the man. Cuts and bruises riddled his abdomen and his knuckles were bloodied. He definitely was in a fight before he was killed. She could feel that something was off about this man. There was a sense of darkness about him, similar to that of the Malignin but different enough for her to note it. His presence all but confirmed that this was the area that Aroc and Sainte had to be in. Jasmine examined her surroundings, looking for any signs of where they may have gone.

Soon her eyes fell on the foliage on one side of the path. Some bushes had been bent and limbs broken as someone had pushed their way through them. Jasmine left the dead man's side and made her way towards the edge of the path. Before she could take a step further, her ears picked up the sound of someone walking closer. Stumbling clumsily through the brambles.

"Aroc," she tentatively said. There was no answer. Jasmine readied herself, not knowing what to expect. The calming surge of power ran through her veins, reminding her that she was more than capable of defending herself.

But what, or rather who, came out of the brush was no danger to her. She was the most pitiful woman Jasmine had laid eyes on. She was pale of skin, dressed in raggedy, bloody, muddy clothes. Her left arm hung limply by her side. Cloth had been tied around her bicep for a wound, apparently, but blood had long ago soaked through. It now dripped from her fingertips. Her other arm clung to a low hanging branch, the only thing holding her up. She seemed unable to have the strength to lift her head.

As if in slow motion, she began to fall. With a start Jasmine ran to her side and saved the poor girl from meeting the ground.

"Come, I have a wagon just over here. I'll help you there," Jasmine said as she put the girl's good arm over her shoulders. She more or less dragged the girl to the wagon. Her feet trailed behind her and she moaned quietly. With a little bit of struggle, Jasmine finally got the girl in the back of the wagon and laying down, covered with a blanket.

"Time to get a look at your arm," Jasmine told her. As she began to unwrap the cloth she asked, "Who are you?" The girl did not reply. No matter, she continued her assessment. Once fully unwrapped, Jasmine could see the extent of the damage.

She had been cut in her bicep, all the way to the bone. Probably broken but there was no good way to tell how bad out here. It is a wonder it was not cut through. Jasmine doubted the girl would ever have control over that arm again. The wound was inflamed and warm to the touch, but all in all Jasmine believed that this woman would survive, with some help. She always had salves with her and applied some to fend off the infection.

With the ointments touch to her wound, the woman stirred. Jasmine imagined it stung quite a bit. The girl opened her eyes and looked around groggily. It was a good a time as any to ask her some questions.

"What is your name?" Jasmine inquired. This time she got a response.

"My name… is Iris," she said weakly. "Sainte found me… I took him to the cave…" she was unable to say anything else before she closed her eyes, passed out once more. Jasmine wanted to ask more questions, but she knew she would not be

4

getting anymore from her anytime soon. At least she now knew to look for a cave. She quickly finished wrapping Iris's arm with some clean cloth, made her as comfortable as possible, then decided it was time to go hunting for this cave.

Jasmine set out in the direction that Iris came from. Iris's trail was not hard to backtrack since it was still fresh. She walked as fast as the brush would allow, eager to find her friend. Almost an hour had passed when Jasmine heard what sounded like crying. She cautiously followed the sound as she pushed her way through the latest bush that snagged at her. Soon a cave entrance loomed before her, and a few feet from the cave was a man sitting on the ground, hunched over something, sobbing.

As Jasmine crept closer, unbeknownst to the man, she saw that he was holding a person. A lady. Aroc.

"Sainte," she whispered. He lifted his head, but other than that he did nothing else. She softly stepped in front of him and knelt down. He turned his head toward her and she gasped. It looked as if he was crying blood. "What happened?"

"I killed her... I killed her to save myself. She told me to..." he managed to say between sniffs. "The Malignin... Ellie... Aroc. I can't go on..." he started to shudder on the verge of breaking down into tears. Snot rolled from his nose.

"Sainte, are you alright?" a stupid question, an obvious answer. Jasmine blinked back her own tears. She had to hold herself together right now, there would be time to grieve for Aroc later. "Tell me what happened. I have to know," she said more forcefully.

Sainte took a few deep breaths as he gazed back down at Aroc, hands clutched around her tightly. When he looked back up at Jasmine she realized just how wretched he looked. Blood was caked onto his face and around his eyes. His eyes themselves were so irritated she could not tell if they were red because of the blood or because of crying. His clothes were ripped nearly to shreds and his fingernails were broken.

"I heard that Ellie was here," he said with a raspy voice, "I came this way quick as I could. When I was close I found Miqel about to kill Iris. I… I didn't know what else to do other than stop him. I killed him. I checked on her after, and did what I could, but I don't know if it was enough. Iris was in and out of consciousness but managed to point me in the direction of this cave where Ellie was. I left Iris out by the path as I made my way here.

"When I found the cave I entered with little hesitation. I don't think I could've stopped myself if I wanted to. Ellie was here, I couldn't stand to wait any longer. This was my last chance to save her. I'm not sure how deep I went into the cave before I finally found her. No more than a few seconds passed before I was jumped by Malignin.

"They held me aloft, completely and wholly at their mercy. At her mercy. But they didn't kill me, no. What was in store for me was far worse. Ellie walked up to me and said…" he took a breath, "She said horrible things. She said she was pregnant with my child."

Jasmine's insides froze. She regretted asking him what happened. If she heard no more it would be too much, but it was now her duty to know. She had to pass on this information. "Go on."

"The Malignin… mated," he spit out the word in disgust, "with her. I tried to look away, but then they tore off my eyelids and held my head in place. I was forced to watch. I couldn't stop it. I couldn't help her," after those words he slumped over even more. He had stopped crying at this point, he probably had no more tears to spend. This man in front of her was not the Sainte she knew from before. He was merely a shell. After a moment he continued to speak.

"When they were finished, she gave birth to something… Something terrible. I could see the love she had for it in her eyes. But it killed her. Just like that. She's dead.

Everything I had done up to that point… pointless." He paused for a few seconds then continued, "I was sure I was next to die. My time was up. But then Aroc showed up. She said there was only one way to get out of there alive. I had to kill her. She asked me to… So I did.

"A great white light burst from her. It blinded me. When I could see again, the cavern was empty. I was alone. I don't know how long I stayed in there holding Aroc. Somehow I remembered Iris. She needed me. I carried Aroc out of the cave. I found Iris outside, she must have brought Aroc here… I don't know… but I told her to go back to the path without me. Help would eventually come for her. I don't know if she made it…" he trailed off.

"She did," Jasmine said comfortingly. "She is alive. I got her. Not in good shape, but she's alive." At her words Sainte was visibly relieved. "Sainte," she began again, more than a little reluctant to ask, "what else did Ellie say to you?"

"She… She said that the White Wyverns locked us in with the Malignin. That we're locked in a small portion of land cut off from the rest. She said that Aroc lied about almost everything… I don't really know… It's hard to recall…" Jasmine put a hand on his shoulder to stop him. To comfort him.

"That's ok, I don't need to know anything more," she had heard enough to confirm her worst fears. "You have to come with me, Sainte. I must bring you to the Council."

Sainte did not know what she meant by the Council, but he knew that he did not want to go. He could not resist Jasmine even if he wanted to in his current state. In defeat, he gazed back at Aroc. His vision was getting worse by the second. Jasmine could not help but feel a pang of sorrow for the poor man.

In a last-ditch effort Sainte looked in the direction of Jasmine, she was now nothing but a blur in his eyes. "Please, don't make me go with you," his voice was a whisper, "I'm so tired. I won't tell anyone anything. Just leave me... Leave me alone," his voice broke at his last words.

Jasmine knew what was expected of her, she knew what she was supposed to do, but this man in front of her had been through so much. More than what one man should be put through. He had done what he could, everything in his power to right his self-blamed wrongs. She could not in good faith put him through anymore. Sainte just stared at her helplessly, waiting to see what she would say.

"I won't take you," she relented with a sigh, "but before I leave you, at least let me clean up your wounds. I may even be able to do something for your eyes, and then we can bury Aroc together."

"Thank you," he said.

"C'mon, let's go. I'll help you carry Aroc back to the wagon. I have my supplies there, and, if you like, you can say goodbye to Iris." Jasmine stood up and helped Sainte to his feet. Then, as promised, together they made their way back to the path. Iris was still asleep, much to Sainte's relief. He was not sure he would be able to handle any more questions she may have had for him.

He looked at Miqel's corpse, sorry for the way things had ended. The first man he killed. Staring at the body brought back the memory of the three of them, watching the sun rise together. The memory was so vivid he could almost feel the warm embrace of the sun on his skin. Jasmine grabbed his arm, startling him out of his reverie. She guided him to a spot where he could sit and wait as she prepared her ointments.

Sainte sat still and silent, the only noise that accompanied him was Jasmine rummaging through her supplies. Vials clinking and tapping together. A short while later he heard her approach him. At this point his vision was all but gone, only able to see blurred objects if he squinted.

"Hold out your hand," Jasmine said. He did as he was told and a vial was placed in his fingers. "This poultice should keep your eyes moisturized. As long as you keep applying it, it should keep your eyes from drying out. It will also help the recovery of your eyelids, but, as you probably know, they will not grow back. My guess is you'll probably have to apply some hourly, but really just put some on when you think you need it.

"When you need more, it is a simple thing to make. What you have is half water and half liquid from the plant Alon Zirnia. Do you know it?"

Sainte nodded, "I know of it, yes."

"Good, now go on. Try it out." At her request, Sainte dropped a few drops in each eye and immediately felt a cooling sensation. After only a few seconds his vision began to restore, almost as good as it was before.

"Thank you," he said in disbelief.

"You're welcome, I'm just glad I could do something for you. Just be sure you always have some, I'm not sure how long it would take for you to totally lose your sight. Now, let's see about your other wounds."

He shook his head, "None of my other wounds are physical. Get me a wash rag please, and then let's be about our business."

11

After Sainte had cleaned his face and minor scratches, he and Jasmine moved Aroc to a secluded area far from the path so that it would not be disturbed. Together they dug her grave, and once deep enough, gently lowered her now wrapped body down. Once buried, they stacked rocks on the grave to mark it as such. Side by side they stood silently, each paying Aroc their respects.

"You're sure you want to do this, Sainte? Go off by yourself?" Jasmine asked him, "I know Iris would be thankful if you were there for her. You would be safe with me."

"I'm sure. I'd probably only bring her heartache. I'd be a constant reminder of what we once had, and how we can never be that way again. This is the best thing I can do for her. For me," he said as if he tried to convince himself of it. "Take care of Iris, please."

"Of course."

"And tell her I'm sorry."

"I will, Sainte. Goodluck, with whatever you end up doing. Wherever you end up going. And be careful, you know as well as I that the trouble is not gone. Not all of it. Not yet."

Sainte nodded and tapped his pocket to make sure that he still had the vial. Then, without another word to Jasmine, he walked away into the woods.

Jasmine lingered at Aroc's grave site, sorting through her thoughts, before eventually making her way back to the wagon. With every step she took she tried to convince herself that letting Sainte go was the best choice she had. At least she knew it was the best one for him.

ONE

Kial stood on the protective parapet that surrounded Munich and surveyed the barren fields that spanned across the field. Farmers tended to it, desperate to try to get some crops, any crops to grow. Peng stood beside him but instead looked into town. It was now the fourteenth morning since the sun had risen in a row. They did not know what Sainte did after he left them, but they could only assume that this was because of him. The Malignin were still around, however. Some of their night patrols caught sight of them, but they seemed to avoid all people. The sun may have been back, but Kial had a feeling that all was not as right as it may have felt.

Peng shuffled around and Kial anticipated his voice before he spoke.

"What're ya thinking, Kial? You're awfully quiet these days."

After rummaging around his thoughts, he finally said, "Things aren't quite right. The sun has been rising and setting, it doesn't seem to be leaving anytime soon, but I taste an unease upon the air. Something's still not right," he looked across the plains towards the Shinta village which was only visible by the smoke rising at this distance. Peng clucked his tongue at his friend's words.

"Relax a bit. The sun's out, crops are growing again, or at least trying to, and animals are getting back into their regular schedule. Even if you're right, ya shouldn't be wasting this time. Use it to rejuvenate yourself, ready yourself for whatever you think is going to happen. Spend some time with your wife and kid."

Kial shook his head, "You haven't been around long enough yet to know, but that's what they're waiting for. For us to let our guard down. I should speak with Madelaine about what to do with Franceska if, when, things go sour."

"That's what who is waiting for? You see, there's nothing else out there that wishes to harm us. Not now, at least. The Malignin are still around, aye, but they're no threat anymore. I'm sure Madelaine has her hands full enough with raising

Franceska without having to worry about being attacked. You're just being paranoid."

"Now is not the time to get complacent," Kial said. "Besides, Malignin are still about, I don't care if they're attacking or not, they're not to be forgotten. Not to mention that butcher that went crazy and killed everyone, what was his name? If it wasn't for him, we never would have formed that party to go seeking answers elsewhere."

"The butcher? I don't know his name. He's long dead, no bother now. When you're mad that ya haven't had a good night's sleep in forever because your thoughts're keeping you up at night, don't say I didn't tell ya," Peng said with a smile. "Come on, relief's here. Let's go get some breakfast. Or are you too paranoid for that too?" he asked sarcastically.

Kial allowed himself to smile, "Nay, that I can do. Maybe after I'll look into the butcher a bit, if you want to help me?" He just smiled as Peng shook his head.

"We just talked about this. What about Madelaine? Your daughter, Franceska, misses you too, I'm sure."

He dismissed him with a wave of his hand, "Madelaine understands, and Franceska will understand when she's older."

Peng just shook his head and said, "I'll pass. I haven't a mind to go digging a hole when there's no reason for a hole to be dug."

They spoke briefly to their relief, passing on what little information there was, then walked to the stairs leading into Munich. The sounds of town life echoed up through the barren stairwell as they descended. People were finally starting to get back into the routine of their lives that they had known before the Dark Days, starting to wake up early and go to bed late.

As they reached the bottom a familiar voice cut above all the commotion. It was Jasmine, and she did not sound pleased. Their current conversation would have to be put on hold, for now.

"What do you mean I need a permit to take these supplies from Munich? I write the permits, *I* do," she did not sound pleased at all.

Peng and Kial shared a look, then headed towards her. The small woman was standing with her hands on her hips and on the tips of her toes, almost face to face with one of the guards assigned to gate duty. He had to make sure that, for the time being, Munich kept the supplies the city officials deemed necessary. That included medicinal supplies. Unfortunately for him, he had apparently not researched who needed a permit and who did not.

"I'm sorry, missus, I cannot let you go without the appropriate permit citing which medicines you can take," the guard was trying to explain to her.

"Hey, Jasmine, what's going on?" Kial interjected. The woman turned a heated gaze onto him, but it cooled when she realized who entered her conversation.

"This…" she gestured crudely at the young man, "guard does not realize that I do not need a permit. I *am* the permit. After explaining myself to him, he still insists that I get one."

Kial had to give the man credit, he stood his ground, but when he saw Kial he snapped to attention. "Let her pass. What she says is true, she writes the permits for the medicines. If she says she needs to take these out, then she does. Remember her face, and do not question her again. For neither her nor I will be this kind next time."

The guard rendered a quick salute, then stepped out of Jasmine's way. A little red to the face but otherwise undaunted.

Jasmine hoisted her pack, "Thank you Kial. I was quickly growing weary of this man. Now that I have been duly delayed, I must be on my way."

"Sure thing. Where you heading this time?"

"Oh, uh, going to Iris. Got some stuff she was running low on last time. Thank you, boys. You two have a good day," she said as she turned to walk out the gates.

"We will, bout to get some breakfast," Peng said to her back. "You have a good day as well."

Jasmine heard them start chatting about what to get for breakfast, but they quickly got out of earshot. She continued on her way to the Shinta village, a slight smile on her face. She always liked running into those two. They held a rare positivity of this world that she did not run into often.

She was thankful for their intervention as well because the medicines she carried would not have been approved by the town council had they known what she was up to. Jasmine felt bad for holding the truth from Kial and Peng, but they would have tried to stop her had they known her intentions. Iris was tired of being held up at the Shinta village. Iris was going to leave the village and had asked Jasmine to bring her some medicines for her travels.

Jasmine could not blame the girl for wanting to leave. She herself never wanted to stick around awfully long in the smoky village. This was the last time she was going to see Iris for who knew how long, and if the boys had known this they would have undoubtedly tried to stop Jasmine letting her go or joined up with Iris. Which was exactly what Iris did not want.

So, the as of yet undiscovered White Wyvern continued on her trek to the Shinta village, with no more disturbances.

It was about an hour's walk before she was entering Iris' tent. Chests were opened and mostly empty. Two satchels sat on the cot in the middle of the room stuffed with random odds and ends. It had seemed she had already packed all her bags with her essentials, and the last thing she was waiting on was Jasmine.

"About time you showed up," Iris greeted her with a smile. Her left arm was in a sling and swathe across her chest, the left sleeve of her shirt hung limp and empty. She had not regained control of that arm, and it seemed that she had come to terms with it.

"I have things I have to do too, you know," Jasmine said as she unshouldered her bag. "How're you going to carry all this?"

"What do you think I've been doing when you're not here? I've been training on horseback again. Got my own now. I'm not carrying this all by myself."

"The Shinta are going to let you take one of their horses?" Jasmine was incredulous. "That's unheard of. They've only ever let me ride one of them. Once."

"Well, yeah… It's not just any horse. It's Tal's horse. When they found out he… died… they got ownership of it. They have no need of it, so they gave it to me. I guess it's because I was his friend, or something," she trailed off.

Jasmine thought it best to lighten the mood, "Well, that's amazing. It's an honor you should not bear lightly. How soon are you going to leave? I can help you saddle your supplies."

"He's the buckskin stallion tethered outside, named Dawn. You probably saw him on your way in."

"He's yours?" Jasmine just shook her head. "Good luck with him. Beautiful, but he seemed like he could be a handful."

"Oh, I've already ridden him. We're pretty in tune with each other," Iris told Jasmine taking joy in the woman's disbelief.

"Well good for you. I guess I'll go see about attaching this bag on him. How much more room does he have?"

"This is it," Iris said gesturing to her two bags in the tent. "I just finished packing this morning, haven't got anything on him yet."

Jasmine raised her eyebrows at such little supplies that Iris was bringing with her, despite the tightly packed satchels, but this was her choice. She could not help herself but support the girl. "Alright," Jasmine started, "let's get at it then." Jasmine shouldered her bag once more and grabbed the two bags on the cot. The women walked out of the tent to Dawn who stood patiently waiting.

They loaded the bags quickly with no trouble. Before it was even midday Iris was sitting atop Dawn ready to go. Some Shinta women had come and gone, saying their goodbyes to Iris. Seemed she had grown on them. Laureen showed up lastly.

"Iris, thought you were going to leave without saying bye?" she said looking up at her.

"Wouldn't dream of it, Laureen. If you hadn't come by, I was going to go looking for you."

"Well, here I am. I'm glad to see how far you've come from when Jasmine first brought you here. I'm sorry I couldn't do more for your arm."

"It's quite alright, you've done more than enough. I don't know that I'd be emotionally ready to leave right now if not for you. I'll miss you," Iris told her.

"Where are you going to go?" Jasmine asked.

"North, I suppose. I've heard good things about Thissaren. A rather small seaport town and warmth. That's all I need to hear at this point."

"All good things," Jasmine agreed. "If you ever need anything, seek me out and I will help."

"I know you will. Thank you. For everything you've done. I wouldn't be here if not for you. I can only guess as to what else you've done that I don't know about. Until we meet again, Jasmine. I hope that we do. White Wyverns watch over you."

Jasmine smiled at her last sentence; the poor girl had no idea. No one ever did. "Thank you, and the Wyverns guide you. Safe travels."

Iris nodded through some unexpected tears. Jasmine had been there for her through her healing process. Helped her every step of the way. But now it was time to move on, as all things must. The world was returning to normal, and eventually everyone had to catch up. Now was her time.

With a final wave, Iris galloped away on Dawn. She had no intentions of stopping until she met dusk.

"How do you think she'll do?" Jasmine asked Laureen as they stood side by side, watching Iris ride away.

"She'll be fine. She's strong. I'm sure there will be struggles ahead of her, but nothing worse than what she has already faced," Laureen said. "Have you spoken to the Council recently?"

"A little bit, just by messenger. I've told them a little bit more about my plan to see how receptive they might be."

23

"And?"

"They're apprehensive, but they'll allow me to try. They say I have three days to find Sainte Nore before they begin the Sever. What they don't know is that I've always known where he's been."

"How?" Laureen asked with genuine surprise.

"Nadrian," she said.

TWO

Darkness swallowed Sainte and his vision disappeared in the blackness. He groped around himself feebly, desperately, hoping to feel something, anything. He heard something, a soft brushing sound, and whimpered in fear. Something was slowly approaching him. The steps came closer, and finally it revealed itself. It was Ellie.

She looked so beautiful. Her pale, unblemished skin as it was when she was still in the Mountain. Her curly black hair softly bounced as she came to an abrupt stand still.

"Sainte," her voice washed over him like a cold wave. "You lied to me. You let me be taken. You let me die. All you had to do was not let me die."

"I tried," he said.

"Not good enough. You can't do anything right," she took a step closer. "Now I'm dead, and it's your fault," her face began to contort and stretch. Sainte tried to move, to run, but he could not. Her skin tore and ripped, revealing the bulging head of the abomination that she gave birth to.

The thing wore Ellie's skin in tatters. It let out a wail so piercing it felt like Sainte's ears would burst. It grabbed his head and squeezed. Sainte was sure he would die, the pressure becoming unbearable. Inevitable. Death. The abomination squeezed harder; he felt his skull crack right before the…

Pop.

Sainte woke himself from his slumber by his own screams. He sat up quickly, chest heaving from the night terror he just had. The same one each time he fell asleep, which was not much. His eyes stung from being dried out. He had to learn how to sleep all over again without eyelids, only recently being able to fall asleep for more than five minutes.

He groggily rummaged through his pack, looking for the poultice that Jasmine had made for him. He was getting low and would have to make some more soon. He scrunched his face up, the longer he was awake the more pain his eyes were in. Where was the damned vial?

Finally, his fingers grazed across the smooth glass. He scooped it up, uncorked it carefully, then dripped two drops into each of his eyes giving him immediate relief. He rolled his eyes around, spreading the cool moisture to the backs of his eyes. Sainte sighed audibly and sat back on his haunches. His gaze lingered over his sad excuse of a campsite. The fire had long ago smoldered out, his bedding was a pile of leaves he pushed together, and the only other company he had was of his pack.

He stood up and stretched, joints cracking with the movements. His posture was not as it had used to be. Shoulders sagged forward, his head was not held as high, permanent bags had settled under his eyes some time ago. With a sigh he scooped up his pack and slung it over his shoulders, as ready as he was ever going to be to continue his pointless wandering through these woods. He ran a hand through his greasy, unkempt hair.

After he and Jasmine had buried Aroc, Sainte continued walking north. He did not want to risk going back to Guardstin and running into anyone he knew, if it even had anyone living there anymore. Today he was going to reach Bethrune, his home village. He would see how his parents were, if they were still alive. He was not going to hold his breath, but he had to know what became of them during the Dark Days. It had been almost a year since he had contact with them.

He had no plans on what he was going to do after Bethrune, and that scared him. Sainte wanted, needed, something else to focus on so his thoughts would not wander to the cave. He

27

was afraid of what he might do to himself if he could not escape those thoughts. No matter, he would have to figure it out after Bethrune. Maybe he would find his parents and together they could figure something out. It all depended on his parents.

Whatever the case, it was time for him to start moving. He slept in so long the sun was almost at the peak of the sky. This was a later start than he had wanted, but if he kept up a decent pace he should reach Bethrune before evening.

So off he went to his home for the first time in he almost forgot how long. Probably close to five years. His childhood girlfriend, Violet, popped up into his mind as he wondered about all his family friends that he had not seen in so long. While he was in the Blades of the Night his parents kept in touch with him, but as the months turned to years, the letters sent back and forth slowly dwindled down to one a month, sometimes less.

But Violet, they wrote each other fervently until a little over a year ago. She stopped after she told him that she was going to be wed within the year. It hurt him, but he knew that whatever they may have had ended long ago, before he joined the Blades. He wondered if she was still here, or had she moved? Foolish thoughts. Of course she would not still be there. Not after the Dark Days. That is, if she was even alive.

A gentle, warm breeze blew by Sainte and rustled the newly budding trees, reminding him that not all was as bad as it could be. The sun was out, the ground was dry, the plants were growing. Not that it lifted his mood, however, but it could be worse. He took comfort in that thought. Somewhat.

He was both eager and reluctant to reach Bethrune. Scared to have hope. Scared to not have it. Scared to see what would come after, but he already had an idea. His day continued with all these thoughts circling in his head. It was relatively quiet. Some bugs had started to return to the lands of Crearia after the Dark Days. Not many animals had, yet, but they were coming back slowly as the vegetation grew back.

The mountains passed him by in a blur, as had the entire two weeks since the sun started to show itself again. This day was no different. He would have been easy pickings for any bandits in the area, but they would not have found anything of value on him. Before he knew it, when he looked into the sky the sun was well on its way descending to the horizon, and Bethrune was almost visible, cradled in its valley.

Sainte found himself quickening his pace, eager to be done with this journey. He soon found the usually worn path, now overgrown, winding itself around the rocks that jutted from the ground leading to his old home. Not far now, just around this turn and it would reveal itself to him after all these years. He took a deep breath and readied himself for the worst.

There it was. Bethrune. Mud hardened buildings standing as they were when he left. It looked almost exactly as it had when he last saw it. But it was clearly abandoned for some time. No one walked the streets. The wind howled through the solitary homes, making it sound as if Bethrune was calling out for a long-lost life. Maybe someone was still here though, hiding, waiting for the world to return to normal. Maybe that someone would be his parents. Sainte could not leave without checking.

Once he entered Bethrune, he walked the paths he once wandered at a young age. Old forgotten memories rushed back. He could almost see the familiar faces walking through the deserted village. Of neighbors he helped, friends he played with, chores his parents commanded of him. Running with his friends between buildings playing tag, hiding with Violet from her parents.

Violet. He could remember how it felt holding her hand.

He consciously made his way to his house, tracing his footsteps from long ago. Any hope he had of finding anyone hiding away in his town was quickly fading. Any hope of finding his parents was already long passed. Suddenly aware of how alone he was, Sainte found himself standing in front of his old home.

Gingerly, he walked up to the front door and pushed it open. With a breath he stepped inside and took a moment to look around. It had been empty for a long while, cobwebs hung in the corners and weeds began to grow through cracks in the floor. There was no point in going further into his old home. There was nothing there for him. He turned around and left. For the past two weeks Bethrune is what kept him going. He had hoped, however faintly, that he would find something, someone, there. Now was different. Now he had nothing else to do, no one else to go to.

The once familiar houses seemed to float by him as he absentmindedly made his way ever closer to the great oak tree that grew on the outskirts of the fields around Bethrune. The one where he and Violet had spent many a long night under. He guessed it did not really matter which tree he chose for this, but it seemed right. It was a strong tree.

Before he knew it, he stood at the oak tree's base. He slipped his pack from his shoulders and grabbed the poultice for his eyes from it. One last time, he dropped several drops into his eyes and let the empty vial slip from his fingers. Then he grabbed the rope from his pack. The end had already been tied in a noose, having tied it two days after Aroc's death. He climbed up the tree, rope in hand, his mission set in his lidless eyes. It reminded him of being a kid again, climbing the trees for fun, feeling the excitement of seeing the world from a new perspective. This was not fun now, though, it was just a thing that needed doing.

He stopped, about halfway up the tree, seeing this as good a spot as any. Meticulously, Sainte tied the loose end of the rope around a branch. He tugged on it hard a few times for good measure, making sure that this knot would hold. His eyes looked at the knot, then followed the branch to its tip and rested on the sun, now setting upon the horizon. The sky was a brilliant shade of red, with the mountains as a beautiful backdrop. Without wasting any further time, Sainte slid the noose over his head and took a deep breath. He was determined to finish watching the sun set, one last beautiful sight before the nothingness that awaited him.

He stood up on the branch in preparation, legs suddenly jelly as the realization set in. Sainte took a breath and steadied himself. Now that he was standing, the branched of the oak tree block his view of the sun. He shuffled his feet to get a better view.

And slipped.

A cry barely escaped his lips before Sainte slammed into a branch on his way down, slowing the fall. Apparently, he was slowed enough that when the noose tightened and caught around his neck, it was not with enough force to immediately break his neck. Instead he flailed his legs around wildly, feet searched for a solid surface to gain purchase, fingers grasped the taut cord around his neck to no avail. His lungs struggled to fill with air, but none got in. He gurgled in his attempts to draw in a breath. Why did he fight against death so much now? This is what he wanted, he just hoped it would have been a little quicker. He could feel his head start to build with pressure as his blood had nowhere to go. Eyes burned as his vision began to cloud over and darken.

Strength started to seep out of his body. Fingers that once grasped the rope tightly loosened up and his arms dangled to his sides. Legs slowly slackened without care. It was getting hard to think clearly now, and not being able to breathe was suddenly not bothering him so much. Just as his lungs began to spasm in their last attempts to get air of any kind, the rope snapped, and Sainte fell the remaining five feet he had left to the ground.

His legs buckled immediately under him and he rolled to his back. The jarring landing knocked some consciousness back into him and his hands finally grabbed the rope around his neck and pulled it over his head. This entire time his lungs worked but did not draw in anything until his throat was unobstructed.

With a loud gasp, mouth wide open, oxygen was finally sucked into his starved body. It hurt to breath, but that did not stop him. His unblinking eyes stared up into the tree that he had chosen to be his grave, and they rested on the rope that was now hanging loosely. It was a clean cut, not ragged like from a tear as Sainte had suspected. Suddenly a foot stomped down next to his head and someone leaned over him into his point of view.

"Long time no see, Sainte Nore. Shield, or rather ex-Shield, of Crearia."

Eyes wide open, Sainte struggled to suck in air and looked up at Nadrian. Surely, he was hallucinating. He had not seen Nadrian since before Ellie was taken. He rolled over onto his stomach and forced himself to his hands and knees. A coughing fit took him over. Felt like his throat had been crushed. Felt like? It had been crushed, he thought to himself stupidly.

After what seemed like ages Sainte finally had his breathing under control, though his throat still ached. He sat back on his haunches and looked at the man who had been watching him silently this entire time, his eyebrows were raised and a hint of a smile was on his face.

"What're you doing here? How did you know where I was?" Sainte rasped.

Nadrian ignored his questions, "What were you thinking? Hanging yourself? And badly at that."

"I wish I was dead. I wish I died in that cave with Ellie and Aroc. I don't want to keep going on," Sainte shrugged, thinking those questions had rather obvious answers.

"Jasmine told me where you were. That you might need some help. Glad I found you when I did."

"Jasmine? She told you? You're a…?" Sainte stopped as the realization dawned on him.

"A White Wyvern. Aye," Nadrian nodded. "There are more of us here than you realize. Now that you know some of what we did, there is not much point for us to help you without you knowing."

"What'd you cut me down for? Jasmine said I could go. Are you going to bring me to wherever it is that she wanted to take me?" Sainte eyed the man he once confided in. "She said I could go."

"No, that is not my goal. My only goal here is to try to convince you to keep pushing on. Don't kill yourself," he said with some disgust. "Such a weak thing to do. Jasmine and I are the only White Wyverns who know where you are, that you are even alive, as far as I know. For now, we intend to keep it that way. All we ask is that you do something for us."

"What more could I do?"

"Find a weapon, a sword. It has wondrous, terrible properties. Find it, and you will be able to kill the Abomination with it. Without it…" Nadrian shuddered, "I don't want to say what the White Wyverns are capable of doing to try to put the Abomination down."

Sainte thought about it. It did not seem like such a tall task, but he knew there was more to it than Nadrian was letting on. A powerful sword? How much more powerful could swords get?

"Why me? Why don't you get it, or another Wyvern? Or any other person?" he questioned. There it was. The troubled look of having to explain the consequences of what was asked of him. "And what do you mean a powerful sword? What makes it so powerful?"

"Good questions, all of which I have answers for. The sword is protected by something. A being from the ether world guards it, a demon. We placed the demon there to guard it to keep not only humans away, but to mostly keep fellow White Wyverns away from it. Our powers have no influence over the being. It would consume us, kill us. If we were to get past the demon, somehow, the power of the sword would never satiate us. We would be wholly at its mercy. Whichever Wyvern wielded the sword would be on an endless journey for power, killing anything in their way."

Sainte stared at him, eyebrows raised, "Is that all? What makes you think I could wield such a weapon?" the disbelief was clear in his words.

"It was made for you. Well," Nadrian corrected, "made for those who were born without our power," he gestured at Sainte up and down.

"Why? What does it do?"

"There were troubling times. We made it to fight against an enemy that you did not know existed, the Cult of Bal'Shere. We were losing against them as their powers were unchecked, unbalanced, unpredictable. We recruited the aid of humans and gave them weapons like this sword. They proved to be highly effective. This remaining sword consumes the soul of those it kills and transfers it to the wielder, giving them a temporary boost in strength. Then the soul is gone, forever, as if whatever it came from never existed," he looked at Sainte expecting a reply, but Sainte just sat in silent comprehension. Nadrian continued, "Once the battle was won, we destroyed all the weapons but the sword. This sword we saved just in case a repeat of events happened. We hid the sword and set a demon to guard it from anyone who would find it, to guard it from fellow White Wyverns.

"Now is time for the sword to reemerge, to prevent a repeat of before. It must, the only other option will result in the destruction of Crearia. Instead of a land where people can thrive, it will turn into a mass graveyard. A desolate prison for the Abomination."

Sainte had thought that nothing else would be able to move him after what he had been through. He did not really care if anyone else died, but if the whole of Crearia died? He had an urge again, a small one, but an urge nonetheless. Maybe he would die trying to get this sword, which would be a blessing that he would keep to himself. However, he was still skeptical of Nadrian, and Jasmine for that matter. They were White Wyverns, they had agendas of their own and could quite possibly be holding some truth from him. Not to mention the sword, if what Nadrian said was true, scared him. How could he wield such power?

"Please, Sainte. Without you, everyone will die. Jasmine cares about you, I care about you. We don't want to see you dead, but after this if you decide to decline me, then I won't stop you again. Do this, find the sword, and save everyone in Crearia, get your revenge. Hurt those that made you like this. Or you can give up, climb back into that tree, and hang yourself the right way. I won't intervene."

Sainte sighed. He had nothing left to live for and felt he had no other option. Nadrian was now offering him one, a way onward.

"I'll do it. I want you to know I'm not doing it for anyone else but me, though. If I die while trying to get this sword so be it. I don't rightly trust you, and I feel like you're not being completely truthful to me, but right now I don't care," he paused. "What do I do after? If I do succeed in killing the Abomination?"

"You can do whatever you want after," Nadrian replied. "Thank you, Sainte, for doing this. I don't know what awaits you, but…"

Sainte held up a hand, "It doesn't matter. Can't be much worse than what I've already gone through. Where do I start? How do I track down this sword that's so well guarded? Do you know where it's at?"

"Well, yes and no. I know of two locations it might reside. There is an island north of Thissaren, it's not large, but that is the first location. There is a lake in the center, and I have reason to believe, if the sword is there, it will be in a cave near the lake.

"The second location is in the mountains of Deshiere, but that's as much as I know. Yes, I know, these are very far apart and the mountains are vast, but our books on this particular matter are not informative, to say the least. I must ask that you do not tarry, time is not something that we have much of."

"It's a month's worth of travel from Thissaren to Deshiere mountains almost nonstop. I don't know how long we have, but it better be long enough for travel," Sainte said shaking his head.

"I am well aware. So you better be on the move, now. Oh, and before we part ways, I did the pleasure of bringing your sword back to you."

"That was destroyed," Sainte began, thinking of the sword that was destroyed while fighting Miqel.

"Not that one. Your grandfather's, I believe. I found it in the rubble of Ellie's home, that is why it took me so long to finally meet up with you." Nadrian shuffled through his bags he had behind him and turned back around holding Sainte's sword that was lost the same night Ellie was. Nadrian handed it to him and watched as Sainte drew the blade from the sheath.

"No rust, looks almost freshly forged."

Nadrian smiled, "I took the liberty of cleaning it up for you, bloody dirty blade, covered in soot and mud. I hoped you wouldn't mind."

"I do not. Not at all," Sainte sheathed the sword once more. "Thank you, Nadrian. I don't know what else to say."

"Nothing else need be said. The fire in your eyes is thanks enough. It's good to see that again. Right, well, you'd best be on your way. I have a pack of food and some fresh vials for your eyes. Jasmine said you might need them," Nadrian tossed a pack to Sainte.

Sainte shouldered the bag, "Thank you. I'll move as quick as I can." He shuffled in the bag and found a vial. He uncorked it and dropped a few drops in each eye. Then he stood up and buckled his sword to his belt. "Goodbye, Nadrian. Will I see you again?"

"Oh, I don't know. But I will be seeing you, whether you realize it or not. Good luck Sainte Nore, Shield of Crearia. Where will you be going first?"

Sainte thought about the question, "I suppose I'll go to Thissaren, and from there to the island. It's closer from here. Let's hope that this sword I am seeking out is there."

"Be careful, I don't know exactly what awaits you when you find the sword."

41

He shrugged his shoulders, adjusting the weight of the pack accordingly. "I will be, always am. Goodbye, Nadrian," he said once more. He turned and started walking back to Bethrune, back to the path that would take him around the mountains and north to Thissaren. The way was dark. Time had been lost to him while speaking with Nadrian. No matter, time meant little to Sainte when he could barely sleep. He was more afraid of his nightmares than whatever he would face in his waking hours.

THREE

Munich had not seen very much destruction in the Dark Days, save for the butcher who went crazy and managed to take down several people before being killed himself. Kial had heard what happened to the other towns, mainly Guardstin and Elion, and if a murderer amok was the only bad thing that happened to Munich then he would consider that a good thing. The butcher was still a mystery that bothered him, and seemingly no one else. Peng was curious about it too, but he had not the mind to ruffle anyone's feathers.

It bugged Kial. A lot. That butcher was one of the main reasons their band had been formed and left to find help, only to return with just him and Peng. For it to just be blown away on a gentle breeze was curious. The butcher, whom Kial did not know personally, was a long resident of Munich, and Kial had made it a personal mission to figure out why the butcher snapped on the first Dark Day.

He raised his fist and knocked on the wooden door. Three times, one after the other, firm. Also, the third door he knocked on since breakfast with Peng. He had not yet been home but told Madelaine about his plans the previous night.

The first two homesteads yielded him no answers, so this was the last one he would try. If he could not get anything from here, he decided he would drop this personal investigation.

The same fist that knocked laid to rest on the head of his warhammer. Kial was dressed in his guard garb still, hoping that he might get some more information if people thought that he was on official business. It did not seem to be working. His head rolled side to side, stretching out his neck. He was getting older and it seemed as if his body was ageing faster than him. Maybe Peng was right, maybe he should get more rest. He almost knocked again when the door opened.

A woman answered the door, graying hair. She looked to be about sixty, twenty years or so older than Kial.

"Good morning, miss," he said.

"What're you here for? I didn't break any laws," she said as she crossed her arms, immediately suspicious.

Kial smiled and laughed, trying his hardest to put his best foot forward. "I know. I just have some questions for you. About your husband."

"He's dead, what more could you want? His killer's dead, too," her eyes narrowed.

"Again, I know. I'm just trying to figure out why. Why did the butcher…" Kial damned himself, why could he never remember the name?

"Flotier?"

That was it. "Yes, Flotier. Why did he kill your husband? Why did he kill all those other people?"

She scoffed at his question, "I don't know. What's it matter?"

"What if he was part of a group? There may be more. Was he hired to do this? Did he have someone in mind to kill, or would anyone do? I just want to know what made him do what he did, so I can try to prevent anything like it from happening again," Kial explained.

"I don't know what you want from me. I got our meat from that butcher a handful of times. Barely knew him, probably wouldn't have even remember his name had he not murdered my…" the woman's strong façade faltered. Her eyes teared up as she almost said it, but she quickly regained her composure. "Had he not murdered those people. If you'll excuse me, I have a lot to do today." She shut the door.

Kial turned away and sighed. He did not mean to upset her. Maybe she was right, too little too late. There was nothing else to be done about Flotier. After all, the man was dead. Kial walked away rubbing his temples. He had decided that this wild hunt for reasoning behind the murders was not worth his time. If no one else cared, why should he?

He walked with every intention of going back to his home, seeing his wife and daughter, and getting some sleep, but before he could even get twenty steps away from the house he was yanked into an alley. Strong hands grabbed him and shoved him against a wall, holding him there. The man was hooded and his face wrapped in a dark cowl so no features could be seen except for his brown eyes.

"You would do well to stop asking questions, Kial. There are some things better left unanswered. I'll only tell you this one time, there won't be a next. Move on with your life, help the people of Munich, of Crearia, rebuild. But this, what you seek, is not for you to know."

"Are you threatening me?"

"I will do what must be done." The man then shoved off and ran away. Kial had no intentions of following him. But now he had every intention of finding out more about Flotier.

After straightening himself out, Kial returned home for the first time that day. When he entered, he saw his wife with her back to him, stirring a pot that was over a fire. He walked up behind her and encircled her in his arms.

"About time you came home," she said at his touch.

"I had a few things to do after breakfast with Peng," he said, squeezing her before letting go. "What're you making? It smells delicious."

"Deer stew, with potatoes and carrots. Won't be ready for some time. Franceska's been asking about you," Madelaine said.

"Where is she?"

"Her room, I think," Madelaine said. Almost if on cue, Franceska came running into the room.

"Dad," she said as she embraced him in a hug.

He hugged her back before saying, "How's my little girl doing?"

She leaned back and looked up at him, "I'm not a little girl anymore, I'm already nine years old."

"You'll always be little to me," he smiled.

"Glad you're back, dad. You were gone a long time today."

"I believe I'll be having longer days here soon. Why don't you go play with Catty? I'm sure she'd like to," Kial suggested.

"Can we go out and play with sheep in Mister Granush's fields?" she asked.

"Fine by me, make sure her parents are ok with it," as soon as she heard that she turned and started to run away. "And ask Mister Granush too," he called after her.

After Franceska was out of ear shot, Madelaine asked, "How'd your first day go asking about Flotier?"

"Does everyone remember his name but me?" Kial said sheepishly. Without waiting for an answer he continued, "It was interesting. Already been threatened."

She stopped what she was doing and turned to him, "Threatened? Kial, I thought you said this was just something you were looking into, not a big deal?"

"Madelaine, it's fine. Means I'm on the right track, asking the right questions," he tried to brush her concern away. By the look on her face it was not working. "I'll be fine, no one dares do anything to a guard of Munich, the whole town would be after them."

"Won't be any good to me if someone has you killed. I was worried about you doing this, and now I'm even more worried. You should leave it be, everyone else has."

"I can't do that now, it's just starting to get interesting," he said making light of her worries.

She sighed heavily, "I know I can't stop you... Just remember you have a family, alright. Don't forget that."

"How could I?"

Jasmine sat with her elbows on the table and her chin rested on her clasped hands. She had arrived back in Munich after seeing Iris off from the Shinta village. Now she waited for Eringar. He was taking his time getting with her, he was supposed to meet her in Raven's Feather Tavern by now. She had denied a refill of her mead two times now. Had she known he would take this long she would have gotten another.

The tavern was one of the more well-kept drinkeries in Munich. One of the bar wenches would go and sweep up every hour, and the owner made sure to point them in the direction of tables that needed cleaning. Not to mention the drinks were more expensive than any commoners would like to pay for, so that kept most of the troublesome folk out. This is why Jasmine had chosen this place for many of their meetings. The few customers that were in it were too self-important to care about anyone else.

The door swung open, and, finally, Eringar strutted in. He pulled down his hood and he had lost the cowl that he wore the last time Jasmine saw him. She sat up straight and his head swiveled towards her movement. Pulling out a chair he sat down. Seeing a new customer, a wench hustled over quickly.

"What'll it be, sir?"

"An ale, please."

"We have several. Morten hails from Sanctin, and several come from Mountsville. Also, a sweeter one that some like is…"

"The first one," he cut her off. "The first one is fine." Seeing that he was clearly annoyed, the wench gave a curt nod then turned her gaze upon Jasmine, "And for you, missus?"

"Nothing more, thanks." The wench smiled politely and left to get Eringar's order.

Jasmine waited for him to begin speaking, but he just looked at her and smiled. "Well?" she held her arms out. "How'd it go? I didn't invite you here to hang out over drinks."

"You mean this isn't the beginning of a romantic relationship?" Seeing at how unamused she was, he continued,

"Jasmine, how do you think it went?" he asked with a confident smile.

She sighed. She hated dealing with this man, but no one else was willing to do what she asked. "That's why I'm asking you how it went? Because I don't know. If anyone else would have done this, trust me, I would have picked them." She knew the only reason Eringar was willing to help Jasmine was because he fancied her.

"If anyone else did it, it wouldn't have gone as well as it did. You sent the right man. If your plan works out, then everyone must remain as they are, ignorant. They cannot know that the White Wyverns are here with them. And I am the best at keeping secrets."

"Say that a little louder, please, I don't think everyone heard you," Jasmine said sarcastically.

Eringar ignored her, "The man, what was his name?"

"Kial."

"Aye, Kial, he won't keep poking around. I made sure of it," he leaned back with a smile as the wench brought his mug of ale. "Thanks."

Jasmine waited for the woman to be gone before she spoke. "You didn't hurt him, did you?"

"You care too much for these people. First you send Nadrian after Sainte, then me to do your dirty work against Kial, but with the stipulation that he is to remain unharmed. There are many who say you're getting soft. Too soft to listen to anymore. You're lucky the Council gave you any time at all for what you did. You better hope it pans out as you planned, for your sake."

"You didn't answer my question."

"Hmm? Oh, yes. No, Kial is not hurt. He's fine. Maybe wounded his pride a little, but I do believe I got the point across."

"Good, thank you," Jasmine nodded and leaned back, satisfied.

"What do you plan to do if, against all reason, this man does continue to question? What if he finds out that Flotier was only doing what we all should have done?" he asked slyly.

Jasmine paused to think the question over, "I don't know. But it won't come to that. I'll figure something out if I must."

"Well, you better. You're on thin ice with everyone right now. As your friend, I'm telling you all it will take is one bad move, something that makes the Council just a little nervous, and they'll begin the Sever. No more talking them out of it. This is your last chance." At this point Eringar was leaning forward, drink forgotten, face serious.

"I like you, Jasmine. I don't want you to fail. I must admit, I don't care for…" He leaned back and looked around, then pointedly at the other men in the tavern, "But I like you. So I want you to succeed."

Jasmine almost blushed. Almost. She had been turning Eringar down a long time, and now would be no different. "I have to go. Thank you for what you did. If I need anything, I'll contact you. Until then, keep doing what you've been doing."

"I'd ask you to stay and enjoy a drink with me, but I doubt I'd convince you. So instead, just keep in touch, eh?"

"We'll see, Eringar. Don't push your luck." She stood and shot him a smile, "See you later." She walked out of the tavern and headed home. It was getting late, she was tired, and she had things to do in the morning.

FOUR

With every step Dawn took, Iris' left arm was jostled and shot a jolt of pain up her shoulder. Despite having mostly healed, it seemed it would pain her for the rest of her life. She cursed her gimp arm, not for the first time.

She wished her arm was the only thing bothering her right now. Having been on Dawn for the better part of five hours, her rump was sore, her thighs were chafing, and her back was stiff. It was about time to take a little break, get on her feet, walk around, and stretch out her aching muscles. She did the math in her head and came to the conclusion that it would take about six days to reach Thissaren.

She guided Dawn over to the side of the path, dismounted, and threw the reins over a low hanging branch. Iris raised her good arm over her head and stretched, her back cracked a few times and relief flooded into her body. After walking in a few circles, she looked around. She was deep in Litewood Forest, made up of mostly pine and oak trees. If she continued north, she would soon come to the small mountain range known as the Mouth of the World.

In the middle of those mountains laid Bethrune, Sainte's hometown. She had no intention of going through the mountains, instead deciding to stay on the east side of them and continue north. Dawn waited patient for her to mount once more. There was about two more hours of daylight left, then she would make camp.

Time passed uneventfully and quietly, and soon evening was upon her. Iris found a flat wooded area and stopped Dawn there. Soon she had a fire going and her blankets laid out in a makeshift bed. She settled down by the fire and pulled out a mix of berries she was given before she left.

With a mouthful of berries, she poked at the flames with a stick sending a shower of sparks airborne. Her thoughts strayed to her recent past. She remembered it, mostly. Like a dream, she knew overall what happened, but specific details eluded her. She remembered when Miqel was trying to kill her, and Sainte killing Miqel by smashing his face, but how she got to that road she did not recall. Iris shook her head; it was all over now. That is what she had to keep telling herself.

After relaxing by the fire for some time and reminiscing on better times, she decided it was time for bed. The sun was down, the stars were out, and the night life began to make noise. It was loud but comforting to hear once more. Soon she was laying down, getting ready for blissful sleep. As she was about to drift away, she heard a faint noise. Snapping twigs as something walked ever closer to her fire light. Iris slowly sat up and reached for her dagger with her good arm. Her eyes darted left and right, skin started to sweat in fear. Then she saw it.

A Malignin. Immediately she could tell that something was off. This one was walking upright, not prowling on all fours as they normally did. It did not even seem to notice her. When it got about twenty feet from the fire it stopped then started to make a wide berth of it. Iris felt some relief at that but did not take her eyes off it. The fear was still there. It was just one Malignin, that she knew of, but it could still kill her if it wanted to.

Suddenly it stopped walking. The beast threw its nose into the air and sniffed. Apparently, it caught a whiff of something. Then it looked at Iris. Straight at her. Yellow eyes glinted in the firelight, thin, needle-like teeth jutted from the top and bottom jaw, black skin shined as if the thing had just crawled out of a lake.

Goosebumps crept across her skin, too afraid to do anything except stare back. Stare into the eyes of the thing that started her down the path of right where she was. She was full of equal parts fear and hatred. Each emotion fighting to make her attack the thing or run away, but also each so strong they made her do nothing. Nothing except stare back and meet its gaze.

After what felt like an hour the Malignin slowly looked away. It continued to amble on, aimlessly it seemed to Iris. She watched it walk away until she could see it no longer. It was odd seeing one by itself, she could not recall if she had ever seen a Malignin just meandering around by itself. She stared in the direction it went long before she finally laid back down to try to get some rest, but it never came.

When the sunlight began to creep through the limbs and leaves of the trees around her, Iris sat up. After seeing the Malignin so near all she accomplished through the night was tossing and turning. She stood up and slung her pack over her good shoulder, then untied Dawn and climbed into the saddle, eager for these next few days to be over. She could hardly wait to sleep in a bed again with four solid walls in place of the tent furs she had become so accustomed to with the Shinta. The ache in her arm throbbed up in down soon after Dawn began to trot, she could hardly wait for that to go away, if it ever did.

To try to pass the time and take her mind off the pain she began to wonder what she would do when she reached Thissaren. How would she make a living there? Hopefully, she would be able to get a job at all. Maybe work at a tavern as a barista? Or a cleaner for someone's home? It was a port city so there were a lot of trade ships and tradesmen. Perhaps she would try to become a hand for a ship, that would be interesting. She shook her head at the notion, it was something simple she wanted. A ship hand was not that. Maybe she could be hired to clean the ships out while they were at port? She was sure she would be able to find something.

The Mouth of the World slid by on her left. It was a small mountain range both in length and in height. The smallest mountain range in Crearia, actually. It was made famous by the vegetation that grew there. For reasons still unknown, the wood from trees that grew within the mountains would not burn. Instead travelers would have to make do without a fire or gather a lot of small brush to burn. Iris had never been to Bethrune herself but had heard that they would buy wood from people passing through. She should have asked Sainte about that, she thought to herself. It was then Iris realized how lonely she felt. She missed talking to people, to her friends.

"At least I have you," she patted Dawn on the neck. The horse did not reply.

The days began to go by quicker. Occasionally she passed by a traveler, but no words were ever exchanged, just a curt nod or two. She barely looked at them. Sure, she was lonely, but she was also cautious of strangers out here. Thankfully, none bothered her, and she did not run into any bandits.

Soon the Mouth of the World was behind her, lost on the horizon. The slightly used path she rode on continued north and should take her just around Nuse's ruins, the old king's castle. It was on her fourth day of travel when the old ruins loomed up in front of her. The white rubble a stark contrast against the green grass. The castle once had been huge, spanning across acres. Now it was nothing more than a pile of rubble. If one wanted to, they would be able to walk through the remains and have an idea of the layout, but Iris felt she did not have that kind of time.

Instead she urged Dawn forward just past the ruins and made camp for the night, looking forward to her last day of travel.

Iris woke up early, before the sun rose. She was surprised that she actually got some sleep, some good sleep apparently as she felt more rejuvenated than she had since she began her journey to Thissaren. Without wasting any time, Iris had a quick breakfast consisting of bread and the rest of her mixed berries, then she packed up her blankets, slung the pack over her shoulder, and rode towards her final destination.

There was quite a bit more foot traffic now that she neared the city. She passed by a few carriages full of tradeable goods, no doubt, and was passed by some lone travelers, mostly men, looking for work aboard some ships she assumed. There was plenty of good paying work to be found aboard a trade ship if you were hard working, or so she had heard.

Before long she looked upon the open gates of Thissaren and of everyone entering and leaving the city. It was still early afternoon when she passed through the gates. From what she had heard, Thissaren had largely remained unaffected during the Dark Days. No Malignin made their way this far north, they had all stayed to the south of Bethrune. That was one of the main reasons she wanted to go north, was to get away from everything that reminded her of those times.

Without thinking on it anymore, Iris ushered Dawn forward into the city. Forward into what she could only hope was a brighter future than what her past held.

The main road made a straight line through the city, starting at the gates and leading straight to the ports. It was the only road, that she had noticed, that was cobblestone. All the other smaller roads that branched away were merely packed dirt. People on horseback and carriage dominated the cobblestone rode, while people on foot made their way to their destinations on the sidelines and dirt paths.

Iris watched everyone with cautious eyes, this was a new town and she was not sure how prevalent pickpockets would be. There were not as many people around as she had expected. Tradesmen voices were heard over the bustle of everyone's movement. At least trade seemed to be picking up a bit here.

That did not matter right now, she told herself. First and foremost, she must find a job. She had plenty of food and water yet, but no coin to her name. Iris knew of one place where one could always find a job, the local tavern. For now she put Dawn into a slow gait and followed the flow of traffic. The tavern would be at a busy spot, no doubt somewhere close to the port.

Soon she found out that she was correct. The tavern, appropriately called Barmaids and Booze, was located on the waterside just a few blocks away from the port. In fact, she could see the port from the entrance of the tavern. The noise from the tavern was so loud she heard it before she saw the sign for it. She doubted the tavern was ever quiet, what with ships pretty much constantly coming and going.

Iris found a hitching post nearby, tied up Dawn, and made her way into Barmaids and Booze. If she thought the ruckus was loud outside, the ruckus inside almost made her dizzy. After almost a month of being in the Shinta village and then traveling by herself, the yells and banter were almost overwhelming.

Almost every single table was full of men of various ages and various facial hair. The one thing they all had in common was weathered skin from being out in the sun and wind almost constantly. Tobacco smoke lazily wisped around the ceiling, but the smell of it permeated everywhere. It was hot inside, with each table having at least two lanterns lit.

Wenches with their breasts nearly busting from their tops quickly bustled to and from tables with mugs both empty and full. Two cooks in the back yelled at each other, but Iris only knew that because she could see them, not because she heard them.

After taking all this in mere seconds, Iris took a deep breath and walked between the tables to the bar. She pushed herself between two drunk men who did not even react to her, then waved down a bartender.

The woman walked in front of Iris and said, "What'll it be, honey? Food, drink, wench, or a combination?"

"None of that, I'm looking for some work. Was wondering if you've heard of anything?" Iris asked.

The woman looked her up and down, eyeing her slung arm, "Dunno if many men would want you with that gimp arm, and you can't hold very many drinks in one hand. Dunno of any other work you'd be able to get as a one-armed woman."

"I don't want to be, er, a bar maiden. If you had anything else?"

"Honey, I've got nothing for you. Now, I'm going to have to ask you to buy something or leave, we're busy 'nough as it is."

Over the noise a woman's cries could be heard, Iris and the bar tender looked over to the noise. A man was grabbing and pulling at a bar maiden's clothes, trying to pull her on his lap. He had a stupid, drunken grin on his face.

The bar tender cursed under her breath and quickly made her way over there. Iris watched as she slapped at the man and tried to, unsuccessfully, pull his hands away from the poor girl. Iris was about to leave but an idea came into her head.

She made her way over to the scuffle as the man seemingly got annoyed by the bar tender trying to interfere and he slapped her with one hand while still hanging on to the other girl.

"Let her go," Iris demanded as she came up to them. The man ignored her and pulled the other girl into his lap. She struggled halfheartedly. Having enough of the man's idiot smile, Iris cocked her right arm back and punched him in the jaw with all her strength. The man's head snapped back and then forward, chin to chest. His arms slumped to his side and a trail of blood dribbled from his mouth onto his shirt.

Two men that were sitting at the table stood up at Iris' action, but before they could do anything four other men came over in support of Iris.

The woman the now unconscious man was grabbing at stood up and hurried off towards the back, face flushed. The bar tender turned on the remaining two men at the table.

"Get this bastard out of here," she told them. "Better not see you lot back any time soon." Begrudgingly, they grabbed their friend and drug him out. The bar tender watched them to make sure they left and did not return. The four men who had came over all went back and sat down, then the bar tender turned to Iris. "Thank you, that was unexpected. My name's Grenda."

"I'm Iris, and no problem. I'd hope someone would do the same for me. How's your face?" she asked as a red handprint started to show on Grenda's cheek.

"It's fine," she waved it away, "not the worst that's happened. You were looking for some work, Iris? I think I may have something for you. Follow me, back to the bar."

Once there, Grenda said, "I like how you handled that. Quick, easy, no fuss, no one hurt. Well, except for that fellow but I don't care about him. I could use help watching the girls, making sure they're treated right and get payment from the clients before they bring them to bed. I can't promise great pay, but you will be paid. You'll have free meals, drinks, and a place to stay."

"You don't already have people here for that?" Iris asked.

"Sure I do, but never for long. Most of the time they get picked up by the ships for better pay. I don't expect many ships would want you aboard so hopefully you'd stick around for a while," Grenda explained.

"I'll take it," Iris said.

"Excellent, consider right now your first day."

"Where's the room? Can I put my stuff there? And I have a horse tied up outside, the buckskin outside."

"Here, hand me your bags, I'll put them behind the bar and I'll send someone out to bring your horse to the stables. I'll show you them and where your room is later on."

Iris handed her bag over and made sure to see where it was placed, then turned around and looked over the large tavern. She was tired from all her travels and would have liked to rest, but she was excited to be starting something new. Something different.

FIVE

Sainte trudged through rainy days, sunny days, nighttime, with barely any sleep. He worked his way through the Mouth of the World, stopping only when he wanted to, and even then it was never longer than an hour. Even with his almost constant moving it still took him a week before he was out of the mountains. It took another week of walking through the hillside before he finally arrived to Thissaren.

Now he stood outside of the gates of the port town, watching everyone come and go. Thissaren was unique as the walls of the city were not really walls, but the backs of buildings built so close together there were no gaps between each one. The only places where there were gaps, they placed the gates, but only one gate was being used at this time, the others were too small to be of any use so they remained closed and locked.

Thissaren was not a city that was well prepared for any kind of assault, not that they needed to worry about it. There were only four port cities, and it was one of them. No one wanted to risk the destruction of a city built around trade, much less trade by ship.

Weary of his travels, Sainte made his way into the city unhindered, though a little cramped. The gates were open for all to enter or leave as they pleased. They had armed guards, but they were only there to keep the peace in the case of any unruly persons. His first priority was to find an inn, get a room, and get some much-needed rest. Although he hated to do it, he knew his body needed sleep after the two weeks of travel.

As he walked through the town he began to wonder if he would even find an inn. There were plenty of small taverns and local shops. He started to worry that when he found an inn it would be full since there were so many people. Traders pushed their wares around in carts and attempted to sell their trinkets to any who would listen. It was like Thissaren had already forgotten about the Dark Days. The people who lived here seemed to turn a blind eye to the decimation of the Southern towns. It almost made him feel angry.

Some people around him were smiling at each other, laughing even. How could they be so ignorant. So much loss happened so recently, and they did not even care. Everything he did for them and these people could not care less. They did not know what suffering was. He was not almost angry. He was angry.

"Hey, you there!" a vendor shouted. "I've got some new cloaks for you, yours looks rather dirty and worn out." Sainte snapped his attention to the man. He was a pudgy fellow, short with stringy hair. His cart was full of cloaks.

"I don't want anything." Sainte said, having to consciously hold his anger in check. It had grown considerably. He drew in a breath and let it out, "I do have a question."

"Everything comes with a price, sir."

Ignoring him Sainte continued, "Where are the inns here?"

"A price. Buy a cloak and I'll answer your question."

"I don't have any coin," his words came through gritted teeth.

"A trade then, perhaps?"

Sainte had to take in another deep breath and exhaled slowly. Gods his eyes hurt, "What would be adequate?"

"Show me what you're willing to part with and I will show you what that can get you."

Sainte thought about it. He did not have much. He could give up his dagger now that he had a sword, "How about this?" He pulled it out.

"Aye, that could get you some these. Fine weave, they are. Durable, and good to wear in warmth or cold. What do you think? Which one do you like?" The vendor gestured to the left side of his cart. There were reds, blues, greens, blacks.

"I'll take a black one," they exchanged goods. "Now, my question. Where's the nearest inn?"

The vendor tucked the dagger away, "Not from around here, eh?" Sainte did not answer. "There's only one inn, near the port. There used to be several, but they all got bought out one by one and are now owned by one wealthy, lucky man. Just follow the main road, cobblestone, and it'll take you to the ports. Turn left and you'd have to be daft not to miss," the trader said while making wild gestures with his hands that did not coincide with his directions.

Sainte tucked the cloak under one arm and left without saying anything else to the annoying man. He would have been angrier, but he had to admit that he was in need of a new cloak. He took his old one off and tossed it aside in a pile of trash, then replaced it with his new one.

He made his way to the port, head bowed, keeping to the side of the main road. The less people he looked at the better, he could barely stand seeing everyone acting as if the events of barely three weeks ago never happened. To help keep his vision focused on what was solely in front of him he put his hood up. More than a few people made faces at him when they noticed his eyes, and he figured the less attention he drew to himself the better. So, in this way he eventually found himself at the port. Turning left, sure enough, were the signs for the inn.

To call it an inn was an understatement. It was an establishment, about three blocks long. The building was in fact several buildings. The inn had apparently bought the surrounding businesses out and combined their building with it. This inn was now a tavern and a brothel. A big one at that. When Sainte entered, he took down his hood and looked around. The inside was huge. The walls that had once separated building from building had been torn down, support columns now in place. There were at least thirty circular tables in the room, almost all of them full of people. Sainte looked around for a minute before he found one that had room. There was only one other man at the table. He walked over through the pipe smoke that filled the room.

"Seat open?" Sainte asked gesturing to the bench across from the man. He was an older gentleman, long scraggly grey hair and a face that had not been shaved in what looked like since he was a lad. The man barely looked up from his drink. Sainte took that as no one sat there. He sat down and almost immediately a woman was standing by his side. She laid her hand on his shoulder, causing him to flinch. He had not been touched by another person in a long time. The feeling was almost foreign to him now.

"What'll it be, ser?" she asked. "Come in here for drinks, company of a woman, or both?" It was hard for him to hear her soft voice over the music that the band was playing and the cacophony of the drunk's voices. She was a pretty woman. Curly brown hair, with eyes to match, and a homely face if she was not doing such a terrible job at hiding her expression when she noticed his. She was on the skinny side, she probably worked more than she ate, and her dress was a little tight, revealing more than her fair share of skin.

"My company then, eh? Follow me," she sighed as if it was always the ugly ones that wanted to sleep with her. Sainte looked down at the table, not realizing how long he stared at her in silence. She grabbed his hand, but he pulled away.

"No, thank you," he finally said, "I'll take an ale. Some food, if you have it."

She visibly relaxed at his words, relieved she would not have to spread her legs for him. "Aye, we have pig stew today. That'll be eight gold," she held her hand out for the coin and saw him hesitate. Her face now showed annoyance. "No coin, no service. Get out you dirty bugger, can't 'ave you soiling everyone's day," her attitude changed immediately. Apparently, she dealt with homeless often. Sainte did not move.

"I've traveled far, I'm tired. Is there anything I can do for some food and a room, forget the ale," he said that as nicely as he could muster. The woman's attitude brought up the anger that he had pushed down.

"Nay, there's not. Get out," her voice started to raise. "Go on!"

Some of the surrounding people began to look over at the commotion. Just what Sainte needed.

"Get-" but before she could finish the sentence, undeniably the loudest one yet, she was interrupted.

"No problem here, I've got him covered," a man called out and walked up, well dressed, black hair slicked back. He looked to be nearing his forties. "Eight gold, you said? Here," he shuffled around his right pocket and counted out some coin, "Here's ten, keep the two for yourself," he winked at her.

"Thank you, ser. I'll have his ale and stew right out." The woman's attitude had changed quickly, once again, upon payment. She took his coin and bowed low, showing off more than she needed to, and left.

"No one sitting here?" he asked Sainte as he was already sitting down. Sainte saw no reason to reply. "Name's Aldred Malum. Who did I just pay for?"

"Sainte," he told the man curtly, not looking at him.

"Mate, what happened to your eyes?" Aldred asked hiding the disgust in his voice badly.

"A fight."

"Hate to see the blokes you've been fighting."

"Yeah," damn his eyes burned. "'Scuse me." Sainte rummaged around his pockets for the vial. He brought it out and dropped some of the fire quenching liquid into each eye. He rolled his eyes around to spread the coolness. Aldred had watched in respectful silence. By the time Sainte finished the woman returned with a mug of ale and a bowl of stew. She placed each down in front of Sainte.

"Anything else for you gentlemen?" she smiled.

"No, thank you, that's all for now," Sainte said. The woman smiled at Aldred and glanced at Sainte, who had already begun to eat the stew, and left the two men.

"Bold of you to come in here with no coin. This place is known for being strict on the penniless."

"I'm new here, just arrived today. Didn't realize the hospitality of this place," Sainte said between mouthfuls.

"What brings you to this great city? Not much to do here unless you're in the boating business."

Sainte thought about how much he should tell this stranger. This stranger who had taken interest in him for no apparent reason.

"Why'd you pay for me?" he asked instead.

Aldred shrugged, "A little bit of kindness, a little bit of boredom. Sometimes the poor have some good stories. I'm trying to find out yours."

Straightforward, it seemed, "I'm trying to make my way to the island just north of the ports."

"Why? There's naught there but rocks. No animals, no plants worth a shit."

"I'm looking for something, heard it might be there."

"Ah, haven't seen one of your kind in a while," Aldred leaned back with a knowing smile. "You're looking for the sword?"

Sainte was taken aback, "Yeah, how'd you know?"

"It's a town legend around here. Many have gone there looking for it, mostly kids, some more serious folk, but nothing's been found. I've never seen someone so, destitute, come looking for it. How do you plan on getting there? The seas between the port and island aren't exactly suitable for swimming."

Sainte shrugged, "I was hoping to catch a ride over."

The man who was sitting at the table before Sainte snorted and sat up, "A ride says ye? I'll take ye wherever ye want. S'long as there's payment for me." He looked at the two other men at the table with lidded eyes.

"I need a ride to the island just north of here. It's a short distance, I believe. How much would you require for that?" Sainte asked. He did not care who took him to the island, as long as he could get there and back without dying.

"Short trip, aye, but foolish. Reef makes for dangerous sailing, dangerous waters. Five hundred-coin, one way. Round trip seven hundred."

"Seven hundred?" Sainte scoffed. "That's insane."

"I need coin for more drinks, not to mention putting meself and my ship in danger. I don't sail often anymore, so I need to make a lot of coin whenever I do to make it worth it. Take it or leave it, ye won't find anyone else to do it at all."

"Sainte, I'll pay the man. All I ask is you take me along," Aldred interjected.

"Why would you do that?" Sainte asked. This stranger was far too interested in his affairs, and far too willing to pay.

"As I mentioned earlier, I'm bored. I have the funds to pay for this, no problem. Let me go with you. It'd do me well to get out of this town for a bit."

Sainte took a long drag out of his mug. The smoke in this tavern was starting to sting his eyes again, time for another drop. As he thought about Aldred's offer he pulled out a vial and dropped a few drops of the soothing liquid into each eye.

"Fine, I don't guess there's any harm in it," Sainte consented. He had to get to the island somehow. Aldred smiled. "What's your name?" he asked the drunkard.

"Earl, Earl Bansford at yer service."

"When can your ship be ready, Earl?"

"The morrow, early if needs be. Just cause I drink don't mean I don't take care 'o my ship. When's ye wantin' to leave? Morning? Eve? Sometime time 'tween?"

"Morning would be best, I think."

Aldred nodded in agreement. "Might be best to catch some sleep. Earl, I'll have your payment tomorrow morning. I'm only giving you half up front, and the other half upon our safe return. Where shall we meet you?"

"Aye," he waved a hand in agreement. "Outside here is fine, the front."

"Sainte, how about we go get a room? Tonight will be on me."

Sainte had not realized his bowl sat in front of him empty and he just swallowed the last bit of ale. He had not slept a full night in a long time, but it would probably do him well to rest. He followed Aldred as they walked to the bar.

Aldred waved down a bar tender. "I'll take two rooms, one for me and one for my mate," he motioned to Sainte.

"Alright," the woman smiled, "Let me grab the new girl, Iris. Gotta show her how to do this right, messed up the last time. I'll be right back."

Sainte froze. Did she just say Iris? What was she doing here? Was it even the same Iris as he knew? He was not ready to face her, not here, not now. He quickly turned away from the bar and leaned against it with his back. He should leave the bar, but something held him in place. He had to know if it was actually her or not. He put his hood on just in case.

Soon he heard the bar tender return with someone else.

"Two rooms, aye?" a woman said. It was her. He recognized that voice anywhere.

"Aye. What happened to your arm?" Aldred asked.

"It's uh… a long story. That'll be twenty gold for the both of you."

Sainte heard the gold coins clink together as he handed them over.

"Rooms thirteen and fifteen. Second floor to your right, they will be across from each other. Is there anything else I can offer? Will these rooms be coming with full services? A woman and drinks for the night? Get a girl of your choosing and the drinks are free," Iris offered.

"No, I think we'll be alright. Thank you though, I'll let you know if one of us changes our mind. Have a good night."

"You too," she said. "He alright?"

"Him?" Aldred lightly slapped Sainte on the shoulder. "Aye, he's fine. A bit off his face, but that's what we need the rooms for."

Aldred turned away and Sainte followed him back to the table, making sure to hide his face from Iris as well as he could.

"What's gotten into you, Sainte? Acting awfully strange back there," Aldred said.

He shrugged, "Didn't want to unsettle her what with my eyes."

"No matter. Here's the key to your room," he handed it over. "Well gents, I'm going to bed. I'll see you two in the morning." Aldred said and walked away.

"I think I'm going to do the same, Earl. See you in the morning. Remember, sunrise," Sainte told the old drunk sailor.

"Yeah yeah, I'll be there," Earl said as he waved him away.

Sainte shook his head and walked away, towards the stairs to his room. Once up the stairs he turned right and unlocked the door and stepped in, shutting the door behind him. It was rather dreary compared to the large, almost lavish, room beneath his feet. There was one window, nailed shut on the inside, the bed was made but who knew when the last time the sheets had been changed. An unlit candle sat on a rough looking wooden table by the bedside. All in all, it was much better than where he had been sleeping the past few weeks.

He placed his bag on the table and laid down on the bed, letting himself relax more than he had in a long time. It did not last long. There was a knock at his door, softly, sounding almost reluctant. Sainte sat up with a grunt and put a few drops of the liquid into each eye again.

"Coming," he called out. He shuffled to the door and opened it, expecting Aldred or Earl. Maybe a working girl who got it in her head to try to convince him he wanted company. When he opened the door he found that it was none of those people. It was Iris.

She stared at him, mouth agape and eyes wide. Sainte probably looked about the same. So much for not letting her notice him.

"Sainte?" she croaked out.

He let out a sigh before saying, "Come in."

She numbly walked past him and sat down on the bed, her left arm in a sling. "What happened to you? Where have you been?"

He shut the door and turned around, "It's a long story…"

"Why didn't you come to see me?"

"I couldn't. It was too hard," he remained standing by the door.

"I almost died, surrounded by strangers. All I wanted to see was someone I knew, a friend. You weren't there. You were all I had left, and you weren't there."

81

"I knew Jasmine had you, you were in good hands. I needed to be alone. To be away from everyone."

She sniffed and wiped some tears away that had started to fall. Sainte walked over and sat down next to her.

"How'd you know it was me?" he asked.

"You think I can't recognize you from your back?" she let out a quiet laugh. "No, I saw you go back to Earl. Once you went to your room I went over and asked him about you. Told me everything, the drunk fool."

"Not surprising, I didn't really think this through. Didn't have time to. Didn't expect to meet you here. What are you doing here, anyway? The last place I would expect you to work at is a brothel."

"Well, after I left the care of Jasmine and the Shinta, I headed north. I heard that it wasn't hit hardly at all by the Malignin, so I figured I could start new up here. I came here and knew I needed to find a place to work soon. I found this brothel, quite easily mind you, and long story short beat the piss out of a man who was getting too violent. The manager, and the girls took, a liking to me and offered me a job as, I dunno, watcher for them. When someone gets too handsy or violent I deal with them," she explained. "Starting to give me some more responsibility now, actually."

"What about your arm?" Sainte asked. "You're able to handle yourself?"

"With what we did, what we fought before," she shook her head. "Fighting old drunk fools is something I could do with no arms."

"I suppose you have a point," an uncomfortable silence settled between the two for some time, both at a loss for words. Both in a sort of shock.

Iris did not know what to say because there was so much that she felt she needed to say, she did not know what to say first.

Sainte was at a loss for words because he felt there was nothing more to be said.

"So, I hear you're going to the island tomorrow? What for?" she asked.

"Well, I'm looking for something."

"What?"

"It's… complicated."

"Try me," Iris insisted. Sainte sighed.

"I have to look for a weapon. There's more going on than any of us had ever realized. The Malignin aren't gone, not for good."

Iris looked surprised, "Of course they're not gone. I saw one on my way to Thissaren, although it seemed lost. What made you think they were gone?"

"I was there, Iris, when it should have ended. I saw what Aroc did. I saw some of them escape…" he paused. "The White Wyverns are more active than anyone knew, and they are taking action, asking me for help."

Iris stared at him, waiting for the end to this joke. It had to be a joke. Sainte just stared back no longer forthcoming.

"You can't be serious. You know that sounds crazy, right?"

Sainte nodded but remained silent. He knew he had told her too much, he was relaxed with her company once again, speaking more than he had wished.

"You are serious… Let me go with you. I can help, I've heard stories about that island. I might be able to help out looking for whatever it is you're looking for."

"A sword. They're asking me to get a sword."

"Of course they are."

"I don't think you should come with me. It could be dangerous, and I don't want to put you in any more trouble than you've already been in."

"I doubt I could experience much worse than what happened with Mi…" she choked as she tried to say Miqel. "With him."

"No, Iris. I don't want you to get hurt doing anything for me. Not again. Stay here, continue working. It seems like a good place, all in all. When this is all over, I'll come back here. Next time I won't be trying to hide from you. I'll be back here for you," old feelings started to return the longer he spoke with Iris. Memories he had almost forgotten of drinking with her at the Sun's Ale tavern after a night of killing Malignin. An even more distant memory of them together during training for the Blades of the Night before he was chosen to become the Shield for Ellie.

How different might things have turned out had someone else been chosen? He shook his head slightly, unnoticed by Iris. Those thoughts would do him no good. Things turned out how they did and there was nothing that could be done to change it.

"I'm sorry, Sainte, that's not good enough. I'm going to go with you, no matter what you say. Ever since Jasmine had picked me up and brought me to the Shinta village I've had thoughts to… to kill myself, end it all. Now, those thoughts have gotten easier to handle, but they haven't fully left. I don't know if they ever will. I need this. I need to have a purpose again. I need to not feel useless. I'm doing good with these girls here, but they were doing well enough before me, and I assume they'll be just fine without me. No matter what you say, I'll be on that ship with you tomorrow morning. You owe this to me. We were apart for so long before, I can't just let you go again. Don't get me wrong, I'm angry at you for even suggesting that I stay here, but I also still love you," she said sheepishly.

Sainte was at a loss for words, completely taken aback by her response. Maybe he should not have been. Maybe she was right, they had been apart for so long perhaps he had forgotten who she was. He knew that nothing he said would change her mind.

"Truth be told, Iris, I'm afraid of you getting to know who I am now."

"Don't be dramatic, Sainte. You're acting like a girl. We've both been through trauma, more than what a normal person would experience in a lifetime I'd wager. We need each other, we can rely on each other, like old times."

"But it's not like old times anymore."

"Then we'll make new times," she said beginning to get desperate. "I'm not okay, Sainte. I need this. I need you," her eyes began to water. "I don't have anyone. I don't know anyone here. The girls and Grenda have tried to talk to me, to become friends, but I can tell they don't get me."

Sainte awkwardly put his arm around her, "Alright, fine. Come with me, Iris. I won't fight it anymore." Damn her, she knew he had no defenses against her crying. Once the tears started to flow, he knew he had lost this conversation.

She wrapped her right arm back around him and leaned on him, "Thank you." She squeezed him then stood up, "I'd best be going, then. I have to finish up my shift and then have some packing to do I suppose. I'll see you in the morning. Sunrise, right?"

"Aye, see you then."

"If I don't, then I will track you down and I will kill you."

"I believe you," Sainte gave a tired smile. Iris left the room and Sainte finally laid down. He dampened a cloth with some of his poultice, then wrapped it around his head and tried to sleep.

SIX

True to his word, Earl was out by his ship just before daybreak. It was not as large as a trading ship, but not small enough to be considered a personal boat. It had lower deck beneath that would hold ten people comfortably. The ship's name *Mahogany* was carved into both port and starboard side. The lumber used to build the boat showed signs of age, but no leaks had been sprung. He checked his sails and ropes. Frayed, as expected, but they would get the job done. The seas were rough between the port and the island, but the distance was short. He expected he would not even remember the trip, he mused to himself, as he took a swig from his flask. The burning sensation of spirits down his throat was a comfort to him now.

Sailors and traders alike crowded the docks, moving ship to ship. Bartering, prepping, trading stories to friends rarely seen.

The docks were always busy in Thissaren. Earl wiped his nose at everyone, his days of gossip were long over. He had not sailed his ship in probably seven months if he had to take a guess. No matter, it was still floating and it would get the job done. Always had before. Through the dim morning light someone made their way to his ship. He could tell it was a woman from her figure and the way she walked. She stopped just short of the gangway.

"Good morning, Earl. Anyone else here yet?" she called up.

He rubbed his eyes as he unexpectedly recognized the woman, "Iris? What're you doing here?"

"I'm joining you on your little trip. I spoke to Sainte last night and he agreed that I could come."

Earl grumbled to himself. He did not like this, unexpected company. If he knew more people were coming he could have probably asked for more coin. He liked Iris, though.

"Are you going to stare at me all day or invite on board?" she interrupted his thoughts.

"Oh aye, I s'pose. C'mon up. To answer yer first question no, no one else is here yet. Expect they should be soon. I don't have all day," he finished with another swig.

"You don't have all day? You?" Iris scoffed. "You're the only man I know who has all week, much less all day. Either way, if Sainte said he'll be here, he'll be here," she said while she walked up the gangway.

Earl mumbled to himself and continued to check his ship. Sure enough, not even two minutes later, someone was heard calling out for Earl. Iris and he walked to side of the ship and looked down at the dock. Sainte and Aldred were standing by the gangway looking up.

"C'mon up," Earl said.

"Morning," Sainte said once he was on their level. "Glad to see you made it," he directed to Earl.

"I could say the same about you. Was beginning to think you might have flaked on me," the old man grumbled back.

"Well, here we are."

"I see that you didn't tell me about Iris here. Would've been nice to know last night."

"Well, she was a last-minute addition. Happened after we spoke. Hope it's not too much of an issue."

"I s'pose not, lucky fer ye."

"Good. When do we leave?"

"She'll be ready shortly."

"Mahogany, huh?" Aldred asked.

"Aye, that's her name," Earl replied with his back to him as he prepared.

"Is it made out of mahogany?"

"No, she ain't."

"Why'd you name it Mahogany then?" Aldred continued.

"I liked it," Earl snapped at him.

"Huh, you were nicer last night, Earl, I must say."

"Yeah, well I was also drunker. Speaking of…" he took another swig. "Well, that's it," he said as he pulled on a recently tied knot. "Let's go. I suggest you remain seated, trip's likely to be a bit choppy. If you feel like you're going to spew, spew over the side, otherwise yer cleaning it."

Sainte and Iris sat down on the deck near the stern of the ship. Earl unfurled the ship's sails and gently pulled away from the dock. The sails whipped around a moment, then caught the wind. Quickly, if not a little staggering, Earl made his way to the wheel. As the ship lurched forward, Aldred went below deck.

"Guess he's not got his sea legs quite yet," Earl muttered. Off they were, the four of them. The sounds of the dock faded away as they made their way out into more open waters. "I'm guessing this trip will take about an hour. Water's are shallow out in this part, which is why they're so choppy. I don't want to be running into no reef so the going'll be slow."

Unsure if he was drunkenly rambling to himself or to them, neither Sainte nor Iris replied.

"So, Iris, what can you tell me about this island? What have you heard?" Sainte asked.

She shrugged before replying, "Honestly, not much. I've only been in Thissaren for about two weeks. All I've heard are just rumors and stories. Apparently something's hidden there, guarded by a beast. Its lair is near the center of the island, on the bank of a small lake. Least that's what they say. Numerous people have been there, some say they were chased by a large animal, others say they saw nothing living. All stories have one thing in common, they don't actually believe anything of value is there."

"That's it, lassie?" Earl interjected. Sainte and Iris looked at him, surprised he could hear what they were saying. Now that he had their attention, Earl drank some more and wiped his mouth on the sleeve of his shirt. "There's a beast, aye. Some have claimed it has ten legs and three mouths, large as a castle. Others say it has no eyes and slithers around, using some kind o' slime to move, like some kind of giant blind slug. I don't know what's true, but I do know something has taken that island as it's home. Back in my younger days I'd sail by the island quite often, and most times than not I would hear some guttural roar coming from there. I's never brave enough to stop and check it out, but I know some people who have. Most returned, some did not. I know not if it is guarding a treasure, or what you'll find there. I don't care, either, as long as I get my coin."

Sainte listened to him and kept a note of what he said but was not going to believe anything until he experienced it for himself. He hoped this island would be where the sword was at, but he had his doubts. It was too easy, too quick.

They had been on their way for about thirty minutes. The waves white capped and the ship rose and dropped with them. Sainte stared forward with Iris by his side. It felt odd being with someone he knew before everything happened. It seemed like a lifetime ago, but it was only a few months back the last time he had been with her, a remnant from his not so long-past life.

"Land 'ho!" Earl shouted, pointing ahead and slightly left. "Starboard and ahead! Or is it port and ahead?" he shook his head, "I can never remember." He took a long drink from his flask, apparently finishing it as he chucked it over the side of his ship.

Sainte looked to where the drunkard pointed, barely catching a glimpse of what looked like a small cloud in the distance. "I suppose that could be counted as land," he said to

Iris. He pulled a vial out from his pockets and put some drops of the liquid within in his eyes, "Saltwater burns."

"I never thought I'd say this, but I'm thankful Earl's taking us to the island and not you. A drunk leading the gimp," She laughed.

"Watch your mouth, or I might take the use of your right arm too," Sainte retorted. Iris looked at him, hurt, mouth agape.

"I can't believe you'd…" she could not finish the sentence. She laughed, and Sainte joined her. Maybe this would not be so bad, being together again. Together they watched as the island floated closer, not saying much else.

Soon Earl left the wheel and dropped the anchor. The island was much closer, about a half mile away. "You'll have to row from here. Get in the rowboat on the side, I'll grab Aldred and bring him up."

"What do you mean 'you'll'? Are you not coming with us?" Iris asked.

"Oh nay, my dear. I'm staying right here on the Mahogany. Ye'll not catch me on that isle. 'Sides, what if something were to happen to me on there, you think you three could figure out a way to sail back? Or would you row?" He laughed, "Ye can't do that if ya wanted, current'd drag you out. Get in the small boat, I'll be right back."

"Guess the rowboat it is," Sainte murmured. The boat was hung from the side of the ship, a system of ropes and pulleys held it up. Sainte climbed in and helped Iris in. Soon Earl came up from below deck pulling a green faced Aldred.

"How you holding up?" Iris asked as the man slowly got on the boat.

"How's it look?"

"Not great if I'm being honest with you."

"Like you just saw your ma and pop grinding groins," Sainte chimed in.

"I'm glad you two are in such great moods," Aldred mumbled. "C'mon, lets get to land. Quicker we're there, quicker I'll feel better."

"Ya'll ready?" Earl asked. Without waiting for all their replies, he yanked loose a knot and the boat dropped about ten feet into the water.

All three occupants yelled at him the whole way down and abruptly cut short as it crashed into the water. Slowly, Earl poked his head over the side of his ship and looked down.

"We're alright, if you're wondering," Iris called up. Without warning Aldred clambered to the side and heaved.

"Guess I'm rowing," Sainte said. The waves actually helped to bring them in closer to the island. Before long the bottom of the boat was scraping against the rocky black sand. The island was circled by cliffs with small beaches of black sand between. Sainte jumped out of the boat, grabbed it, and pulled it further onto the beach splashing through ankle deep water. The beach itself was small, about twenty feet wide with ragged cliffside on each side. In front of him the cliffs cracked in two, creating a narrow valley they could walk through in single file.

"Alright, anyone have any idea where to start looking?" Sainte asked them as they got out.

"The lake in the center. People have said that there's a cave-" Iris was cut off as a bellow reverberated through the crevice in front of them. "Only one way to go. I say let's go look for this cave, and for whatever made that sound." The three of them tightened up their pack straps, made sure their weapons were ready and in reach, then set off into the crevice. Sainte led the way, feet crunching on the sand.

The steep rocky walls around them began to descend and round out, turning into small hills. Soon the trio stepped from the crevice and the lake was in front of them. The mirror-like surface sat in the bottom of a crater. Wind whipped in from the multiple crevices but did not stir the water. Small trees poked through cracks in the rocky terrain, barely holding on by the roots. Green moss covered the rocks, giving the otherwise barren landscape a look teaming with life. They could see across the lake, it seemed to be as wide as it was long forming an almost perfect circle.

"You guys see anything?" Aldred asked.

"Not yet. Let's walk around. I don't want to spend all day here if I can help it," Sainte said. He took the lead and started off to the right. He looked behind him to see Iris' back to him, struggling with something. "What're you doing?"

"Hold on… There," she stepped aside revealing a stack of stones, "so we know this is where we came in at."

"Smart," Aldred said.

"Come on," Sainte began again. The island was quiet, other than the slight howl of wind, but that was no surprise. There was not much reason for any birds to come here, and there were not many animals that could make the swim here. There was however life in the lake. Occasionally a fish would break the surface of the water, causing ripples to spread out and quickly disappear.

The only sound that broke the air was the occasional growl that seemed to crawl out from the crags of rocks. It was near impossible to pinpoint the exact location of it. It was near midday when they found a cave. It was nestled a short distance away from the lake hidden behind some large rocks. The ground leading into the cave was scraped clear of moss, so something came and went enough times to stop anything from growing there. Fish bones were scattered around the entrance, causing them to smell the cave before they found it.

"Anyone have a torch?" Sainte asked peering into the cave.

"I do," Aldred pulled it out from his pack, lit it up, and held it out to Sainte who grabbed it, then drew his sword.

"Didn't think we'd actually have one, thanks. Right, no time to waste," he stepped forward into the cave with the others in tow. There was not much to see in the cave except for more fish bones of varying sizes, some surprisingly large. The ceiling was just tall enough for them to walk upright. The cave walls had scratches in them and dripped with water. They did not get more than twenty steps into the cave before a hissing sound reached their ears from ahead. Movement could be heard further in front of them, but nothing reached the firelight yet. It sounded like something was sliding against the rocks. Sainte stopped and held the torch up higher when a pair of eyes glowed at them from ahead.

A scaled grey snout entered the light, followed by a bony head with horns lining the sides of it like a crown. The head itself was about three feet long, Sainte could only guess that length of the entire thing was close to twenty feet. The horns, the longest being about eight inches, came together near the back of the head and followed the spine to the tail. The reptile hissed again, showing short and numerous sharp teeth. A clawed foot crept forward, and Sainte noticed the feet were webbed.

Sainte took a few steps back and bumped into someone. "Back up," he snapped. Never had he come face to face with a giant lizard. "Quick, but slow. Don't startle it," he stayed facing the creature, always holding the torch up. He held his sword with the tip pointed at the ground but was ready to attack should the need arise. The three of them crept backwards, and the giant lizard kept pace. Light from the mouth of the cave revealed the rest of the creature's body, showing that it was about the length that Sainte had guessed. Its tail seemed to flare out on the top rather than come to point, almost resembling a fin.

Once all three were out and the creature still slowly following them, Iris asked, "What do we do?"

"Run?" Aldred offered. "I don't know how to fight this thing."

Sainte's mind raced, but he could not think of any other option. "I suppose, take the same path back as we took here. Ready?"

"Aye," Iris and Aldred replied in almost unison.

"Go," as Sainte shouted he threw the torch at the giant lizard, turned, and ran following Aldred and Iris. As he ran, he was careful about his foot placement on the slick, moss covered rocks. He did not wish to trip, and if he did, he did not want to accidentally stab himself. The lizard could be heard behind him, scales sliding over rocks, clawed feet scrambling for a foot hold on the sharp ground. It was slower than he realized as he looked back and saw they were gaining ground on it.

It took everything in him to not fall from the mossy rocks. His feet slipped with almost every step; his sword added another layer of difficulty to running but he dared not put it away. He was just beginning to wonder if they had run past their rock stack when he saw Iris dart into a crevice. Aldred was next and Sainte was right behind him. Together they caught their breath and looked behind them. Soon the scaled head appeared and pushed into the small ravine, but it was not large enough to fit its shoulders in. The giant reptile clawed at the rocky sides that blocked it from its prey. They were showered with spittle that flew from its open maws and small rocks tumbled down onto them. Once it realized that it would not be able to reach them, it stopped its frantic clawing and instead watched them with a curious eye.

"Well, what do we do now?" Aldred asked.

"We go back to the ship. The sword is not here," Sainte said. "Wasted trip."

"How do you know that?"

"Because it's not guarded by a giant lizard, it's guarded by a demon. I don't think this creature would remain here if there was a demon inhabiting this rock that you all call an island. From the looks of all the bones, this creature has been here for a while."

"A demon? You expect me to believe that a demon is guarding a sword? Would've been nice to know that before I came with you, wouldn't you say Iris?" Aldred looked at her and it seemed she did not even hear him, "Iris?"

"Greldan, greldan dracogins," she muttered to herself staring into the large eye of the reptile. "They haven't been seen in, I don't know, a hundred years. They were all thought to have died out," she gazed at the reptile that gazed at them hungrily and still tried to pry itself into the ravine. "It's beautiful. How did it get here?"

"We'll talk about it later, now's not the time. Let's go," Sainte said as he pushed Aldred and Iris forward towards the black sand beach their rowboat was at. "Aldred, keep moving," he said. He took one last look back at the greldan and locked eyes. With one lust huff the greldan withdrew its head and lumbered back to where it came from. It did not take them long to get back to the rowboat. Aldred climbed in and helped Iris. Sainte pushed the boat back into the water then hopped in himself.

"Damn waste of time," he muttered to himself. Iris seemed to still be enthralled by the greldan that attacked them. Sainte rowed back to the ship that bobbed on the water in the distance. They sat in silence, only the sound of the waves sloshing against the boat could be heard.

"Hey, what's that?" Aldred said pointing to the left of the small boat. Ripples in the shape of a 'V' were heading towards the boat. As they watched it get closer a grey snout broke the surface of the water and snorted, blowing out a mist of water from each nostril. It was followed by the eyes of the greldan. The swish of its tail sprayed water behind it as it propelled itself towards the boat and rammed it.

"Shit," Sainte said as he grabbed the sides of the boat to steady himself. The walls of the boat got dangerously close to sinking under the water but rocked itself back steady. "Get your fucking weapons out," he said incredulously as neither Iris nor Aldred did anything. He drew his own sword and his eyes darted around the waters looking for any sign of the approaching creature. Seeing none and noticing that Iris and Aldred were holding their swords, he dropped his own and resumed rowing. "If you see that thing attack it, we're done if we get in the water," Sainte rowed as hard as he could, and they began to gain some speed.

"Here it comes," Iris shouted alerting Aldred. Together they held their swords like spears. As the greldan approached for another ram they began thrusting their swords into the water. Apparently, they had hit it because the boat did not rock nearly as bad the first time and a shade of red clouded the water for a few seconds before dissipating.

"Keep it up," Sainte encouraged between breaths. Maintaining the rowing speed was increasingly difficult, sweat dripped into his eyes and seared mercilessly without him able to blink it away or add his drops. He gritted his teeth and continued to row despite his burning muscles. He looked behind him to see how far the ship was and put it at about fifty yards. He hoped Earl saw them coming and was ready for them. "Earl you bastard, better not be blacked out. Better be sober enough to pull us up."

The boat rocked hard, this time water lurched into the side, but not enough to sink it. How much more damage could this boat take before the greldan broke through the bottom or managed to tip it entirely? No one wanted to find out. Sainte spotted the greldan a distance away, turning around. The top of the head was above water, as well as the spines along its back. The tail was beneath, but the water above it churned with each powerful swish. There were noticeable cuts on its face, but it did not seem to care. It was hungry, it was resolute.

Iris and Aldred saw it coming back as well and readied themselves. When it got within distance they stabbed the water, looking ridiculous, and then seconds later there was a loud crack.

"Shit," Iris said, "it cracked the bottom. We're leaking. Hurry up Sainte."

"I am," Sainte said through gritted teeth.

"Earl!" Aldred shouted through cupped hands, "Earl, we're coming back. Toss the ladder!" A few seconds went by then, "I think I see him. Yeah, there he is. Toss the ladder!" he yelled again. "There we go, it's down. Now we just have to get there."

Sainte continued to row as hard as he could, he kept going until he hit the ship. Finally, they made it.

Aldred grabbed the rope ladder and began to climb up, sword already sheathed. Iris sheathed her sword with a worried look.

"I don't know if I can do that," she said as she looked at her arm.

"Yes you can, you have to. Go, now. Hurry up," Sainte urged her.

She wrapped her good arm around the rope between two rungs and then stepped on. She pulled herself up, sliding her hand up the rope and wrapped it on the rung above. Sainte watched her slow ascent with growing concern. Where was the greldan?

The answer came almost as soon as he had the thought. The giant lizard's head burst through the floor of the small boat, nearly knocking Sainte overboard. The creature thrashed about, throwing him to the floor. Desperately Sainte grabbed a hold of the bottom of the rope ladder, barely able to pull himself up and put his feet on the bottom rung, merely inches away from the snapping maw of the lizard. Iris' feet were on the rung above his hands. He meant to tell Iris to hurry up, but all the came out was a grunt as he held himself just above the thrashing creature.

The rowboat began to get ripped apart from the creature, unable to handle the assault any longer. Sainte pulled himself as high as he could, face nearly in Iris' ass.

"If you could hurry up, that'd be great," he called up to her. Aldred was already on the ship, leaning over the edge reaching down towards Iris. One more rung and she was high enough to grasp his hand and be pulled over. Sainte clambered up as quickly as his aching muscles allowed, helping hands grabbed him and pulled him onto the safety of the ship.

He was breathing heavily as he flopped to his back on the floor, relieved to be out of that tiny boat.

"I never had a reason to hate the sea, I do now. Earl, please take us back to Thissaren. I'm tired," Iris and Aldred sat down next to him, backs against the parapet, breathing quickly and deep.

"Bossy lot, ya'll are, ain't ye?" Earl replied, clearly unfazed by the events that just transpired. "Sank me boat, ye did…" he walked away from them mumbling under his breath. Once he was at the wheel and unfurled the sails, he called out to them, "Ye'll pay for that rowboat."

"You'll get your damned gold when we get back to port in one piece," Aldred replied. Sainte slowly sat himself up and leaned against the parapet with the other two. "Think he forgot I was supposed to pay him before, maybe I'll get away with only paying him half of what he demanded."

"What next, Sainte?" Iris asked, not caring about Earl's payment.

"I'll go to the mountains of Deshiere."

"Makes sense," Aldred said.

Sainte glanced at him, "What does?"

"Oh, that it's so far away. Makes sense that it'd be halfway across the land instead of in the next town over," he explained.

"I'm going with you, Sainte. I don't want to be split up before, we work better together," Iris said. Sainte offered no argument.

"So will I," Aldred said.

"I don't think-" Sainte began.

"Won't hear it. I went through this with you. I'm interested to see how this ends. Who knows, you might be needing someone with coin along the way. I have plenty of that."

Sainte was too tired to argue. For now, he did not care. He could feel the weariness wafting over him, before he let it overtake him, he put some drops in his eyes, then leaned back and relaxed. The rocking of the ship put him into not a sleep, but the closest he had been to it in a long time.

SEVEN

Making his way to the top of the wall Kial thought about how to convince Peng to help him find out more about Flotier's attack. On one hand he thought Peng would be more than willing to help him once he found out he had been threatened, but what if that still was not enough? He would have to bring up Ivan and their whole band who went out to look for answers. Finding out why it happened is what they would want them to do.

As he reached the top of the stairwell the early rays of the rising sun warmed his face. He could hear Peng speaking to the guards they were relieving already. Kial followed the voice and found them at a corner leaning against the parapet. Peng saw him and stood up straight.

"Kial, about time you showed up. These fellows had a long night and are eager to get some breakfast," he joked with a smile.

"By my calculations they still have about fifteen minutes left. I can come back later and you can say that again, you'd be right then."

"Told you he wouldn't like being screwed with this early. We appreciate you coming now, Kial. Peng here don't know how to keep his mouth shut," one of the guards said, Kial recalled his name being Ravrick.

"It's all good. I'm not going anywhere else. You two go on, Peng and I are good. Anything to pass on?"

"Nay, quiet night. Nothing of note that we saw," Ravrick said.

"Right, you two go on and get something to eat. See you later," Kial told them. They nodded and left, already arguing about where to grab breakfast. "How was your night?" Kial asked now turned to Peng.

"It was fine, slept good. Wish I could've slept in a little later, but alas here I am. What about you?"

"I slept fine," Kial waved away the question, "but I have been up to some digging around. I was asking some people about the butcher, Flotier."

"Of course."

"I wasn't getting much at first but get this. After I left the last lady I spoke too I was dragged into an alley and threatened by someone. He said if I don't stop asking questions, he'd make me. Someone doesn't like what I'm doing."

"Well, probably leave well enough alone, then. It doesn't hardly matter now."

"Aye, it does. Obviously, it does. If it didn't matter I wouldn't have been threatened. It matters to someone. Help me, Peng. Something isn't right, and I want to find out. I don't want to do this alone, but if you won't help me, I'm not going to stop. I've got a feeling that this is important, questions need answers."

Peng sighed, "You're really starting our shift out with this? All I wanted was a nice, easy day. No problems, a few jokes, and end it at a tavern with a nice ale. Now you're asking me to play inquisitor on our off time." He took a few moments to sort out his answer, "Fine, I'll help you. But only because you were threatened. No one threatens my friends and gets away with it."

"Thank you, Peng. I knew you were curious too, you're just too lazy to do anything about it. All you needed was a little push."

"Don't push me too much, I might change my mind. So what's first then?"

"I was planning on going to the butchers, where Flotier worked, after our shift. Haven't been there yet, and I think it would be good to stop by and ask a few questions," Kial explained.

Peng let out a long sigh, "Sounds good to me, let's just grab an ale afterwards at least?"

"I think I can do that," Kial said.

The rest of their shift went by uneventfully, Peng and Kial passed their watch on to their relief and descended from the wall. It was nice to hear the sounds of life floating through the city once again. Everyone they knew were in high spirits, basking in the sunlight and no longer fearing that the sun would not rise anymore. The evening banter was full of laughs and tavern music and drunken yells were already starting before the sun fully set.

"C'mon Peng, we have to get to the shop before it closes," Kial called back to his lagging partner. The going was pretty quick as the streets were beginning to thin out as the evening crept on. It did not take them long to get to the shop. The door was still propped open with an old brick, and there were flickering lanterns lit inside.

They walked inside to see a darkly stained counter, hooks lining the wall, and cleavers stuck in the back of the counter waiting for use. No meat was hung up, presumably put in a cooler for the next day of sales.

"Hello? Anyone here? Door was open," Kial called out. There was some rummaging around that was heard in the back, then a head full of hair poked out from behind a corner.

"Oh, hello. Didn't expect anyone else, sorry. I put all the meat up already, if you want something you'll have to come back tomorrow. You can tell me what you want now and I'll set it aside for you in the morning," the butcher said. He walked around from the corner to reveal a lanky body. He looked to be in his late teens.

"Not here for meat, though I'm sure it's good. We're here because we have some questions about your former master, Flotier," the young butcher's adams apple was visibly moved as he gulped at the name. "What was your name?" Kial asked.

"Er, Bruntishian Leancheshiner. My friends call me, uh, Brutey for short."

"Brutey, fitting," Peng smiled. Kial glanced at him, hoping he understood that his eyes said to keep this official.

"Right, Brutey, my name's Kial, and my friend here is Peng. Would you be willing to sit with us for a bit? Answer some of our questions?"

"Sure, I suppose so. I have some chairs in the back if you like?"

"Right here's fine," Kial said looking around at the few chairs that were set out for waiting customers. He sat down on one and motioned for Brutey and Peng to join him. Brutey's eyes darted around and he licked his lips often. "What's wrong? You seem nervous."

"Aye," he affirmed, "you're here to ask about Flotier. Any talk of him makes me nervous. I don't want people to think that just because I was his apprentice that I would do anything that he did. I just want to make a living doing what I love, and that's chopping good meat to sell to good people," Flotier ended that rant slightly out of breath, not realizing he spoke without taking a break.

"No need to worry, we have no reason to suspect anything about you. We just want to try to find out why Flotier killed all those people, and how. We just want to figure that out to try to prevent anyone else from doing the same thing. Now, how long did you know Flotier?" Kial asked. It did not seem like Peng had any questions, and he was not sure he wanted Peng to talk all that much.

"I knew him about five years. Became his apprentice when I was twelve, I did. My parents knew him because he's where they got their meat their whole lives and suggested I work with him," the teenager explained.

"Did he ever lose his temper with you, or anyone else?"

"Nay, never. Even when I made bad cuts or forgot to put meat up and spoiled it he'd make me do extra clean up or some such, but he never laid a hand on me, barely ever raised his voice."

"Do you know if he perhaps liked ale a little too much?"

"No more than you or I. I know he didn't like working with the headache, so he rarely drank enough to get fuddled. At least, that's what he told me. I had no reason to not believe him."

Kial let out a sigh, "What I'm trying to get at, Brutey, is there anything you know about him that might explain it? Did he meet with anyone in secret, did he have any herbs or spices that messed with the head, did he do anything at all, ever, that you thought was strange? Anything at all?"

Brutey sat in thoughtful silence. Kial could tell the kid was trying to think about something, and he appreciated him that much more for trying. He was just beginning to think that this might have been another loose end when he spoke up.

"There is one thing, though it could be nothing…"

"What is it?"

"There was a guy that would come in, at least once a week but I remember once he came in about five times. He never bought any meat, just came in and always spoke to Flotier, alone.

114

I only ever said a few words to the man. First I figured he was a supplier, a cow farmer or some such, but he never brought anything either. Maybe they were just friends, I dunno," he shrugged.

"What was this man's name, Brutey? This could be important, try to remember," Kial urged. Peng sat quietly listening to the two speak.

"I think it was Aron… Eringir… Eringar. That's it, Eringar. I never caught a last name, never thought to ask."

"Peng, remember that name. I'll try to, but my memory's not as good as it used to be."

"Course, that's why I'm here isn't it?" he replied snidely.

"Do you know anything about this man? Or perhaps was there anyone else that paid similar visits without buying anything?"

"I'm sorry, that's all I know about him. He has brown hair, looks to be a bit younger than you. If there was anyone else that came in often as he did without looking for meat I didn't notice them, sorry."

"It's alright. Thank you, Brutey. I think you helped us out more than you realize. I don't think I have any more questions right now. If I think of some more, you'll see me again, hope that's alright?" Kial asked the boy. To be honest, he could not think of any more questions because he did not think he would get many answered.

"That's fine, I guess."

"Peng, you have anything for him?" Kial asked.

"Nah, I think you asked everything I would've. Thanks for the help, Brutey." With that the two men stood up, gave a slight wave goodbye to Brutey, then left the store. The sun had set by now and the streets were largely deserted and dark. Every fifty paces or so a torch was lit and hanging from a sconce in building walls, but that was the only light around. Voices from various taverns could be heard being carried throughout the allies, but that was the only noise around.

"So, Eringar huh?" Peng said.

"How do you find a man, easily and quickly, in this town?"

Peng shrugged, "I suppose just ask around. Eventually you'll find someone that knows him. Don't think it's a very common name."

"I guess, let's think on it. For now, I'm going to go home, see Franceska and Marianne, and then bed. The sun is set and I'm getting tired. No point in asking anyone now, they're probably all too drunk to give us any kind of sensible answer," before he began to head home, Kial paused. "I wonder when the last time he saw him was?"

Peng stopped walking as well, "You wanna go back? I'm sure we could catch him before he left."

"Shit, I suppose so," Kial turned around and walked back to the butcher's shop just beyond the corner. "You gonna come with?"

"Why not? I'm already here," Peng replied as he followed him back. They rounded the corner and the door was still propped open. Faint lantern light flickered through the windows. The two men walked in and interrupted a very unfortunate scene.

A man was standing over Brutey, bloodied hands seemingly just let go of a butcher's knife sticking from the boy's chest.

"The fuck-" Kial said completely taken by surprise at the sight.

Peng, however, was the first to react. He rushed the man, the murderer, and tackled him around the waist. He did not go down, however. The man kneed Peng with all his might, and in that one motion all of Peng's breath was crushed out by his ribs. His grip loosened around the man and he was thrown off with a grunt.

Kial finally snapped out of his surprise but was too late. The man shoved past Kial, tripping him to the ground as well. Peng was already up and followed the man out of the shop. Kial picked himself up and ran over to Brutey to try to save him, but he could see that he was already dead.

"Fuck," he rubbed his face and dropped down on a chair. Peng came back a few minutes later.

"Lost him. Bastard's fast, trailed him a bit, but turned a corner and he was gone. How's he?" he motioned to the body, but he already knew the answer.

"Dead. How long were we gone? Not even five minutes?"

"Don't matter now. You think that was Eringar?"

"I dunno. Maybe. Who else could it have been? Brutey seemed a good lad, didn't seem like someone who would get mixed in with trouble, not like this. Could've just been a good old-fashioned robbery, just happen to happen right after we left. Either way, did you get a good look at him?"

"Aye, I'd be able to pick him out of a crowd. Guess we should go alert the guards, get them here and get an inquisitor or constable out here. You want me to go?"

"Aye, I'll stay here with him. Make sure nothing else happens."

"Alright… Nothing we could've done, Kial. I'll be back in a bit," Peng said. With one last look at his troubled friend he left to go tell the guards of the murder.

Now alone, Kial sagged his head into his hands. He was warned and now someone was dead. If this was meant to deter him, however, it had the opposite effect. Finding this Eringar was now the foremost goal that he had. It was obvious he was a danger and needed to be stopped, and Kial would see to it that he was.

A rigorous knocking woke Jasmine from her deep sleep. She groggily wrapped herself modestly in her nearby robe and stumbled to the front door. Whoever was at her door still had not stopped knocking.

She threw the door open, "What?" A bloodied Eringar pushed himself past her. "What are you doing? What happened?"

"I did what I had to," was all he said.

Her blood ran cold as she thought of the worst-case scenario, "Did you kill Kial? Peng? Both of them? What did you do, Eringar?"

He shook his head, "No… It was Flotier's apprentice, Brutey or something. They were talking to him, asking him questions. He told them about me, told them my name. He knew too much and said too much, so I did what I had to do. I cut him off, he can't tell them anything else." He explained quickly, breathlessly.

"Shite, Eringar. You stupid… ugh!" Jasmine stared at him incredulously. "How could you be so stupid? Wait… What happened? Why did you run here? Why do you seem so anxious?"

"They saw me. They came back, and they saw me right after I did it. They know my name and now my face."

"Idiot… You have to get out of here, out of Munich. Go back to the Council." He stared at her blankly. "Now! Before I kill you myself," she crossed her arms, looked up, and closed her eyes in thought.

"I just have to grab some things…"

"No, you do not. No doubt they are already on their way to tell the guards, they will be guarding all the entrances even more than they have been once they know there's been a murder. You leave right now," she left no room for argument. "I never should have trusted you with anything. Too foolish, don't think things through," she paused and looked at him. "Leave! Are you deaf?" she snapped. Eringar, without another word, spun to leave. "Wait," she called out. "Clean yourself up," Jasmine through a towel at him. "Toss it in an alley, can't have you walking around bloodied up."

Eringar left as he wiped his hands on the towel, head bowed in embarrassment. Jasmine had a tone that belittled you and cut to the core.

Knowing that she was not going to get anymore sleep tonight, Jasmine sat down at her table, grabbed a decanter of wine, and poured herself a tall glass. She would spend the rest of the night thinking of how to clear up Eringar's gigantic mistake. After taking a rather long sip, the tired White Wyvern swallowed the mouthful of fruity liquid and sighed.

"What exactly were you two doing at the butcher shop last night?" Ser Matrigard, the Major of the town guard, asked Kial and Peng. They had been summoned by him the next morning to give him a detailed account of how they happened to be the first two men to discover a recently murdered body. His office was rather dull, one empty desk sat just in front of a small window, and Scr Matrigard himself sat in a small chair. It would have been a comical sight had the circumstances been different.

"We were looking into Flotier, seeing if there was anything about that instance that had been missed. After speaking to Brutey-" Kial began.

"Brutey?" Ser Matrigard interrupted.

"The lad that was killed," Kial explained. He continued once the Major nodded, "After speaking to him, we have reason to believe that Flotier may have accomplices. There was a man that goes by Eringar who visited him often, but never bought any meat. Not once."

"And?" the Major asked. "He could have been anyone. A friend. Family. A family friend. I'm sure Flotier had friends before he lost his mind. The case was closed, Kial and Peng. What you two were, are, doing is just digging up a dead animal. It's dead. End of story."

"What about the man that murdered him? We saw him, we can recognize him. What's going to happen to him?" Peng said this time.

"We are going to look for him, of course. And if he is found he will most likely be set to the executioner's block, or perhaps the gallows."

"Don't you think it odd that Brutey was killed right after we spoke to him? Do you not think that is a coincidence? Wouldn't that make you think he was being watched?"

Ser Matrigard was clearly getting tired of this conversation, "For all we know you two murdered the boy!"

Peng and Kial were taken aback at his outburst. They stared back at him speechless.

Ser Matrigard sighed, "All I'm saying is the whole thing could be a coincidence. You two were the last to see him alive, aye, but I don't actually believe you killed him. I do believe that a street mongrel saw that the store was still open, he most likely had some liquid courage and decided it would be an easy rob. Maybe Brutey fought back and the mongrel stabbed him, then you two walked in. I don't know. I won't know, and neither will anyone, until this man is captured. He's probably long gone now, if he had any wits about him. Now, you two, I'm ordering you to stop this little side job of yours. Flotier is dead, and so is anything he was involved in. Get back to your duties and no more, but now your duties will be night shift only, until I decide otherwise, as punishment. You're lucky I'm not adding extra shifts to you, I won't be so lenient next time. Now get out of my office."

Peng and Kial saluted without another word, then left the Major. Once the door was shut Peng said, "I know I didn't want to do any of this originally, but you're not actually going to stop, are you?"

"Course not. The Major's more of a fool than I thought if he really thinks nothing more was behind Flotier's actions.

Something not right was going on, and still is. Someone has to find out, someone has to stop it."

Peng nodded in agreement, not having to say anything to confirm that Kial would have his continued support. As they walked out of the Major's quarters and back into the streets of Munich, Jasmine came up to them.

"Hey, heard what happened to you guys last night. Are you ok? Are you hurt?" she asked.

"We're fine," Kial said, "can't be said of Brutey."

"What happened?"

For the second time that morning Peng and Kial explained what they had been up to, and why they had been up to it.

"I feel like it's sort of our fault he got killed," Peng said at the end of their story.

"No, it's not your fault. You didn't kill him, you didn't want him to be killed. The fault lies solely with who killed him. I hope he's able to be caught and pay for what he did… Do you two really think Flotier had some help though?"

"I don't know about help, not with what he did, but there's definitely more to the story than we know. I think it'd be good to find out the entire story, to try to prevent anyone from trying to do what he failed to. How did he do what he did? Why are there not more people questioning it?" Kial said.

"I thought it was said that it had something to do with the Dark Days? That's what the examiner said, he couldn't find anything else," Jasmine said.

"That's it, the examiner," Kial said. "Why didn't I think of him before? He should be the next person we speak to, Peng. But not now, next week probably. We should lay low for a bit, let things settle. Then, maybe we can get some more out of the examiner."

Peng nodded in agreement.

"Do you think that's a good idea? Maybe just drop it. Whatever you're doing has the potential to hurt people, obviously. What happened last night wasn't your fault, but maybe some things are better left not knowing," Jasmine tried to persuade them.

"No, if the truth is bad enough to kill over, it's a truth that must be found," Peng said, supporting his friend.

"Thanks for stopping by, Jasmine, and thanks for giving us something to look into. I'm going to go to home and sleep now, though. We've had a long night and we're bound to have another one now with night shifts. I'll see you then, Peng. Later Jasmine," Kial said abruptly and with a short wave he left.

"Aye, I'm going as well, Jasmine. Take it easy, talk to you later," Peng left to go try to sleep through what little time he had left before shift.

Jasmine now stood alone next to the Major's quarters, berating herself for even mentioning the examiner. What could she do? What could she possibly do without ruining her cover and at the same time convince the two thick headed men to stop looking into Flotier?

If they found the truth, that would potentially ruin all of her careful laid plans, and essentially seal the deaths of every person in Crearia.

EIGHT

Once Iris, Sainte, Aldred, and Earl arrived safely back in Thissaren, they all agreed to take a few days to rest and gather supplies they deemed were necessary for their trip to the mountains.

Iris' first focus was quitting her job, she had not worked there very long, but the girls had grown to like her and looked up to her. She was sorry for leaving them, but there were plenty of other men that were willing to throw a few disorderly drunks out for a bit of coin. Her second plan was to get a weapon made for her. She had heard of something before, and with a few tweaks, she had the plans laid out for it. All she had to do was bring it to the local blacksmith and pay the man to make it.

Aldred had all the supplies he wanted within two days. He was a particular man and wanted nothing but the best, and he had the coin to back it. Luckily for him they were in Thissaren, there were goods from all over the place being sold and trafficked through the town. He found everything he wanted to his specifications. A good, solid long sword and shield to go with it, a well stitched pack, and a brand-new pair of leather boots. He had most of everything else already.

Sainte just took this time to relax before the long journey. He figured he made it to Thissaren with almost nothing, he would continue on like it. Although he did take some time to buy a new canteen, some dried meats, and a map of Crearia. During his down time, he studied the map and figured out the best route to the Deshiere Mountains. The straightest way was to cut through the Marshes, but he did not like that idea. The Marshes were swamp land, waters poisoned by the ground. The animals in that land, the few that survived in it, became infected with that poison and were therefore no good to eat and all had venomous bites. On the other hand, to go around the Marshes would easily add forty miles to their journey. This would have to be discussed with Iris and Aldred.

The second night back they met at the tavern. Sainte walked into the ale room from upstairs. He saw that Aldred and Iris were already seated at a table and joined them.

"Evening Sainte, you ready for tomorrow?" Aldred asked.

"Ready as I'll ever be. How about you two?"

"Oh yeah, I'm finished here at Barmaids and Booze and I have my bags packed and loaded up on Dawn. I've also got a surprise for you tomorrow. Well, not for you, it's mine, but I'm excited to show it off. I'd say we're ready for tomorrow morning," Iris said.

"I'm good too, no horse for me, but my bag is packed. Not sure if my feet are ready, but they're going to have to be. Got some new boots to help them out," Aldred said.

"Good, good. I'm all packed and ready to. So, I was thinking about the best way to the mountains," he pulled out his map and laid it open on the table. "The quickest route is, obviously, as the crow flies. A straight shot is about a hundred-twenty miles, but that will bring us straight through the Marshes," he pointed at the marked spot. "If we go around the Marshes that'll bump our journey up to about two hundred miles and add, I don't know, probably about a week to our trip. I was wondering what you two think would be best?"

"I vote go around. The Marshes are dangerous, poisonous, filled with animals that we can't eat, not to mention the venomous bite that all animals have there, and water we can't drink. Too risky. I say we skirt around it, but limit the times we rest," Iris suggested.

Aldred shook his head, "I think we should go straight through. If you need to find this weapon as quick as possible, then we shouldn't add any unnecessary length to our journey. People go into the Marshes all the time and are fine. Aye, the animals are dangerous there, but they are just animals at the end of the day. As long as we leave them alone, they'll leave us alone. As long as we prep before going right in, we will be fine. I'll even stock us all up on supplies before we go in, so we have plenty of drinkable water and eatable foods, as long as we stop at a post before entering."

Sainte thought about what each of them said, "I think we should go through as well... I don't like it, and if I wasn't in a hurry to try to find this sword, I wouldn't suggest it at all, but," Sainte shrugged. "It is how it is. I have to go with Aldred here, Iris. I don't think I can afford to waste any time. Especially if he's offering to stock us back up."

Aldred slapped him on the back, "Good man. I think it'll be for the best. We just have to be cautious, but that doesn't seem like it's too hard for you all to do."

"For what it's worth, I still think we should go around, but if you two are set on pushing through I won't argue it any further," Iris said. "Your votes outnumber mine."

"Thanks, Iris," Sainte said. There was a lull in the conversation as they all focused on eating their meals they ordered and drinking their ales. "How did they take you leaving your job here?"

Iris looked up correctly assuming he was asking her, "Oh, alright enough. The turnaround on my position is pretty quick, so they weren't very surprised. A few girls were a little upset, they liked having a woman stand up for them for once. I think they looked up to me, saw that they didn't necessarily have to be tavern wenches their entire lives. I doubt any of them will do anything about it though, have to admit it is easy money. I'm sure they already have a replacement for me, I was no big loss."

"Well, you may not be a loss for them, but you're sure a gain for us," Aldred said wholeheartedly. "I'm excited for this little journey, learn more about each other and myself."

Sainte was still not sure what he thought of Aldred, but if nothing else could be said of him he sure was eager. The longer he stayed around him, the more felt familiar, he could not quite place it. "Hey, Aldred, I know we've known each other for just a few days now, but have we ever met before? Maybe you've been down to Guardstin before?"

Aldred looked at Sainte, almost seemed surprised, "Er, I've been there once. Didn't stay long. Didn't really feel welcome there, I don't think anyone I spoke to liked me for some reason. Only stayed one night, all I needed to stay anyway. I don't remember you; I feel like I would had I met you. Why do you ask?"

"I just, I think you remind me of someone, but I can't quite place it. Doesn't matter, sorry you didn't feel welcome there. Guardstin was quite a rugged town, to say the least, but it had a certain allure to it."

"Aye, it was, it did. Full of the Blades. White Wyverns watch them," Iris toasted in respect. She held up her mug of ale. Sainte bumped his up against hers in agreement.

"Oh, aye," Aldred hastily, almost reluctantly, joined them before they all took a swig. The tavern was beginning to come alive with drunken sailors and traders. A wench stopped by their table, chest glistened and brown hair stuck to her forehead with sweat. Her face was flushed from running to each of her tables, but that did not stop her from giving them her best smile.

"Anything else for you lads and lass… Iris," she corrected as she saw who sat at the table.

"It's alright, Gweniver," Iris said. "I think I'm done for the night, don't know about these two."

"Aye," Aldred and Sainte said in unison.

"Let me get this," Aldred said, "No problem. I'll pay the tab. I'll see you two in the morning, 'bout an hour before sunrise." He stood up and followed Gweniver to the bar to take care of the payment.

Sainte and Iris stood up and walked together to the second floor, their rooms being next to each other on the same side of the hall. Outside they stopped to talk.

"What do you think of Aldred?" Sainte asked.

"I was about to ask you the same thing. He seems nice enough, but I can't get a good read on him. He hasn't done anything to make me think poorly of him. He just seems like a good spirited, if naive, rich boy. Do you think it's a good idea to bring him with us?"

Sainte shrugged, "I don't know. If he's offering to pay for everything, I think I could suffer his company. Don't think he'll be much good in a fight, though."

"Don't know how good I'll be in a fight, a real one that is," Iris said nodding towards her limp arm in a sling. "Hopefully with what I had made that'll change."

"What'd you have made?"

"I'll show it off tomorrow. I think it'll be hard to miss."

"Either way, I'd wager you'd be better than him," they laughed shortly together. "I think he's a good head, but that's it.

I'm fine with him coming, long as he stays not getting under my skin. We should go, before he comes and hears us talking about him. I'll see you in the morning, Iris. For what it's worth, I am glad you're coming with me."

"Good night, Sainte," was all she could think to say. She did not know how else to respond to that.

Sainte was the first to wake up, apparently, as he sat down at an empty table in the morning. He had his sword strapped to his side, his cloak on, and his pack slung. The tavern was quiet, but it was beginning to stir. Many tables had men and women still slumped over them, but a few were groggily sitting up. Fewer still were picking their way out the door to their ships to begin the day's work.

Soon Aldred came down and sat down with him with only a slight nod as greeting. It was not long before Iris came down as well, three packs on her back barely holding on. She was noticeably without a sword, even though she had one when they went to the island. The two men stood up and met Iris halfway to the door.

"Need any help?" Sainte asked once outside.

"Nay, I'll be fine. We have to go to the stables to get Dawn, I'll be putting this all on her."

"Oh right, almost forgot about our equestrian," Aldred said. Iris and Sainte shared a look at his odd choice of words but said nothing. It was not a long walk, and thankfully Iris had told the stable hand the day before to expect them, so Dawn was brought out as soon as she arrived.

"Thank you," Iris told the boy. She gave him some coin as a tip and then grabbed the reins of her horse. She tied the bags onto the saddle, tugged on them for good measure, and nodded in affirmation of the good knots. "Alright boys, I think we're about ready. Just one more thing."

Aldred and Sainte watcher her rummage around one of her packs and pull out odds and ends, equipment made from mostly wood and some metal. Iris methodically attached the pieces to herself. It was almost like armor, but there was a wooden arm that folded up tight across her chest and could extend. Then, she attached a boxy looking crossbow to the end of the arm. Without saying a word, she showed off her weapon. With her right hand she pulled the crossbow out from her chest, the wooden arm extended out with it and locked in position, effectively holding the crossbow for her. She let out a triumphant laugh and looked at Sainte.

"What is that?" Sainte asked, eyeing the contraption.

"I made it, sort of. I figured I'd need a weapon of some sorts, and I was never great with sword when I had two arms, so I figured I'd ditch it. I made this up, it holds the crossbow out in front of me. The crossbow itself is a repeating crossbow, this box on top holds the bolts, and I just push the lever forward and back to load a bolt, then I just squeeze the trigger," she was practically beaming at the end of her explanation.

"That's brilliant," Aldred said.

"As long as it works," Sainte added.

"Oh, it works. I was sure to test it out before I paid the blacksmith. I'm excited to use it against something real," she said with a glint in her eyes.

"Clever, Iris. Excited to see what that can do, too. You all ready?" Sainte asked. They all nodded.

Together Sainte, Iris, Aldred, and Dawn walked out of Thissaren. For most of the morning the travel was mostly in silence. Occasionally there was small talk, but Sainte and Iris did a lot of catching up the last few days in Thissaren, and Aldred seemed not much in the mood for talking, which was the complete opposite of Sainte and Iris expected.

"Hey Aldred, what's going on? A lot quieter than last night," Iris observed.

"Oh, it's nothing."

"C'mon, if you want to get to know everyone better that takes some talking," she insisted.

He sighed, "Well, I'm uh, a little nervous. I've never done anything like this before."

"What do you do, Aldred?" Sainte asked curiously.

"Well, I was a hide tanner in Lenshire before I caught my wife screwing one of the guards over there. I left her, sold all my leather cheap, took all the coin I had and went to Thissaren. I was there for about a week before I started to work as an advisor for hire. A buyer would hire me to inspect goods, mostly leathers, before he bought them. Quality inspector I was, made good coin too. Not a very exciting job, but it was good for the time. Then I ran into you, Sainte, and now here I am. So, long story short, I'm quiet because I'm nervous."

"Hmm, hope you're good in a fight. I'm sure we'll be in some," Sainte said, doing nothing to relieve the man's nerves.

"I've been in some bar room brawls," Aldred said with a laugh, trying to ease himself. "Fighting's a young man's game, but I'm not necessarily old yet."

"Hope that's good enough. We'll see," Iris said giving Sainte a sideways smile. She thought he was just messing with him, but she could tell Sainte was not playing. He was trying to figure this man out.

"How long till we reach the Marshes?" Aldred asked, trying to change the subject to one more comfortable for him.

"I'd say two or three days as long as we keep a good pace, start days early, end them late," Sainte said.

"How do you two know each other? I don't think either of you have told me."

Sainte and Iris shared a look, "We were both Blades of the Night. We actually worked together, went through the training together. We got separated during the Dark Days," Sainte explained.

"What did you do in the Blades? If you don't mind me asking."

Sainte dropped some of the cooling liquid into his eyes before answering, thankful Iris was letting him decide how much he wanted to say. "I was the Shield for the Barrier. Iris assisted me outside of the tunnel. Every night we fought the Malignin."

"I wouldn't change it for anything, either," Iris added.

"Wow, so you two have been through it, huh? Must've been hard through the Dark Days," Aldred said somewhat callously.

Neither Sainte nor Iris replied. The conversation faltered for a while, instead they continued on in silence. The sky was clear and a breeze wafted lazily by, the world was greener now than it had been in long time. Plants were growing back in force, taking back what ground they lost during the long night. The well-worn path they traversed on even had some budding weeds. Life in Crearia was on its way back to normal but had not quite reached it yet.

Normally the road would have been clear of plants due to the heavy foot traffic of traders, movers, farmers. Some recovering still had to happen. Crops were being grown, but none ready to harvest. Animals had grown lean; farmers were trying to fatten them up to be profitable enough to butcher.

Throughout the day they passed some homesteads that looked abandoned, yards were unkempt, and fields were empty of livestock. The families had either died or abandoned their homes for the safety of a walled city. There were a few that had some people out beginning to work on the yards, families returned in hopes of getting something going but they had a daunting task ahead of them.

The sun began to set, turning the sky a vivid array of yellows, oranges, and reds. They continued on through the sunset, and only stopped walking about an hour after the horizon took it. It was dark when they found a flat spot just off the road and set up a small camp there.

"Think we have to worry about any Malignin?" Aldred asked.

"I don't think so. I haven't seen any for a long time," Sainte said.

"I saw one about four weeks ago when I was heading to Thissaren but haven't seen any since. I haven't heard anyone talk about seeing any either. I don't know what happened to them all, but you'll have no complaints from me if they're all gone," Iris said.

"Can't help but feel a little nervous out here, in the open. What about bandits?" Aldred said.

"Stop worrying. If bandits come by then we'll deal with them. Until then, no point in worrying about it. I'm gonna start a fire," Iris began gathering some sticks together.

Sainte rolled out his blanket and laid down, using his pack as a pillow. Dawn had been tied to a nearby tree. Aldred stopped pacing and finally sat down as flames came to life at Iris' small fire.

"So, Sainte, you were the Shield? Then that means you knew the Barrier, huh? The only person to talk to her. How was that?" Aldred asked.

It took Sainte a moment to reply. He was not bothered by the question; he just did not really know the best way to describe her anymore. "She was nice. Really nice. I felt bad, you know, lying to her about almost everything. She never questioned me about what I told her. Of course, she would ask about stuff but never once thought that what I told her strayed from the truth. She trusted me."

"Where is she now? Is she…?"

"She's dead," Sainte replied.

"Oh, I'm sorry. I didn't know. I still don't fully know what went down," Aldred poked at the fire sending up a small flurry of sparks.

"It's fine. Nothing to be done for her now."

"For everything you two seem to have gone through, it seems like you've found some ways to deal with it."

"Ha, can't speak for Sainte, but I am not as good as I make out to be. Some things just don't leave you, you know?" Iris said.

"Aye, some things you just can't really deal with. Some things stay with you, and you just have to do the best you can," Sainte said, thinking about how he had tried to take his life. He felt bad about it. Bad that he had tried to. Bad that he had failed to. He took out a piece of jerky and chewed on it. "I think we best try to get some sleep. We'll have another long day tomorrow, and hopefully we reach the Marsh. Think we will as long as we keep up the pace. We'll resupply at an outpost, stay the night near there, and the next day enter."

"Should anyone stay up and keep watch? Just in case? Maybe take turns or something?" Aldred asked.

"Nah, I doubt we need to worry about anything here. Anyway, I don't sleep much anymore on account of having no eye lids," saying that reminded Sainte it was about time for some more drops. Thankfully, the wind was blowing the smoke from the fire away from him. "Just sleep, Aldred. I'm going to try. We have to get up early, before the sun rises. I'll be sure to wake you if you're not up on your own," Sainte said after his eye drops.

"No arguments from me," Iris said as she laid down and stretched. She turned over onto her side and closed her eyes.

"Alright, I guess I should try to sleep. Don't know how much I'll be able to with my nerves, but I'll try," Aldred said as well, laying back.

Finally, all Sainte was left with was the crackle of the fire. His eyes looked up to the night sky at the thousands of stars that dotted it. He doubted he would be able to sleep even if he wanted to. Now, thanks to his eyes, his sleep was borderline wakefulness and slumber. And whenever he did reach that state he was plagued by nightmares, tortured by his failures and regrets.

142

He stared up at the stars, and the stars stared back.

"This is our baby, Sainte," Ellie whispered. She was sitting on her knees on the ground, her back was to him and she was surrounded by darkness. "Won't you come look at him?"

Not able to resist, Sainte crept closer. He could see over her shoulder now; the babe was swaddled in a cloth. She moved so that he could see the child's face. He breathed a sigh of relief, it was a normal looking, napping baby. When he got to her side, however, the baby opened his eyes and looked at him. Where the eyes should be were empty, black voids. A shadow crept from around the eyes and devoured the head. The skin got tight around the baby's head and tore away, revealing an inky smoke. The child, his child, opened its mouth and released a deep piercing cry that reverberated around inside his head.

Sainte took a horrified step back and Ellie looked at him smiling. Slowly her throat started to bulge as something rose inside of her. She tilted her head back and opened her mouth. Something bulbous and read popped from between her teeth. Her cheeks billowed out and tore apart, blood leaked from the fresh wounds. With a force her guts began to be expelled from her, tearing her bottom jaw from the top.

The baby had grown, now standing over Ellie. It was a black shadow with a humanoid form. The voids where the eyes should have been were endless. The mouth was wide open, the scream had not yet ceased for even a second. It took a step forward, towards Sainte. Ellie was no longer moving but remained on her knees with her head back. Her intestines pooled around her.

Suddenly Sainte felt something strange inside him as he gazed at the Abomination that towered over him. He had fallen to his knees, but he did not remember it. Something was rising in him, something solid yet soft. It pushed up into his throat, he could feel it bulging, wanting to rip through his skin. With horror in his eyes, his head was forced back, jaw contorted open wider than humanly possible. He felt it sliding across his tongue. He tasted it, the intestines that were once in his abdomen were coming out of his mouth. He could no longer breathe; he could do nothing but feel as his insides were being pulled from his body.

Sainte stared at the Abomination.

And it smiled back.

"Sainte," Aldred said, rocking him. "Sainte, wake up!"

Sainte suddenly shoved Aldred to the ground and sat up gasping for air. He was drenched in sweat and his eyes burned something unholy. Everything was blurry, he could see nothing. Forms blended in with the shadows.

"Ah," he groaned. "My eyes," he used his hands to cover his eyes, damnit they burned. "My vial, give it to me," he managed to say.

Iris scrambled over and looked for it. It took her a few seconds before she found the glass vial a few feet from Sainte's blanket, "Here, here. Hold out your hand."

Sainte tilted his head back and with shaking hands dropped the liquid into his eyes. He rolled them around, spreading the cooling liquid. After about thirty more seconds his vision started to clear and the pain began to subside, but not totally dissipate.

"You alright?" Iris asked. She sat near him, she wanted to put a hand out, to hold him, but felt he needed some space more than he needed contact.

"Uh, yeah," he was slow to reply. "Just a… Just a nightmare. Have them pretty often, now."

"I'd say that was a bit more than a nightmare. Started out moaning, then that turned to a scream," Aldred said. "Sounded like someone was gutting you."

Sainte did not answer but stretched instead, "How long were we sleeping?"

Iris looked to the horizon, "If I had to guess probably four hours. I'd say about two hours before the sun begins to rise."

"Should pack up and go," Sainte said. "We should try to reach the Marshes today to stay on schedule."

"I didn't realize we were on a schedule?" Aldred said.

"Aye, as quick as possible. That's our schedule. If I'm right, we should reach the Marshes by the end of today, and that'll give us all day tomorrow to try to make it through them. I don't think we will, but it'll be close. I'd like to start in them today, but I don't think we'll have enough day light left for it to be worth going in."

Aldred did not reply as he rolled up his blanket, grumbling to himself.

Iris looked at him annoyed. He knew that they were going to have early days and long nights. Not to mention that he was almost double their age and acting half their age. She rolled up her blanket and packed quickly. Sainte was finished with his by the time she finished, and then they waited on Aldred. Seeing that he was the last prepared, he tied off his blanket to his back, then shouldered it, apparently ready to go.

146

"All good?" Sainte asked.

"Aye," Iris said. Aldred just nodded.

"Good, let's go," Sainte stepped off towards the Marshes.

Crickets were chirping, getting their last voices heard before dawn, before the birds woke and looked for breakfast. There were trees around them, spread sparsely apart. Small creatures, squirrels and other rodents, shuffled around them as they heard the trio walk by. Some curious enough to stop what they were doing and stare at them for a moment before scampering away.

Sainte could not help but feel a little better than he had when he awoke. The sun was now shining, warm on his skin. He relished that feeling, not realizing how much he missed it during the Dark Days. The wind gently brushed his skin softly, not cold and harsh like it did in the fog. And the sounds he heard, life all around him, was a stark difference to the silence that was brought on by the release of the Malignin. How much more serious could the White Wyverns, Nadrian and Jasmine, think it could be? Surely Aroc's sacrifice subdued the threat of the Malignin and the Abomination.

The day continued and their pace did not lessen. The sun had just begun to set in the evening, but still had some time left before the horizon took it, when they could see a small spire in the distance. The white stone tower was undoubtedly part of the defenses set around the Marsh. This particular lookout was called Defensun, if Sainte recalled correctly. There were four of these large lookouts around the Marshes. One to the north, the south, the west, and the east.

Another hour went by before they approached the gates to it. There were two men standing guard in full suits of armor. It was simple armor, but effective. Built for battle, not for show. They each held a spear in their right hands and had a longsword strapped to their waist.

"Halt. What is your business here?" one of them asked as they approached.

"We seek to enter the Marshes. Tomorrow morning though, tonight we would ask to have shelter here," Sainte said. "If you have any supplies, such as water to fill our canteens or any dried foods we would be willing to pay for it if you can spare us some."

"What are your reasons for entering the Marsh?"

"We just wish to pass through, we are on our way to the Deshiere mountains and seek quick passage. We do not have the time to go around the Marsh."

"Why can't you spare the time to go around?"

"That is our business."

After a moment the guard replied, "Fair enough, it is not forbidden to enter the Marshes. Why come through a post, though?"

"As I said, we seek provisions before we enter. Defensun was the closest entry point to us," Sainte told him.

"Ser, this is not Defensun. You're about five miles north of it."

"We are?" Sainte asked, surprised. Neither Iris nor Aldred had anything to say, both had thought they were right on track to Defensun. "Well, either way we would like to stay here for the night and resupply, if at all possible."

"Aye, you can stay for the night. I'll have to get with the others, but I believe we'll be able to separate with some food and water. Our shift out here is almost over, will be in two days. I think we have plenty to spare for three people. Come on in."

"Trusting lot, they are," Aldred muttered to Iris as they walked into the small encampment.

"They don't have to worry about anyone bothering them, they're the only ones keeping the poison in the Marsh in check. What good would it do anyone to hinder these people from doing their jobs?" Iris replied.

Aldred did not respond, instead he took in the encampment. There was the tower, of course, about four stories high. Then there were three buildings, one was obviously a barracks for the men stationed here, one had to be the bathrooms, but he was not sure what the last one was, maybe food storage. There were three more guards sitting around a fire, and no one else that he could see.

"Hey, how're you doing?" one of the men said. They were cooking a small rodent on a rotating spit.

"Alright, a bit tired after two days' of travel. You have anywhere to put up a horse for the night?" Sainte asked, motioning towards Dawn.

"Oh aye, we've got a hitching post just there, outside the barracks."

Iris led Dawn to the post and tied her up.

"We've got some grain too, if you want for her. It's in there," he pointed to the third building.

"Thanks, I'll get some for her later," Iris said.

"Go on, have a seat, we won't bite. Don't get many visitors around here, nice to talk to some new faces."

Sainte was skeptical, why were these men being so nice? But before he could deny them Iris was already joining their small circle, and then Aldred sat down. Sainte followed suit and sat next to Iris.

"So, what brings you three here, to the edge of the Marshes?"

"We're just trying to reach the Deshiere mountains fairly quickly, didn't feel like taking the long way and going around," Iris said.

"Aye, I get that," a different guard said. "These Marshes are dangerous though. The water is no good to drink, kill you in about two hours. The animals themselves have, somehow, become accustomed to it, but it renders them uneatable. All of them harbor venomous bites as well. There're wolves, crocodiles, deer, panthers, snakes to just name a few. All are more aggressive than normal. I've been attacked by a deer in there before and if it wasn't for my armor and my partner, I'd be animal shite long ago."

"We know, but they are just animals. For the most part you leave them alone and give them a wide berth, and they'll do the same to you."

"Aye, that rings true everywhere else but in the Marshes. If you've never been then you'd do well to heed our warnings," one of the other guards spoke up.

"We'll keep that in mind, thanks," Iris said.

"The two guards out front said that you might have some extra food and water we could buy from you?" Aldred said.

"Oh, aye. I suppose we have some extra. Gaulin, fetch them some jerky and bread," the oldest looking guard said. "If you want to fill your canteens go for it. We have plenty of water so need to pay. For the food stuffs I'd say seventy coin will suffice, ten coin for each of us here."

"Sounds fair to me," Aldred said as he pulled out some coin and counted it. "Seventy, here you go," he handed it over.

Gaulin came back with four loaves of bread and three strips of jerky, "There's tapped barrels of water in the barracks, to your left as you enter. You can sleep wherever, but there are four empty cots in the barracks as well you're welcome to," he told them all.

"Thanks," Sainte said. He distributed the food amongst himself, Aldred, and Iris. "I think I'm going to go grab a cot now, we'll have an early morning. Thank you, men, for your hospitality." Sainte stood up with his pack and headed into the barracks.

Iris and Aldred stayed up a short while longer, talking to the guards. They learned about some ruins, rumored to be King Zith's old castle, in the Marshes that the guards generally did not go near. They said the ruins were northwest in the Marshes, and the way they were going was more southern so they should not have to worry about it. The guards did not explain much about the ruins, only that any time a patrol went near or through them something bad would happen.

After that Iris and Aldred retired too, each found an empty cot on either side of Sainte.

Sainte woke up first, as was normal. He dropped fluids in his eyes and grabbed his canteen and the other two's and filled them up as quiet as he could, not wanting to bother the guards. After the canteens were filled, he put them back near the packs then went outside. The sky was still dark as the sun had not yet risen. He stretched out his arms and stood on the tips of his toes and relished the cool morning air. He had a good night, last night. At least, good enough that he did not remember any nightmares.

He took a breath then went back in the barracks, slightly surprised to see Aldred and Iris both up, putting their packs on. He nodded his head quietly in greeting as he went and got his own pack. Once outside the barracks Iris went to Dawn to untie him. Before she went to sleep last night, she was sure to place some grain out for her.

"You guys ready?" Sainte asked as Iris walked up with Dawn.

"Guess so. Let's get this over with," Iris said. Aldred nodded in agreement, apparently still too tired to talk.

They walked into the Marshes. About an hour went by before they noticed anything really different. The ground was soggy, with each step their foot would sink just a little bit. That is when they noticed the smell. It was putrid, smelled like decaying flesh and dead fish. Soon there was water around them. It had an almost purple hue. Mist hugged the ground, thickest over the waters. The trees were all short, the tallest being about six feet high. The leafless limbs reached to the sky like fingers, skinny and desiccated. Right now the sky was cloudless, but it felt overcast. Occasionally there would be a splash as some unknown creature moved in the waters that now surrounded them in little pools.

The day dragged on and they walked in silence, even Dawn seemed to keep his snorts to a minimum. No one saw a creature, but they heard them. There were worn down paths, either game trails or patrol paths, but Sainte and the group were told to stay on the most worn one. It was the most common patrol path and would lead almost directly south and west. They should be out of the Marshes early the next day.

Their canteens were drunk out of sparingly, and the food was eaten one bite at a time. They only made short stops, no more than was absolutely necessary. The entire day went by with no incident, no animals seen but they knew they were around because of the constant sounds. At least there were no bugs to bother them. The guards had said that bugs could not survive in the Marshes, could not live long enough feeding off of the toxic land to become immune like the animals had.

As the sun started to descend, they noticed they were passing by what looked to be old, cracked columns. The columns stuck out of the waters in rows of four. There were some walls that had mostly crumbled with time, but still tried to stand their ground.

"Did we stray from the path?" Sainte asked as he slowed to a stop. "I don't recall the guards mentioning any other ruins."

"Not that I noticed," Iris said, "and the only ruins they told us about were King Zith's."

"I don't think we are where we should be," Sainte said looking around nervously. He turned around and looked down the path from where they came.

"There were many paths, I could see where we could have taken the wrong one," Aldred said.

"I don't like this," Sainte looked at the sun. It was getting low. Would not be much longer until darkness overtook the Marshes. He did not want to be wandering around here in the dark.

"Maybe we should stop here for the rest of the day? Looks like we could get a little protection from the elements if we go on a little bit, I think I see some walls that have not yet fallen completely," Aldred suggested.

Sainte looked where Aldred pointed and saw that he was right, three walls stood together. There was nothing overhead, and one wall was completely gone, but what was left should be good enough to block the wind. "I don't know…"

"The guards said the ruins are in the northwest of the swamp, right? That means we're close to being out of the thick of it still, just not where we expected to get out. As long as we get out of here on the west side, somewhere, it will still bring us to the Deshiere mountains. We aren't where we expected to be, but it should be fine… I think," Aldred explained. Iris and Sainte looked at him uncertain of his explanation. "Look, I guess I'm just tired of walking through this sponge of a land. We can do whatever, I'm just not looking forward to walking around here at night."

"Maybe he's right, Sainte? Camp here for the night, get another early morning and we'll probably be out of here before midday," Iris said.

After a sigh, Sainte agreed. "Come on then, let's go there," he motioned to the walls a short distance away, "and see if we can find any dry spots for our blankets." They could not. The ground was too saturated. Once they had their blankets laid out, they found that if they in the same spot for too long water would seep through. There was nothing to be done of it, so they just accepted they were going to get wet.

Before long they had a small fire crackling, Dawn tied up just outside the three walls, and had a small supply of sticks broken from the craggy trees. Even though the fire was small, they all took some comfort from the heat, though it did nothing for their soggy bottoms. By now the sun had set and it was dark, strange sounds could be heard beyond their view, but for now nothing had bothered them.

"I think that we should have someone keep watch here," Sainte said. "It'd be foolish of us to not."

"I agree," Aldred said.

"Aye," Iris nodded. "I'll be first up, no problem."

"No, go to sleep, both of you," Sainte said. "I can hardly sleep anyway, and when I do I'd rather be awake. I'll watch all night and wake you come morning."

"You sure about that? All night?" Aldred asked.

"Yes, no problem. I'll wake you if the need arises."

"Thank you," Iris said. She was obviously very tired if she did not argue with him about it. Instead she just laid down on her moist blanket.

"Thanks," Aldred said as he did the same.

Sainte nodded back at him. He nestled with his back to the wall and faced the opening, staring out into the darkness. Nothing could be seen, but there were many splashes. Strangely, it seemed like none of the animals in the Marshes made noises other than what they made when they walked.

An unknown number of hours went by and Sainte remained vigilant. All was peaceful within the three walls. He kept the fire going and occasionally looked at Iris as she slept and remembered their times together, about their time during training. Of the time they had slept together and almost got caught. He had not thought about that in a long time. He had practically forgotten it had happened when he was the Shield. He slightly shook his head, now was not the time for those thoughts.

He looked at Aldred then and was startled to see that Aldred was looking back at him. "Alright there, Sainte?" Aldred asked.

"Aye, didn't expect you to be staring at me, is all."

"Have been for some time now."

"Er, a little strange, don't you think?" Sainte asked.

Aldred shrugged, "What're you thinking about?"

"A lot."

"The Barrier? Ellie?"

"A bit, aye," he answered slowly. "Why do you ask?"

"I have been too. Quite a bit, actually," the way Aldred spoke now was different. Sainte could not quite grasp what was strange about him though.

"Why?"

"The way you remember her and the way I remember her is different. Quite different indeed," he was more precise than normal. Before he seemed nervous, sort of skittish. But now he was firm, seemed indifferent to where they were at.

"How do you remember her?" Sainte was thoroughly confused. "What're you getting at? No one spoke to her except for me."

"Oh, she was scared," Aldred ignored his questions. "So very scared and in pain. She was aware the whole time, you know? The things I did, the things I made her do. She cried, a lot," Aldred was sitting up now. "She begged me, pleaded to me, to end her life. It was pathetic."

"What are you saying?" Sainte said, fear rimmed his words. He stood up and drew his sword. "Who are you?"

"You don't remember? We've met once before. You know who I am. In the caves. You were one of the first people I had ever seen, in a long, long time. You witnessed my coming into this world," Aldred stood up too, not caring that the point of Sainte's sword was now poking him in the chest, drawing blood.

"What? How?" Sainte took a step back and found that he was up against the wall. His knees were weak as memories of the cave came back. Terrible memories.

Aldred drew himself up and although he was Sainte's height, seemed to leer over him. "I am King Zith. But you've been calling me the Abomination, and you have something of mine. I mean to get it back," Sainte stared in horror as Aldred, King Zith, grew in stature. The skin stretched grotesquely around his face and his features were distorted to the point where he was no longer recognizable. Soon his skin could not take it and sloughed off revealing the Abomination underneath. It was everything Sainte saw in his nightmares and worse.

The eyes were bottomless pits, the mouth was agape with a guttural sound echoing out from the depths and it seemed to suck in all light. The hands, fingers now dark and long, reached for Sainte and almost wrapped around him, but he swatted them aside with his sword. The Abomination did not seem to mind, perhaps even let it happen.

"Sainte?" Iris asked as she groggily sat up. He had almost forgotten about her so wrapped up with his fear was he.

"Run!" he screamed. "Get out of here!"

Her eyes opened wide when she finally was able to take everything in. She scrambled to her feet and fumbled her crossbow out in front of her with the harness. She managed to load a bolt and fire it off at the Abomination in one quick motion. The bolt plunged into the dark flesh of its back. The Abomination did not move. It almost seemed to smile.

"Where's Aldred?" she called out.

"It's him," was all Sainte said, but his words were drowned out by splashing from the Marshes. Something, lots of somethings, were running towards them. Dawn was heard just outside the wall as he let out a scared whinny that was cut short. Iris jumped over by Sainte's side, away from the only opening. Together they held their weapons at the unmoving Abomination. In what little firelight was left they saw what rushed them.

Malignin, lots of them. They formed a wall at the opening, cutting off any escape they could have hoped for. Where had they all come from? The Abomination stepped closer. Sainte took that opportunity to attack and plunged his sword deep in its chest, buried it almost hilt deep. The Abomination seemed unaffected and swatted Sainte back into the wall.

161

All his breath had been knocked out of him, but he had managed to keep a hold of his sword, yanking it from the horrible thing. Iris cried out for him as the Abomination crept closer. With one large hand it grabbed a hold of Sainte's head fingers wrapped completely around. It lifted him up, his toes barely brushed the ground. Iris released another bolt into the dark arm, but it did nothing. Sainte gasped through ragged breaths as his head was squeezed, the pressure becoming unbearable.

Suddenly, a bright flash of white light blinded him and Iris. He was dropped to the ground and caught himself on his hands and knees. He stood up quickly and rubbed his eyes trying to clear them, hand still grasped his sword. When his vision returned, he saw that he and Iris were joined by someone else.

"Get up, Sainte. Run, I'll hold them off as long as I can," a man said. The voice was familiar, but he was so disoriented he did not know who it belonged to. The man had his back to Sainte and Iris and held a shining staff aloft. The Malignin had cowered away, but the Abomination seemed to rise up at this new threat.

Darkness emanated from it, almost enough to snuff out the light, but the man held the staff higher and shouted. Sainte looked away from the light and reached out to grab Iris. He pulled her up beside him and saw her blinking to try to clear her own vision.

162

"Go, now! Both of you run," it was then Sainte realized he knew who was talking. It was Nadrian.

Not having time to argue or think about anything other than running away, Sainte saw that the wall to their backs had been knocked down. Who did it or when he did not know, but at this point it did not matter.

"Come on, Iris," he grunted as he pulled her along. He still had his sword out with no time to put it away. Together they trudged through the Marshes in the night. Flashes of light followed their backs for a long time, but neither dared look back. Nadrian could be heard screaming at the Abomination and Malignin, but his words were lost in the mist.

NINE

Four days had passed since Bruntishian Leancheshiner's death. Kial and Peng had continued with their nightly guard duties and did nothing more as had been their orders. Fights were beginning to break out amongst the population of Munich as many survivors from Guardstin had sought refuge there. Since Guardstin had been destroyed during the Dark Days, they had no homes to return to, and Munich barely had enough housing to keep them all covered. Temporary tents had been set up just outside the walls of Munich for them, but they were getting impatient waiting for more housing to become available.

Some self-appointed leaders had begun trying to figure out if they could start building permanent houses in place of the tents, therefore expanding the boundaries of Munich. Some of the Council of Munich were for it, but others were against it. Before any building could occur, an agreement had to be made.

All of this going on had led up to this moment, in the tavern, where Peng and Kial were holding two men apart.

"Bunch of over-rated boys with swords you lot are. If you were any good none of this woulda happened," the older bald man said as Peng held him.

"If you coulda done better why didn't you join the Blades then? Oh, that's right, yer fuckin' scared," the younger man said. Kial held this one.

"Both of you shut the hell up. You're too drunk to stay any longer. Go home," Kial told them.

"I don't have a home to go to. I've been living in a damned tent for better part of two months," the Blade said.

"Then go there, I don't give an arse," Peng snapped. "We can't be letting you two continue on as you are. Either go sleep this off or we'll be tossing you in a cell for the night, maybe longer depending on how much trouble you give us."

"Course ya don't care, you're not the ones sleeping in a tent," the Blade shrugged out of Kial's grasp. Kial let him go as he realized he was not going to try to fight anymore. The Blade staggered out of the tavern and into the night.

Peng let the bald man go after a moment to let the Blade get a head start. "Go home, if we catch you out again, we'll put you in a cell, I mean it," he said to him as he left.

After the two men left everyone else in the tavern began talking and laughing again. They had been watching waiting to see if there was going to be a fight or not.

"You ready, Peng? We should continue our patrol," Kial said. As a form of punishment, they had been put on nightly city patrol rather than their usual wall watch. They had to walk around Munich at night watching for any trouble. It was a position mostly left for new guards as no one really enjoyed dealing with drunks.

Once they were back out on the streets Peng said, "This is the worst. We got newer guys who've been with the guard for five years less than us on our wall duty. All because we were trying to sort out an old case that had not been figured out."

Kial shrugged, "It's a nice change of pace for me. It was getting a little old on the wall. Nothing to do, nothing to see."

"That's the point, it was easy. Here we actually have to walk around and kick drunks out of taverns. Not how I like spending my nights. I like being one of the drunks, not dealing with them."

"We're almost done with it. One more night of this and we'll be back on the wall. That means that tomorrow I'm going to talk to the examiner. You still want to come with me?"

Peng shrugged, "Sure, why not. I'm curious now what we'll find out, if anything."

"Good. I'm planning on going pretty much as soon as our shift is over. Change, eat breakfast, tell Marianne what I'm planning, and you do whatever you need to. Meet at my place about an hour after we're done."

"Sounds good to me," Peng replied.

The rest of the night continued on with nothing significant happening. A few more bar brawls were broken up, but that was expected. The time for shift change came and Kial went home to change and wait for Peng.

"How was your night?" Marianne asked as Kial entered their bedroom. She was sitting at chair brushing her hair.

Kial shrugged, "It was fine. Nothing too crazy, just rowdy drunks." He took his guard garb off and began to put on a fresh set of clothes. "How're you?"

"I'm fine. Going to send Franceska to get another jug of milk for us while I go pick up some pork from farmer Hannidy," she said.

"Good, good. Where is Franceska?" Kial asked.

"Where do you think? Still sleeping."

"Gotta start getting that girl up early and putting her to work," Kial said.

167

"She's fine. What're your plans for the day?" Marianne asked.

"You're not going to like it. I'm going to see the examiner, the one who looked at Flotier," Kial said. He waited for her chastisement.

"I thought you were done with that? I don't know if you should push your luck, how much more could you get away with?" she sighed. "You're too old to be chasing wild geese."

"Peng's coming with," Kial started to say but was interrupted by a knocking on the door. "Matter of fact, I bet that's him right now," Kial walked over to the front door and opened it.

"Hey again, Kial. Long time no see," Peng said.

"Huh, you're on time. That's a surprise."

"I'd hate to keep you waiting. You ready for this?"

"Aye, let's go," Kial said.

"Don't do anything stupid, Peng. And keep him safe," Marianne called out, poking her head out from their bedroom.

"Always, miss. He'll be safe with me," Peng said with a polite smile.

Together they walked to the examiner's building. There was only one in town, as the business was not exactly booming.

Most of the time it was not very difficult to figure out how someone died.

Soon they stepped inside the one-story building. It was rather simple with a large open interior with three tables near the middle of the room. To the right of the room was another door, but it was closed. On one of the tables was a cow corpse. An elderly man with a leather apron stood over it holding a pair of large scissors. He looked up as he saw Kial and Peng enter.

"Good morning sirs, what can I do for you today?" he asked. He set down the pair of scissors and slowly walked around the table to face them.

"Good morning, you must be the examiner, no?" Kial asked.

"Aye, I am. The only one in Munich. My name's Prestom, but most know me only by examiner."

"We have some questions; I hope it's not a bad time?" Peng said motioning to the cow.

"Oh, this? Only thing I have to do today, a farmer wants to know if someone poisoned his steer. I have the pleasure of examining many things," Prestom smiled. "What sort of questions might you have? Interested in this profession?"

"No, sorry. We have some questions about Flotier, the butcher," Kial said.

Prestom sagged back. He now sat on the bloody table, "I didn't tell anyone, I swear." His face had turned ghostly pale.

"Tell anyone what? What's wrong?" Kial asked.

"You two, you work for her, don't you? I said what she told me to say."

"We don't work for anyone. We just have some questions about what you found. Who did you think we work for?" Peng asked, immediately suspicious.

"I've said too much already," Prestom started to regain some color in his face as he regained his composure. "Flotier's death was natural, as natural as being tortured to death can be. That's it, no more no less."

"There must be more. You seem pretty nervous about all this. Who did you think we worked for?" Peng asked the question again.

"She paid me not to say. Warned me that if I did speak any more than what she told me that there would be consequences."

"We need to know. We won't tell anyone else, but something isn't quite right about Flotier. We have to find out, have to try to prevent anything like what he did from happening a second time. Tell us, Prestom," Kial insisted.

"You're not with her, you swear?" the old man wiped his forehead with a bloody hand, leaving a streak of red across it without even realizing it.

"We are not. Who paid you off, and what did you find upon your examination of Flotier?" Kial said.

Prestom took a moment to gather his thoughts, "Well, when I received his body his hands had been cut from his arms. Other than that, there was not much to him. On the outside, that is. Once I cut him open is… Well, I had never seen nor heard of anything like it. His insides, his guts, seemed almost… cauterized, I suppose is the word for it. But they weren't burnt, they weren't blackened. They were white. The veins in his arms were also similar to his organs. I can't explain it, there's nothing I know that could have produced anything like it. No poison, no fire, no trauma," he shrugged. "Soon after I had started examining his body, within the hour, she showed up. Told me, threatened me, about what I saw. No one was to know, not a soul. She was nice about it, but I could tell she was deadly serious. She paid for my silence and told me that she would continue to keep an eye on me, to make sure I obeyed her orders."

"Who is she?" Kial asked.

"I shouldn't say," Prestom shook his head.

"Why? You already told us everything else."

"I'm scared," he admitted.

"I don't know what else to tell you. We can help you, try to. If you want a safe haven we can provide it. We can help you out, but we have to know the name. What if there are more like Flotier? What if they decide to pick up where he left off? There are so many questions that need answers, especially now with what you told us," Kial said.

Prestom sighed, "Damn it all, I'm old anyways, probably don't have much longer left as it is. If you think you can actually prevent anything like what he did from happening again…" he rubbed his temples, deep in thought. "She's the healer, Jasmine."

Kial and Peng were silent as they learned the name.

"No, that can't be," Peng finally said.

"Ah, so you know her. Not surprising, many in this city do."

"It has to be a different Jasmine," Kial started to say.

"Jasmine the healer. The one and only healer I know of that's named Jasmine," Prestom confirmed.

"Why'd she pay you to keep quiet?" Kial asked.

The old man shrugged, "I don't know. She didn't tell me, I didn't ask. I felt like she didn't have to keep me alive, but she did. I suppose you two are going to confront her. As long as you'll be sure to stop anything like this from happening in the future, I'm content with how I spent my life."

"Nothing will happen to you, ok? Yes we are going to talk to her, but we'll make sure nothing happens to you. I'd suggest going somewhere for a few days, hiding out just in case. Let us know where you go and we'll be sure to get you help," Peng said.

"No, I'm going to stay here. Finish this job and keep on going. Whatever comes to pass I'm fine with. I'm not going to hide," he shook his head.

Peng and Kial shared a glance, already feeling guilty for forcing this man to put his life in danger.

"Do what you wish, Prestom. We're going to talk to her tomorrow morning, after we get off shift, do with that what you will. C'mon Peng, we've got a lot to talk about. Thank you, examiner. You've been a lot of help," Kial said as he and Peng left the building.

Prestom did not reply, he just picked up his scissors and resumed his work.

"Why're we waiting for tomorrow?" Peng asked.

"Because we have to think about how to approach her. We know Jasmine, or at least we thought we did. We have to treat this delicately. We'll talk about it today and spend the night shift getting the finer details ironed out."

Jasmine sat down at her table, a glass of wine in front of her. It had been a rather good couple of days since Kial and Peng stopped shoving their noses where they should not have been. She had also received word that Eringar reached the Council, finally. He had gotten a verbal warning about what he did to that young butcher, but nothing else would come of it she was sure.

It did not matter now. All that mattered was that she finally could have a relaxing evening, drinking her wine, and then having a good night sleep. After her glass was empty and she was feeling rather well, she went to bed.

Then was woken up to frantic knocking at her door. She groggily got up and walked to her door, barely aware that it was still dark out. She answered her door and saw that it was none other than Nadrian. He looked rather rugged, dirt smeared his face and his clothes were dirty and bloodied. He pushed in past her without being asked in.

"He's back, Jasmine. I saw him. We were right," he said as he dropped into a seat.

"Nadrian? What're you doing? What're you on about?" she asked as she sat down opposite him.

"King Zith. He's back, and so are the Malignin. He has a human body, but then turned into the Abomination and… released?... the Malignin," Nadrian was speaking fast. He was saying more but his words bled into each other and Jasmine could not understand him. She was faintly aware of someone yelling outside.

"Slow down, Nadrian. What's going on? What's this about King Zith? And who is yelling outside?" she asked as the yelling increased in volume.

"The Dark Days are back; it's almost midday and the sun hasn't risen. The Malignin are back, and so is Zith. He took the body, twisted with human and Malignin. It held him together, and it's worse than we thought," Nadrian said.

Jasmine was beginning to piece together what he was saying, but she was still missing fragments. She knew enough that whatever it was he was trying to say was bad. "Start from the beginning and start slow. You were tasked with following Sainte, where was the last place you saw him?"

Nadrian took a few breaths, "In the Marshes, nearly out. He had a man with him, Aldred I think they called him. He steered them to Zith's ruins in the Marshes, and there he revealed he was truly Zith. The body he was in was what was born from Ellie, Jasmine. He is back, and that body can hold the pieces of

175

his spirit. It seems he has control of it, to an extent, because he let it out and his spirit broke apart and took the shape of the Malignin. Once they were out, he became the Abomination. It almost killed Sainte and Iris, but I intervened. They ran away while I held everything off. I fled when I could. I managed to get ahead of them, but I'm sure I was followed. There's not much time before-"

Before he could finish his sentence there was more knocking at her door. Urgent knocking. She shared a look of concern with Nadrian then got up and cautiously called out, "Who's there?"

"Open up, Jasmine. It's me and Peng," Kial's voice replied.

"What do you want?" she asked as she opened the door. The two men pushed past her uninvited. She was getting tired of everyone forcing their way into her house.

"What the hell is going on, Jasmine? Before you say anything, we know you paid off the examiner. What do you know about Flotier? Were you, are you, working with him? What's going on? Why hasn't the sun come up yet?" Kial asked.

"Everyone calm down," Jasmine said, completely flustered at this point. Kial and Peng looked around and just

176

noticed Nadrian. "I really wish you didn't speak with the examiner."

"Why? Because now you have to kill him? He told us that's what you'd do to him if he spoke to anyone about what he found," Peng said. Jasmine noted his hand was on the hilt of his sword.

Jasmine sat down again, "No, I'm not going to kill him. Not anymore, at least. He's the least of my worries. Yes, I know a lot more than you two do about Flotier, about the entire ordeal. It's just more shit I have to deal with," she put a lot of emphasis on the word *shit*. Her stress levels were quickly building.

"We need answers, Jasmine. We need to prevent a Flotier type of event from happening again," Kial said. "And who's this?" he motioned to Nadrian.

"You can't prevent it, but I can. It's bigger than you know. And it's almost inevitable at this point. You two have been pushing against forces that you have no idea about. I told you to leave it be. This is Nadrian," she said absentmindedly.

"Well here we are. We thought you were one of the good ones, Jasmine. We didn't want to believe Prestom when he told us about you. And now the sun's not up, people are scared and rightly so. You need to tell us what you know," Kial demanded.

At his words Jasmine stood up. She was shorter than both the two men, but the way she held herself she seemed a giant. "I don't *need* to do anything. I could leave you, right now. You'd all die. I didn't have to do what I've done for the past I don't even know how many years," she walked closer to them. "But I have, I've been here next to you idiots all this time helping, healing, guiding. And you come in here demanding things of me that you have no place to demand. You demand nothing from me, I demand it from you."

Kial and Peng took a faltered step back together, feeling extremely uneasy. This was not the Jasmine they were used to dealing with.

"You two get out of my house, or else there's no telling what I'm going to do with you. I've been very busy the past few months, and now I have more to deal with than I care to. Get out of here, and speak of this to no one, or I will kill you both, and Prestom."

The two men were pale in the face by now and completely at a loss for words. The atmosphere in the room seemed to crush in on them. They turned around and hurried out, but as soon as they opened her door, bells began to toll. Warning bells, something was coming. Horns blasted from atop Munich's walls, the sound signaling all the guards to their posts.

"They've arrived," Nadrian said.

The horns seemed to shock Peng and Kial out from whatever hold Jasmine had them under. "Who's arrived?" Peng asked.

"The Malignin. Zith. They're here," Nadrian replied.

"Marianne, Franceska," Kial said under his breath. "Peng, I have to go," he readied his warhammer as he went to run out the door.

"Wait," Jasmine quickly called out. "No, stay here. If you go you'll die."

"My wife and child are out there," Kial said frantically.

"We have to, they need our help up there," Peng said.

"They're as good as dead," Jasmine said. "I'm sorry, Kial. We have to get out of here, you're no good if you get yourself killed," as if in response to her there was screaming atop the wall. Guttural snarls echoed through the city as the Malignin scaled the walls and began their assault. People started to run out of their homes, some lighting torches, some seemed to just be running frantically to nowhere. "We stay together, we can get out of here."

Kial did not listen to her, he ran outside and started down the road towards his home, but he came to a sudden halt.

Malignin were already down the street, prowling around. One leaped atop a man who tried to run.

"Fuck," Kial repeated under his breath. "What do I do?" He was suddenly joined by Nadrian, Jasmine, and Peng.

"We go to the Blades of the Night. They're camped just outside. We bring whoever we can convince to them, then we run. Nadrian, come with me. If Sainte got away, then they should be near the Deshiere mountains by now. We'll have to just hope he continues with what we've asked of him."

Nadrian readied himself for what must be done, "Let's go."

"And we just follow you? What about everyone else here?" Peng asked.

"We can't save everyone else. We can tell people to come with us, but the longer we stay the greater our chances of death are. Come on, we've already stayed too long," Jasmine said. "Peng, drag Kial with you. Make him come," Jasmine commanded. Kial stood staring, hands at his side, fingers barely holding onto his sword.

Peng grabbed his friend by the shoulder and pulled him, begrudgingly Kial's feet followed. Screams could be heard as more Malignin undoubtedly clawed their way through the guards and dropped into the city. Jasmine headed towards the east entrance, where everyone from Guardstin had set up camp.

Nadrian followed her, and after another moment's hesitation so did Peng and Kial. As they ran through the streets together, they called for everyone to come with them. Some people joined; others did not even seem to notice. The screams continued to get closer until they were surrounded by them. Peng risked a glance back as they ran through the streets and saw that Munich was being covered in a darkness deeper than night.

The darkness crept forward, and he saw that the Malignin advanced with it. They crawled on all fours through the streets and killed anyone they caught. Their cries were cut short as were their lives. He looked forward and ran harder.

The east entrance loomed in front of them, the large wooden doors had been cut apart and people ran through them out of Munich. There were some people wearing heavy armor with weapons drawn at the gates on either side, ushering people through. Kial assumed these were the Blades of the Night that managed to get ready in time.

Once they were through the gates the change in atmosphere was very apparent. It was calmer out here with the people from Guardstin. These people had dealt with the Malignin before, and it was obvious. The Blades of the Night were calling to each other, forming quick plans. At a quick glance Kial noted that there were those on either side of the east entrance, directing people through and cutting down any Malignin that ventured too near. Some Blades were at the base of the walls on the outside in case anything clambered over. Then there were even more in the tent city that had been built, ushering people through.

They were also tearing down the tents and piling it all up making a wall of debris. Undoubtedly it would be caught aflame once deemed necessary. There were some people out of armor, who could be Blades but Kial did not know, who were telling people to stay together as best as possible and flee to the Barrier's mountain range. Kial assumed they would group together there and figure out what to do next. He looked at all the faces that fled past him, hoping to find Marianne or Franceska.

"What do we do now?" Peng asked Jasmine as if he read Kial's mind.

"You two go with everyone to the mountains, Nadrian and I are going to stay here. We will meet back up once we are through here," she explained.

"What are you two going to do? What can you do?" Peng asked before adding, "I'm not going with anyone except you, Jasmine. We have too many questions to leave you. What if we never see you again? We need answers."

182

"This is not the time," Jasmine cursed to herself. "Fine, stay. I don't care. Nadrian, are you ready?"

"I'll have to be," Nadrian replied.

"I can't leave Marianne and Franceska," Kial said. "I can't."

"I'm sure they got out, they had plenty of warning," Peng said trying to calm his friend. "You won't be able to find them if you go back, you'll just get yourself killed, and they need you to stay alive, alright, Kial?"

Kial did not say anything, but he had stopped trying to run back into Munich. Peng drew his sword, Kial already had his at the ready. Together they prepared to follow Jasmine and Nadrian, but they did not move.

"What's the plan?" Peng asked.

"We wait, wait for the survivors to come, and then fight the Malignin to buy everyone enough time to seek shelter in the mountains," Jasmine said.

They did not have to wait long. They heard shouts from the Blades and almost in unison the Blades at the east entrance moved together, forming a line blocking the exit. The rest of the Blades in the make-shift camp, now torn down, ran to provide back up. Peng looked up at the walls and saw Malignin scramble over and plunge down twenty feet to the Blades who waited for them.

Seconds after that a clash was heard as the Malignin rushed the Blades at the exit. They held their formation and pushed back, stopping the Malignin from getting through, for now. The defenses would not last long. Kial saw that there were a few Blades that held back who held torches. Their jobs were obvious, to light the fires once the Malignin broke through.

Nadrian and Jasmine strode forward, Peng and Kial followed. The uneasy feeling they had felt in Jasmine's house consumed them once more. Nadrian was the first to move, he held his hands out and in a bright flash of light he held a staff that seemed like it was made of light. He thrust his staff forward, like a spear, and from the tip of it shot out about ten balls of light. They flew forward, harmlessly passing by or through any human, and all hit Malignin crumpling them.

Jasmine held her hands out, much like Nadrian, but three bright glowing orbs of lights appeared over the Blades of the Nights line, blinding all the Malignin. Nadrian continued thrusting his staff, sending light out. The Blades, confused at first by the unexpected help, had a second wind and yelled encouragingly to each other as they cut down the advancing Malignin.

Kial and Peng watched open mouthed as Jasmine then held her hands above her head and lowered them, which in turn brought her orbs down into the midst of the Malignin. She violently clutched her hands into fists and her three orbs then exploded into rays of light, killing all Malignin within the radius. This gave the Blades at the exit a chance to regroup.

"Fall back," Jasmine shouted, her voice clear amongst all the clatter. "Fall back and retreat to the mountains lest you be overrun. Light the fires and flee," at her voice the Blades listened. They ran past Kial and Peng, the ones who held the torches tossed them into the makeshift fire walls which slowly but surely began to be consumed by flames.

Once they were sure the Blades were forming back up and retreating to the mountains, Nadrian and Jasmine began their own retreat with Peng and a reluctant Kial in close pursuit. The debris walls had successfully been fully consumed by flame which held the Malignin at bay. The darkness in Munich had spread to the buildings nearest the east exit. Peng and Kial looked in as the blackness consumed their town and Malignin ran back and forth, seeking refuge from the heat and light.

Amidst all the flame, a darkness crept forward that seemed to eat the fire. A darkness no light could penetrate. Flames licked at it but touched nothing. The spreading shadow came to a halt in the middle of the eastern entrance and Kial shivered as he felt an unseeing gaze fall on them. Jasmine and Nadrian looked back at it as well, Nadrian even thrust his staff, sending four light balls streaking at it. As the light quickly closed the distance they dimmed as they neared the darkness, and completely fluttered out about twenty feet away.

"We have to go, now," Jasmine said with fear. As she ran past Kial and Peng she grabbed their arms. Nadrian ran with them as well, but he no longer held the staff.

Kial and Peng ran with them, quietly and quickly. Neither of them entirely sure they could believe what they had just witnessed. Their anger and cautiousness that they felt towards Jasmine merely moments before had been completely forgotten.

TEN

Iris and Sainte quickly travelled through the Marshes, taking no time to stop. It had been about three hours since they were attacked, and the Marshes showed no signs of ending. The splashes that they made trudging through the muck brought the attention of the nocturnal nightlife, which is not what they wanted.

They had no way of lighting their way since they left their torches in their packs, and their packs were left at the ruins. Each of them had been soaked through with murky, rancid marsh water. It was slimy and cold and smelled terrible. At one point they heard what they assumed was an alligator hissing at them, seemed like it was only a few feet away, before it splashed away. They could only hope they would not run into one blindly.

"Sainte," Iris gasped. "I have to stop. I need a break."

"Fine, but we can't stop for long," Sainte called back. They came to a stop and Iris sat down hard; the soft ground squished under her. She had not realized she still held on to her crossbow that was latched to her shoulder. Her fingers reluctantly let go and she tried to stretch the cramping out of them. She thought about Dawn, Tal's horse. The last thing she had that she remembered him by, and she let it get killed. Her eyes watered at the thought of him.

Sainte, still standing, sheathed his sword as well and looked around, "We can't stay here very long." If he noticed her crying, he did not say anything about it.

"I know, you just said that. I just had to catch my breath and give my legs a break," she said then wiped her face.

"The longer you sit still the harder it'll be to move," he took a few deep breaths and tapped his foot impatiently. "Let's go, this is long enough."

"We've only stopped for seconds, and you already want to go?"

"Aye, unless you wish to die here. I'm not going to. I don't know where the Malignin are, I don't know what foul creature may be stalking us. I'm going and you can come with me or catch up later."

"Why are you being like this?" she asked as she struggled to stand up.

"Because," he snapped at her. He took moment to regain his composure, "Did you already forget what just happened? How we almost died? That thing is out there, after us, after me. I need to find that sword to stop it."

Iris said nothing. He was right, but damn she was tired. She straightened up with a groan, "Here, I'm ready. Let's move on."

The going was slow even though they were moving as fast as they could. Eventually they came to a trail, but they had no idea how long it took them to reach it. The sun still had not risen.

"This must be a patrol route, we must be near an outpost," Sainte said. "Let's stick to it, it seems more solid than the other ground and it must lead out of here."

Iris nodded in agreement, too tired to speak. They kept to the trail and sure enough they saw firelight in the distance after another few hours of walking. It was indeed from an outpost they confirmed as they approached. This one was different, however, they were met by two guards about fifty yards away from it rather than right at the entrance.

"Who goes there?" a man called out.

"My name is Sainte, and this is Iris. We entered the Marshes a few days ago from the eastern side. We just wish to rest and then we shall be on our way," Sainte said.

"Did you get bit by anything, or drink any water from the Marsh?"

"No, although we did have to wade through the water a bit. We ran into some trouble."

"What kind of trouble?"

"Let us in your post and we'll explain to you what happened," Sainte was losing his patience.

After a minute of talking with each other the guard called out, "Follow us, we'll escort you to the post."

The two men waited for Iris and Sainte to reach them, then together walked to the outpost.

"Ser Rogir, we have two travelers that came from the Marshes. They seek refuge, then will be on their way after they've rested," one of the guards said to a man in leather armor. He had stubble around his face and looked as if he had not slept in a few days.

He eyed Sainte and Iris before saying, "Very well, return to your post." The two guards saluted then walked back where they came from. This outpost looked much like the one they had entered from, a large fire burned near the center of the buildings and four men sat around it. "You two are welcome to stay and rest for a while, it looks like you need it."

"Aye," was all Sainte said. He walked past him and laid down on the ground a few feet from the fire but away from everyone else.

"Thank you," Iris said. "I don't think we'll be very long. Just enough to dry off."

"No problem, we try to give anyone who passes through a haven to relax after the Marshes. They need it. Definitely looks like you two need it."

Iris walked over to Sainte then and sat down, "Don't you think we should tell them about what happened? Warn them?"

"I don't give a shite right now. Let me just relax. If the Malignin were following us we would have been killed in the Marshes. Now is the time to rest, I suggest you do it before we leave."

It took everything in her not to slap him because of his callousness, "Fine, but shouldn't we at least talk about what happened? Who was that man that came out of nowhere?"

"It doesn't matter!" he yelled. "It doesn't matter," he repeated again, quieter this time. Some of the men looked at them at Sainte's outburst. "Give me a second," he reached into a pocket and pulled his vial. After dropping the liquid into his eyes, he said, "This is my last vial. I have enough for a day, perhaps, but we'll have to find the plants after we're done here so I can make more."

"Ok… Are you going to answer any of my actual questions?"

He let out an exasperated sigh, "That was Nadrian. I don't know if you've ever met him, but he was the man who I'd talk to occasionally, about Ellie."

"Nadrian? Aye, I remember the name but never met him. What was he doing out there?"

"There's a lot you don't know. I'll explain it to you, eventually. For now just let me in peace. I'm going to try to rest, once we're dry we'll figure out where to go next," he laid down on his side, back to Iris. Apparently, the conversation was over.

Iris wanted to sleep too, but they needed supplies. She walked over to the fire and sat down. All the men quieted upon her arrival.

"No need to stop talking on my account. I just want to get warm and dry," she said.

"How was your trip through the Marshes?" one of them asked.

"Pretty bad…"

"What was it? Gators? Snakes? Wolves?"

"No… Malignin."

All of the men chortled with laughter, "Ain't ever seen a Malignin out here. Heard they was all gone anyways," a different one said.

"Might be some truth to her. Sun's not risen yet. Don't rightly know what time it tis now, I 'sume it's morning, or close to it. What happened out there?" another guard asked. This one had stubble on his face and graying hair but looked to only be in his thirties.

Iris thought about what she should say. She was not sure how much Sainte wished for people to know. Then again, if he did not want her to say something surely, he would have told her, so she ended up telling them of Aldred and their journey through the Marshes. She did leave out Nadrian, however.

"So, you're saying that this Aldred turned into a… monster? And Malignin showed up, killed yer horse, and chased you outta the Marshes? Are they coming here? Should we prepare for battle?" one of the guards asked sarcastically.

Iris shook her head, "If they were chasing us they would have caught us. I think they got distracted by something else. If they wanted to stop us from leaving, they could have."

"What'd they possibly get distracted by?"

"I don't know. All I know is that we made it out, somehow. All of our supplies, food and water mostly, were left behind. If you have any to spare."

"If what you say is true, we have to warn someone," they did not seem to hear what she said about food.

"I expect everyone already knows, or at least has an idea. The sun hasn't risen. The Dark Days are back," Iris said.

At the commotion around the fire Ser Rogir walked over, "Garen, send a raven to Defensen explaining what we just found out. But until we get further word we stay here and keep to our duties. As for your supplies, we can give you a canteen of water each, but only one loaf of bread. We should have a spare blanket or two, and I'm sure we have a rucksack lying around here somewhere." All the men were quiet as they listened to his orders.

Garen spoke up, "Ser, you believe her? It's crazy talk. Probably wolves, most likely. Not been a Malignin here ever."

"Are you questioning me? Do what I damn well ordered, not another word," Ser Rogir said sternly. Garen sulked away to do his task.

Iris watched with an approving eye, then asked, "Do you have a map I could take a look at? Ours was left in there."

"Aye, be right back," he said as he walked into the barracks. He returned shortly with a rolled-up parchment. He sat down next to Iris and unrolled the map, placing a rock on each corner to keep it from rolling back up. "We are about right here," he pointed on the map to a location about ten miles northeast of Defensen. "The Deshiere mountains are about ten or fifteen miles to the west, you can reach them in a day if you travel quickly. The towns Kenston and Riperton are on the other side of the mountains, nothing much on this side."

"Thank you, Ser Rogir," Iris said. Her eyelids had begun to droop, and as the conversation came to an end, she realized just how tired she was. "I'm going to try to get some sleep now, unless you need anything else of me."

"No, no. I think you've been enough help. Get some rest, I'll get someone to place two full canteens at your feet with a loaf of bread for when you wake. Thank you for telling us what happened to you out there. Keep the map, we have plenty."

Iris laid down where she was, not caring that she was on dirt. She thought of Dawn again, regret filled her that she was not able to save Tal's horse. The ground was cool, but the fire kept her warm enough, and before she knew it, she was asleep.

Sainte nudged Iris with his foot, waking her, "Let's go."

She sat up and rubbed her eyes, "How long were we asleep?"

"I don't know, but it's time. I guess they gave us two canteens, bread, and a blanket stuffed in this sack."

"I know, I asked them for it. If you had bothered talking to them at all you'd realize they could help us."

"Let's go," he said, ignoring her last sentence.

Iris stood up and grabbed her canteen. Sainte had already attached his to his waist and ripped the loaf of bread in half. He handed her the other half as he stuffed his in his pocket. She looked around but did not see anyone else, the guards must have retired to their barracks. The fire lazily burned, consuming the last few logs that were thrown on. She shouldered the sack that had been laid by her feet.

"Right, I suppose I'm ready," she said. Sainte started walking without a word, away from the encampment, towards the Deshiere mountains. "So what's the plan? Ser Rogir and I looked at a map before I went to bed, no towns on this side of the mountains. Do you have any idea where to look for the sword in them?" she asked to his back.

Sainte shrugged, "Make it to the mountains tonight. I'll set out some snares and hopefully get some small game, otherwise we'll have to make the bread last. We'll pass through

196

the mountains the following days and see what the towns have to offer. I forget their names."

"Kenston and Riperton. Ser Rogir gave me the map."

"Ser Rogir, eh? Great guy he is."

"Aye," Iris said slowly wondering what his point was. "He is."

"Sure was helpful to you."

"To us. He gave us full canteens and a map. You barely said anything to the man. Lucky he was in a better mood than you."

"I'm sure you being the only woman he's likely seen in a few months had nothing to do with it," he sneered.

"What the hell is wrong with you," Iris said. "You've been in a shite mood since the swamps, bitching about everything. What's gotten into you?"

"Everything!" he shouted. "Or haven't you noticed? The sun isn't rising, again, the Malignin seem to be back in force, the fucking Abomination is out there trying to get something from me."

"Trying to get something from you? What?"

"I don't know. It said it wants something that I have. Changes nothing."

"Changed you."

"If you don't like it you can leave. I didn't ask you to come with me, that was your idea," he said callously.

"Because I thought you'd be happy to be around an old friend."

Sainte sighed, "I was… I'm just so angry. I'm sorry," seemed like he had to force that out. "I'll try to work on it. So much is happening, though, it's hard for me to push my anger aside."

"Good, because I'm not leaving you, not again, even though I've thought several times already since we've been awake. I can't blame you for being mad, but don't take it out on me."

Sainte crossed his arms as they walked, the wind swept across the barren land with nothing to oppose it. The hilly plains moaned around them with lonely oaks spotted here and there. There was no civilization this close to the Marshes, the land was too near the swamplands to bear any crops and there was not enough vegetation to feed any amount of livestock that would be worthwhile.

Iris squinted her eyes as a beam of sunlight pierced the thick overcast clouds. She raised a hand to block the brunt of it, "Seems something's wanting to come back out." She lowered hand as the light was covered by another cloud.

Sainte brought one of his hands to cover his eyes as he looked up, the other reached for the last vial, "I suppose it is." After the drops, he looked at the woefully empty vial, "Going to have to do something about this soon."

"Aye, what do you need for it?" Iris asked.

"Just Alon Zirnia, squish it up and mix it with water. Pretty simply, but I haven't quite got used to having to make it. This was the last bit that Jasmine had made for me," Sainte explained.

"Lucky, Alon is pretty common. Here, might as well take a look there," Iris pointed to a copse of trees a short distance from the path. The sun had already started to sink below the mountains, so the shadow soon covered the two as they foraged around, digging through the vegetation.

"I can't believe I let myself run out of the poultice," he grumbled to himself.

Overhearing him Iris said, "If you had told me when you were low, I could've helped. I saw some Alon a day or two back."

"Getting smart now, are you?" Sainte asked sarcastically. "You could've asked about it."

"You could say that, but no more smart than you were an ass right after the Marshes," she snipped back. "Figured you would've told me if it was important."

He knew she joked, but there was truth to her words. He did not know what came over him the last day. He was mad at her, himself, at everything and he was not able to shake it, until the sun showed itself again.

"Just keep looking, we're bound to find some here," his eyes burned and rummaging around kicking all the dust up was not helping his case at all.

"Here," Iris called out finally, thankfully, "I found some."

Sainte walked over to her picking dirt out from under his fingernails, happy to be done. She handed him a handful of the plant. He dropped the leaves into a small wooden bowl they had and smashed them up with a rock. Then he poured a small amount of water in with the smashed leaves and stirred it with his finger. After that, he took out his vials, he had six of them, and one by one uncorked them and dunked them in the poultice. He tried to keep as much leaf out as possible but did not care all too much about it. He managed to fill four of his vials before the liquid was gone. He scraped out the leaves, then immediately dropped two drops in each eye and breathed a sigh of relief. Iris watched with a passing interest.

"Ah, that's much better. Thank you," he said as he corked the vial and put it away.

"You're welcome. Maybe next time tell me when you are running low and I'll make it for you," she reminded him again. "Didn't realize it was that easy."

"You're going to regret those words," he smiled. "If you see any more of that plant let's just go ahead and grab it so we have some," he rolled his shoulders and stretched his neck.

"Will do, only because you asked nicely. You ready to keep moving now?"

"Aye, let's go. Maybe we can reach the foot of the mountains before complete nightfall."

After continuing on for a few steps Iris said, "You have no idea where to go once we reach the mountains? Only that the sword is located in them, somewhere? That's a lot of area to cover, think we'll be able to find it?"

"Well, we'll find out, won't we? I was thinking that we'd make our way through the mountains while keeping a look out for it, though I doubt we'll get lucky enough to get it. If we get to the other side without finding anything, we'll go to Kenston and ask around. Surely there are rumors or legends of it, or something. If this sword really is as powerful as Nadrian made it out to be, it has to have some kind of trail that'll lead to it. It has to."

"Did Nadrian tell you what to do once you find it? What makes it so powerful?" Iris asked as they walked.

"Only that it can kill the Abomination, he didn't get into specifics, and I wasn't in a great position to be asking questions. I guess if he says it can kill Aldred it's worth it. Though I guess he was never Aldred, not really… Have you heard of King Zith before?" Sainte asked.

"Heard of him, yes, of course I have. Heard much of him, no. All I know is that he was one of the last kings we had over two hundred years ago."

"Yes, him and King Nuse. The last two kings. I've only heard their story a handful of times, but they had a falling out, King Nuse killed King Zith."

"Aye, I've heard that," Iris said nodding her head.

"And what else?"

"Well, that's it really. After Nuse killed Zith, the people turned on Nuse and had him killed," Iris explained.

"That's not it. Aroc and Isaac told me what really happened."

"Who's Isaac?" Iris asked.

"He was a White Wyvern, he helped me, but he's dead now," Sainte paused for a moment after he said that. "Anyway, Zith was killed and he had so much rage, so much hatred, that it took a physical form as the Malignin. They were born through his death and unleased upon the land. The White Wyverns then made the Barrier and the Blades of the Night to protect her from the Malignin."

Iris listened and squinted her eyes in thought when he finished, "I have so many more questions."

"Me too, but the Wyverns aren't very forthcoming with answers, like to keep it all to themselves unless absolutely necessary. I was told some more, but I don't know if there's any truth to it."

"From whom?"

Sainte was reluctant to reply, "Ellie… In the caves. She said that the White Wyverns had portioned off part of the world, trapped the Malignin, along with everyone that resided there, in a corner of the world, nothing allowed in or out. Apparently, the world as we know it is much larger, If what I was told was true. Maybe she was just trying to get me to turn against the White Wyverns. Who knows, I haven't been able to ask about it yet."

"This is… a lot to take in. Do you actually believe that?" Iris asked as she thrummed her fingers on her holstered crossbow.

"I don't know… I don't think it's too far fetched compared to everything else I've learned in the past few months. One thing's for sure, we've been lied to, one way or another."

As the day wore on their environment slowly changed around them. The small rolling hills changed into rocky formations. Grass thinned out to craggy plant life, trees were shorter and their roots strove to grasp onto the rocks. The Deshiere mountains now extended to their left and right as far as they could see, the snow-capped tips barely visible through the mist that shrouded them. Wind whistled through the crevices and cracks, promising a chilly journey through the mountains.

They had not noticed it, but Sainte and Iris had been walking up a slight incline for most of their trek after the Marshes. As they got nearer to the mountains, however, the incline increased and the temperature dropped.

"My eyes are not going to enjoy the cold and the wind. They already burn and we aren't even into the mountains yet," Sainte complained to Iris.

"Hmm, wrap your head in a cowl, perhaps. Thin enough so you can see through, but maybe it will help with the wind at least. I've picked some more Alon so I can make more poultice if you run low again, so don't be shy to use more if you think it's necessary."

"Thank you," Sainte said sincerely. "I think we should be stopping for now. It's getting dark, we're about to get into the mountains, and I think we should set up a few snares, try to get some more food before we're fully immersed in them. I'll set them up if you can get a fire going," Sainte offered.

"Sounds good to me," Iris agreed.

"I'm going to use some bread for the bait, if you don't mind."

"Do what you have to do," Iris said absentmindedly as she went about her task of gathering some wood.

Sainte walked just far enough away to where he could barely hear Iris, then he began to set up the small traps. Earlier he had heard a hawk, or some other bird of prey, screeching overhead, so he assumed there must be some rodents around that they would eat.

He ended up setting four separate snares hoping to catch anything, even a rat would suffice. The bread and jerky they got from the guard post was running low, and they would need plenty of food to get through the mountains. After he set the last snare he returned to Iris, who had a campfire blazing. She had the blanket given to them rolled out by the fire and laid on it, eating a handful of bread.

"How'd it go?" she asked after she swallowed.

"Good, I guess. Set four up, hope we can get something. I'll go check them in an hour or so. How good you think you are with that crossbow?" he asked as he sat down on the bare ground across the fire from her.

"I don't think I'd be much help. I'm sure I can hit large targets, but I haven't had much practice with it and I don't want to waste any bolts," she said. She had removed the harness and had it laying out beside her.

"Sounds like you were just as good with bows," he quipped.

She let out a small laugh then sighed lazily, "I do miss it, sometimes. I liked it, you know. It was something I was good at. I'm sure this crossbow is great, but it holds nothing in comparison to a longbow."

"As long as you don't accidentally hit me with it in a fight, I think it'll do you just as well," Sainte said.

"Very funny, next fight I'll just stay back then, let you do it all. Wouldn't want to accidentally shoot you," she joked.

"I've managed to make it some time without you by my side, I'm sure I could handle it a little longer."

"And look where that got you, almost blinded," she was quick with her comebacks, he missed that.

"Minor wounds. Nothing I can't handle," he brushed it off as if he barely realized he did not have any eye lids.

They continued their small talk for some time before Sainte realized it had been nearly three hours since he placed the snares.

"I'm going to go check on the snares, I'll be right back," he stood up and stretched before heading away. He returned about twenty minutes later carrying a squirrel and a marmot that was about double the size of the squirrel.

"Didn't know you were so good at trapping," Iris said.

"Beginner's luck, haven't set any snares before now for, I can't even remember how long. But they worked, got ourselves some food for a little while longer," he sat down and immediately began skinning and gutting the animals.

Soon the fur was drying out by the fire and the meat was getting roasted over it. The smell made Iris' stomach growl.

"Hungry I take it?" Sainte asked.

"Aye, of course. The bread is fine, but it's not very fulfilling."

"Agreed. We still have to eat sparingly, just in case we don't get this lucky every time," he finished the sentence with a yawn. It was fully dark now, there still were some clouds in the sky, but some stars were able to shine through between them.

"I know. You know, you can come over here. We have only this one blanket, sleeping on the bare ground can't be comfortable, though I suppose this blanket doesn't help a whole lot either," Iris sat up and patted the empty space beside her.

"I didn't want to intrude, and I don't sleep much anyway," Sainte scratched his arm.

"Come on, at least sit over here. I'm probably going to sleep soon, and I imagine it's not going to get any warmer as the night wears on. We can at least try to use our body heat to stay warm, along with the fire." She saw the look on his face and laughed, "Not like that, you moron. I just don't want to freeze to death."

"It is getting a little chilly," he said as he moved over to her. As he sat down he said, "You can go to sleep, I'll stay up and keep the fire going." He threw some sticks in from the pile that Iris had put next to the blanket.

"If you insist," she said as she laid down on her side, feet towards the fire and back towards Sainte. Her back barely brushed up against his leg but was touching enough so that they could both feel each other's warmth.

Sainte sat still for a while, stoking the fire when it needed it, and listened to Iris' steady breathing. Once he was sure she was asleep, he stood up and wrapped her with the half of the blanket he was sitting on. She stirred a little at the movement but did not wake. He took the meat from the fire and wrapped it in some large leaves they had picked.

After he stoked the fire one last time, he laid on the bare ground next to Iris. They were back to back, and although he did not have a blanket, he felt warm next to her.

ELEVEN

Kial, Peng, Nadrian, and Jasmine caught up relatively easy with everyone who had fled before them. Munich was no longer able to be seen, the city had been lost in the night as they ran away. All the townsfolk had gathered together in one large group, no longer moving. Their cries were heard long before they came into view.

Everyone was huddled together, parents holding children, strangers comforting each other. A lone man was standing before everyone speaking. At least there was someone trying to get a semblance of order going.

As they approached, they could hear him saying, "… must keep moving on. We don't have to keep it at a brisk pace, but we can't stay here. I've spoken with my fellow Blades of the Night, many of whom have continued ahead to make sure the way is clear, and we agree that we should continue into the Barrier's Mountains and try to establish a camp of sorts."

"We could go to Mountsville, it's not too far and they could provide some shelter," a man called out.

"We talked about that, but we believe that Mountsville would treat us much like Munich treated the refugees from Guardstin. Not to mention Mountsville is much smaller than Munich," he shook his head. "Of course, you're free to do what you will, but the Blades will be going into the Barrier's Mountains. I'll be heading that way now, anyone who wishes to come follow me." The man began to walk away, slowly, so as to give everyone time to decide. A small group of men, the rest of the Blades, broke off and followed him. It did not take long for people to decide. Soon everyone there, about a hundred people, followed him as well.

"About time someone with sense takes charge," Jasmine muttered.

"We going with them?" Nadrian asked her.

"Aye, I think we should," she answered.

"Don't you think you two should be in charge?" Peng asked. "After what we saw you do back there?"

"No, that is not our place here. We guide, not lead," Jasmine said.

"You also bribe, and lie, and who knows what else," Kial said.

"I regret who my actions may or may not have harmed, but everything I've done has been necessary to keep the majority of people safe," Jasmine said. Nadrian remained quiet.

"I don't even know who you are anymore," Kial said.

Jasmine looked to Nadrian who only raised his eyebrows. She sighed, "We're White Wyverns."

"Excuse me?" Peng said.

"You heard me. We're White Wyverns. Our purpose here is to guide only, push people to make correct choices and help out only when absolutely necessary, as you two witnessed at Munich."

"Why did you pay off the Examiner? Threaten him with his life if he spoke up? Doesn't seem very necessary to me," Kial said. "Didn't let me go get Marianne and Franceska…"

"Now is clearly not the time for this," Jasmine said.

"Of course," Kial shook his head. "Come on Peng, let's catch up. See if we can help out with anything in ways that don't rely on blackmail."

Jasmine and Nadrian watched the two men speed up and join the others. "Do you think it wise you told them about us?" Nadrian asked once Peng and Kial were out of earshot.

"I don't think it matters. I don't think it mattered for a while. Not like you were offering any alternatives."

"This is your game; these are your people. Tell them what you want, I'm just here to support you now, not influence you," Nadrian said rather ironically.

Jasmine watched her two friends, if she could still call them that, as they approached the others. "Give them time to think about what I told them, to think about what they just went through. They lost their homes, their friends and family. They'll come back with questions."

"Will you be ready to answer them?"

"I don't know," she said quietly.

Kial and Peng walked past the people of Munich in silence. They were looking to catch up to the man who spoke in front of everyone to see if he wanted any help from them. Not much of the guard was left of Munich, or at least they did not see anyone they worked with, much less recognized.

"Hey, Kial," Peng said. "What do you think happened to the Shinta? You think the Malignin went after them?"

"I don't know, I don't care. They're far enough away from Munich, maybe the Malignin left them alone, or didn't even realize they were there. I just want to get a small group together and head back to look for Marianne and Franceska. Is that the guy?" Kial nodded to a man a short way ahead of them.

"I think so."

"Excuse me," Kial called out. Several people looked at him, but he ignored them, "You, up there. Blade!" The man finally looked back and paused, once Kial and Peng caught up to him he resumed walking.

"Aye, what is it?" he asked.

"My name's Kial, and this is Peng. We are, were, guards for Munich. I was just wondering what you'll need help with once we reach, er, wherever we're going. You think you'll send a party back to Munich to look for other survivors?"

"I imagine we'll need all the help we can get," was his simple reply. "As for going back, no. Whoever was left wouldn't be able to survive that. I'm sorry."

"Aye, but what kind of help?" Peng asked while Kial fumed at the mans answer.

"I don't yet know," he said irritated. "I'll figure that part out when we get there."

"Where?" Peng asked.

The man seemed frustrated with the questions but took a breath and calmed down. "Some of the other Blades have got back to me. They've found a cliffside on the side of a mountain in the Barrier's mountains. They say it's a naturally defensive position and large enough to build up for how many people we have here, plus many more if anyone else joins us."

"They've already reached the Barrier's mountains?" Peng asked surprised.

"Aye, the Blades do not need to rest as often, and move much quicker. I think it will be another two days, at least, for us to reach their position at our current pace."

"What's your name?" Kial asked.

"Seltrin Rethner, from Diplawn. I appreciate you boys for the offer of help, but right now let's just make sure we all get to the mountains in one piece. Once we get there come find me again and we can figure out what to do."

Kial did not appreciate being referred to as 'boy' as he and Seltrin were rather close in age, but he shrugged it off, "You're not sending anyone back, I'll just go myself."

Seltrin shrugged, "I don't care. Do whatever you want, I'll not be sending any of my Blades with you."

"Kial, you can't go back yourself. You won't make it. Don't be foolish," Peng said. "We'll talk to you again, Seltrin, once we make it to the mountains." Peng pulled Kial with him and slowed their pace. They kept their distance from Nadrian and

Jasmine throughout their travel. Twice Jasmine tried to talk to them, but they did not respond back to her.

Finally, during what everyone assumed was the second day they fled Munich, the sun's rays began to break through the heavy cloud cover. The light lifted everyone's spirits and their pace quickened. That evening they were in the Barrier's Mountains, and the next day about midday they approached the cliffside that they would call their new home.

They had to climb up the mountain, but the Blades that were there before them scouted the area and showed them up the least difficult path. They had cleared out the way for everyone, and already a path was being worn down. Another three hours went by before everyone arrived at the precipice. The Blades that had arrived before them had been busy. Some small stone and wood shelters had already been built for housing and storage. Animal skins were hanging up on the sides drying out, and multiple fires were roasting fresh meat.

Seltrin was greeted by another Blade, they spoke briefly before he turned around to address everyone.

"I know we have just arrived and everyone is probably exhausted, but there's still much work to be done. As you can see some shelters have been made already, and I ask that families with children take those first. For the men I ask that you help build more shelters. If you need help constructing anything ask one of my fellow Blades and they will assist you. For the women I ask that you see to the care of the children and of the food. Pull the meat off the fires when it is done, make stews, or anything really. We need to build our stockpile of food up. There's a small creek nearby, one of us will show you there. Now, we don't know where the Malignin are, we don't know if they'll find us, but we need to be prepared for them. We need to build this up as quick as possible, but I don't think you need me telling you that. So, let's get started," he finished.

Slowly people began breaking away into smaller groups. The few children were led by their parents to some of the shelters. The men began to wander to where the shelters were as well, not to rest but to find a spot where they would begin building their own. Kial saw that a Blade was waiting by the shelters and began to explain where exactly they were planning to build the homes as the men approached. The women who did not have any children made their way to the roasting fires to tend to the meat.

"What do you suppose we do now?" Peng asked Kial.

"Well, let's make us a place to sleep real quick, then we'll see if the Blades need help with anything. We could probably do to make this a more defensible position," Kial said.

"Good, get a place ready for when Marianne and Franceska return," Peng said.

"Don't," Kial said. "They're not coming back."

"You don't know that," Peng offered.

"Let's just go, no talking."

They walked to the Blade directing the building in uncomfortable silence and were given a small area for them to build whatever shelter they wanted. Kial started collecting rocks large enough to stack up and Peng went about collecting sticks to use as well. Eventually they were so into building their meager shelter they did not realize Jasmine had walked up to them.

"Hey," she said, shocking them out of their task.

"What do you want?" Kial asked after dropping a particularly large stone.

"To talk, to tell you the truth," Jasmine said.

"About what? How can we trust you?" Kial said.

"I think we should talk, see what she has to say at least," Peng offered. "We've known her for a long time, Kial, and she has helped us and many others more than she needed to."

"She killed those people," Kial said, slightly raising his voice.

"I did not kill anyone," Jasmine said in protest, with a sternness that left no room for questions about it. She regained her composure, "But I can explain why I did what I did. Whether you choose to believe me or not is up to you."

Kial let out a deep breath, "I don't know. Not right now."

"Come by tonight, we'll be here," Peng said. "Where's Nadrian?"

"He's working on our shelter. He'll be with me tonight. Thank you Peng, Kial. I like you two and the least I can do is explain myself," she sounded genuine.

Kial and Peng ended up building a lean-to big enough for them to sleep under with about two feet between them as they slept. Some of the men who were more inclined had started to build up four walled buildings, but a simple shelter was fine by Kial and Peng's standards. After their shelter was finished, they found Seltrin. He was standing at the edge of the precipice overlooking the mountainous valley about a hundred feet below the cliff. It was evening by now and a cool breeze swept passed the mountains that loomed over their small encampment.

"Evening Seltrin," Peng said as he walked and stood by his side. "What're you looking at?"

"Just thinking about all the possible routes Malignin could take to try to overwhelm us. We have a good position here, high, we can see a far distance, see them and have enough time to prepare some kind of defense, or retreat most likely," he turned to Peng and Kial. "What can I do for you?"

"Well, we came here to ask about defenses, if you had an idea for any and to see what we could do to help with it," Kial said.

"I was thinking of lining the cliffside with stakes angled down to hinder any Malignin that decide to scale them. On either side of our little precipice where it slopes down, we could prop boulders or logs, anything that'll roll. Once they're close enough we can release them and let them do damage for us. Of course, scattered throughout would be multiple fire defenses. Perhaps we could implement fire with the logs," he paused for a moment in thought. "Either way, it'll have to wait for tomorrow, give everyone a break. They did a lot of work today, deserve a good night's rest. Tomorrow we can start on defenses. You two can start on the stakes tomorrow, if you like."

"Aye, we can do that," Peng said.

"Aye," Kial agreed. "Thanks for what you're doing, taking charge and all. We need someone like you in a time like this."

"Ah, someone's gotta do it," Seltrin waved his hand.

"Say, do you know a Sainte or Iris?" Peng asked.

"Aye," Seltrin said slowly, "I do. Sainte's the Shield, or was, if he's still alive anymore. Iris went with him, one of his hands, along with Miqel. Haven't seen any of them since, I don't know, a few months now. Why?"

"We ran into Iris a while ago, helped her out. Miqel was after her, actually. He seemed a bad sort. We left her with a Shinta friend, Tal, but haven't seen either of them since, and Sainte came by Munich for a few days. Helped him out too, went out to get the Barrier. Haven't heard from him since either. Was just wondering if you knew anything," Peng explained.

"No, I don't, but that's interesting. Miqel was after her, you say?"

"Aye, she seemed afraid of him, actually."

"Hmm, odd. They used to almost be inseparable. Some of us Blades say they fled, abandoned us when things got hard," he shook his head. "Say what they will, I would give ten of these Blades here up to have Sainte, Iris, or Miqel. I've seen them fight."

"I'm not sure what you all think about them, but I can tell you that Sainte and Iris, although they may have had their own agendas, thought they were doing what was best. I don't know Miqel, but what little I saw of him," Peng shuddered. "He seemed evil."

Seltrin was deep in thought for a few moments then said, "Whatever happened isn't our problem right now. I suggest you two get some rest, tomorrow's going to be another long day," he nodded his head towards them then headed to his own shelter.

"Right, well, let's go back to our lean-to. I'd wager Jasmine is already there waiting for us," Kial said.

While they walked through the encampment soft sobs could be heard throughout. Munes crying for the loss of their loved ones and of the whole situation. It still had not quite hit Kial yet, he did not feel sad or upset, just a certain restlessness. All he wanted to do was go back and get his wife and daughter, there was no questions on if they were alive or dead.

"If I took you up on your wager I'd be a poor man," Peng said as they approached their shelter. Jasmine was sitting out front with Nadrian around a small fire they had started. She looked up as she heard them approach.

"Evening, I was wondering if you were going to come talk to me or just not show up. I'm glad you two did," she said as she stood up in greeting.

"Said we would, didn't we?" Kial said.

"Hey Jasmine, good to see you," Peng said with a smile.

Kial sat down on the opposite side of the fire as Jasmine, ignoring her outstretched hand. "What're you making?" he asked Nadrian who held meat on a stick over the flames.

"It's rabbit," Nadrian replied as he held it close to his face to examine the meat, then took a bite. "Bit rubbery."

"Ignore him," Peng told Jasmine. "He'll come around. Unlike him, I don't turn on our friends so easily."

"Did you forget," Kial started but Peng cut him off.

"Not now. Let's listen to her. Then you can decide how mad you want to be," Peng sat across from Nadrian. Jasmine sat back down from where she stood up.

"What questions do you have?" she asked.

"To start off, let's go with Flotier. What was his deal? Why are you trying to cover up what the Examiner discovered?" Kial asked without giving Peng any time to ask anything.

"I see you've been thinking about this," Jasmine said.

"Of course I have!" he yelled, then quieter he repeated himself, "Of course I have. Were you the one behind threatening me? Did you pay someone to threaten me? Would you have me killed too?" he stared at her, then said, "Flotier first."

She took a breath then began speaking, "Flotier was, like me, a White Wyvern," she glanced at Nadrian who said nothing. "We exist to help you humans make the appropriate decisions in tough situations. As we are in one now, it is Nadrian and I's job to assist you to get to the best possible outcome. We are not allowed to do so in a way that would result in us being revealed."

"What about back at Munich? What you and Nadrian did, how do you blend in with abilities like that?" Kial asked.

"Well, there are others of our kind here, in every city and town. On this precipice there are five other White Wyverns, not counting myself and Nadrian. If someone performs a feat, then someone else will cause the witnesses to forget. There are multiple ways to make someone forget something they saw."

"How do we remember?"

"Because I shielded you and Peng from the spell that was performed while we walked here."

Kial let out a breath of air in disbelief and closed his eyes, "Alright, what about Flotier?"

"Ah, it's a touchy subject, so I'll get straight to it. If the White Wyverns deem you unsalvageable then we…" she swallowed.

"Yes?"

"We are supposed to kill you all."

Kial scoffed, Peng was shocked into silence. "Kill us all?" Kial asked. "The entire world?"

Nadrian sat back on his hands, seemingly enjoying watching Jasmine act under the pressure.

"Your entire world… as you know it," she shared a look with Nadrian.

"What deems us unsalvageable? Why kill us all?" Kial asked, still not believing a word she said.

"It has to do with the Malignin, if they run rampant on the land. We have to try to do what we can to contain them, and that means unleashing something powerful that we have taken to calling the Severence. Unfortunately, nobody would survive the attack."

"Oh, so you're not killing us specifically, it would just be an accident. Hear that, Peng, they don't want to kill us but they have no choice." Peng did not reply. "You still haven't answered any of my questions about Flotier."

"Yes, he was starting the ritual for the, er, magic. He would have succeeded too, had I not stopped him. I begged with the Council, the other White Wyverns, to give me time to try to redeem the situation so we wouldn't have to resort to the Severence. They did, and everything was going well until now."

Kial stood up, "This is ridiculous. I'm going to bed. You're crazy, can't believe you actually thought I'd believe something so outlandish. Do what you want Peng, believe what you want, but don't try to make me believe any of this." He walked the short distance to the lean-to and laid on his side, back to everyone around the fire.

Peng glanced at Jasmine, then quickly to the fire as she met his gaze. "I don't know, Jasmine. This does seem pretty crazy…"

"Do you not remember what we were able to do at Munich?" she asked.

"I do, that's the only reason I didn't leave like Kial. I think he's in denial, or too stubborn to believe his eyes. I don't really know what to think of you anymore, though. I don't know whether to fear you or be glad you're on our side."

"You can be both," Jasmine offered.

"Maybe… I'm going to try to get some sleep. I'll keep in touch, I suppose, would be hard not to up here. Goodnight Jasmine, Nadrian," he stood up and joined Kial under the lean-to.

"How do you think that went?" Nadrian asked Jasmine quietly.

She sighed, "About exactly as you said it would."

"You think it wise to tell them the truth?"

"I didn't tell them all of it."

"I am aware. Decided to keep the bit about them being the sacrifice for the Severence to yourself. Wise decision, I think.

I doubt the Council would have liked you telling humans about that, but I think there are many things the Council wouldn't like about how you are handling this."

"Why are you talking like this? I thought you were on my side," Jasmine snapped.

"I am, I'm here aren't I? I just think that perhaps a little more anonymity would do you, us, well."

"Everything's going according to plan. Hit a few rough patches, but nothing that we haven't prepared for."

"Yet," was Nadrian's simple reply.

TWELVE

Sainte woke with a start. Immediately he noticed that Iris was not behind him anymore. He sat up in a panic, breaths heaved in and out of his mouth.

"Hey, good morning. Sleep good?" Iris asked. She stood a few feet away by the fire, now merely embers, poking it with a stick. He had no idea how he did not see her.

"I must have," Sainte said, getting his breathing back under control. He absentmindedly dropped some drops into his eyes. "I haven't had a good sleep in a long time, usually I'm not able to fall asleep. When I do I have terrible dreams… but I didn't last night."

"Could've fooled me the way you woke up, but glad to hear it. Thanks for giving me the blanket, but you didn't have to," she said.

"You needed it more than I did. I like the cold, growing up in Bethrune and all I'm pretty used to it," he stood up and stretched, then looked around and saw that Iris had already packed everything up. All she was waiting for was for him to wake up apparently.

"Well, I expect it'll only get colder once we're actually in the mountains. Don't be afraid to use it too, if you want it. It's big enough to cover us both."

"I know, and I'm sure I will use it. Looks like you got everything ready without me. I'm surprised I was able to sleep through you packing up our stuff."

"You say that like we had a lot of stuff to begin with. It wasn't that much, really," Iris laughed. "Ready to go, or do you need more time to wake up?"

"I'm good, let's go," he said as he shouldered his pack.

After kicking some rocks over their fire to ensure it stayed out, Iris and Sainte walked towards the Deshiere Mountains across the rocky, wind-swept terrain. Their going was slow but steady. Midday came and went with the two of them eating only what they deemed necessary. The grey, rocky mountains surrounded them with their peaks disappearing into the grey sky. A light snowfall complimented the crisp air that cut at their lungs. Their breaths huffed out in clouds of vapor before their faces.

"I can understand why the White Wyverns decided to hide that damned sword here," Iris said through chattering teeth.

"Why's that?" Sainte asked, too focused on his shivering to focus on her words.

"Why would anyone in their right mind come here? It's too cold for anything. I hope we can find enough wood to make a fire tonight."

"Definitely a good mountain range," Sainte agreed. "I hope we don't get lost, we can't afford it. As long as we can keep heading west, we should come to a road that leads to Edgevin from Kenston. As long as we can get to that road, we'll be fine. As long as we don't freeze to death before."

"And then once we get to Kenston we… what? Ask them if they've heard of this all-powerful sword that the White Wyverns hid and placed a demon to protect it an unknown amount of time ago? I'm sorry, Sainte, but what is the plan other than to ask around?" Iris asked. She had been thinking about how to find the sword to keep her mind off of how cold she was.

"That's all we have for now. Believe me, I wish I knew more too. Maybe there'll be a White Wyvern there that can help us or point us in the right direction. That's what I'm really hoping for. Every one that I've met thus far has seemed to want to help me in some form," Sainte said hopefully. Iris did not reply and continued to ruminate within her own thoughts.

Boulders from rockslides littered the landscape around them as they were almost within the mountains. They zigzagged between them and hoped that they would not be caught in a landslide themselves. Sainte came to a stop as Iris called out asking for a break.

"How you doing?" he asked.

"Getting pretty steep," she said. "Getting a little harder to breathe, too."

"Aye, air is thinner the higher you get. Was like this in Bethrune as well. I think the ground should level out a bit a little further on," Sainte looked up at the peaks as he said this, but then a movement caught his eye. Three people were slowly making their way down towards them. He was about to ask Iris if she saw them too, but a quick glance confirmed she did.

The men wore mismatched, incomplete armor. They had their weapons drawn and were clearly heading straight for Sainte and Iris. Sainte drew his own sword, and he heard Iris lock into place her crossbow.

"What do you want?" Sainte called out to them, but they did not answer. Instead they broke apart. The man in the middle headed straight on, one went right, and one went left. They meant to surround them.

"Been wondering when you might show up," the man in front said. Each of them stopped about thirty feet away.

"Who are you?" Iris asked.

"We are few of many, the hidden saviors, the ancient Cult of Bal'shere. We mean to free all of Crearia, to continue to do what Ellie wished for us all, before you killed her," he said to Sainte. "She told us everything, how the White Wyverns locked us up. How the Malignin were made to be the scapegoats, hated when all they wanted was to join together to bring down the Wyverns."

"What are you talking about? What you speak of is crazy," Sainte said.

"No more questions, let's kill 'em," as one the three men charged. Iris loosed a bolt with a loud twang, Sainte heard it swish by his head, then watched it suddenly appear in the man in fronts stomach. He doubled over and fell down.

The other two men continued their charge. Sainte saw that the man on Iris' side was nearly on her, so he shoved her out of the way and parried the would be killing slash. They traded blows twice before Sainte saw and opening and bashed the man in his face with the pommel of his sword.

He turned around quickly just in time to see the third attacker mid thrust, which he clumsily knocked aside and punched the man in the face. As the man stumbled back he slashed him from left shoulder to right hip, spilling blood on the freshly snow covered ground. Sainte turned back around to face the second man, but saw that Iris had dispatched of him with two bolts, one in the throat and one in the chest.

Iris joined Sainte once more and looked at the three bodies that now lay around them. One of them still moved, the first she had shot. Together they walked to him. His breath came in in short intakes and out with gurgles. Iris must have hit some vital organ, the man was dying, albeit slowly.

He turned his head up to look at them, Sainte in particular, and said "We strive… to be free. He will stop… you."

"I don't fucking care," Sainte said. He put the tip of his sword on the man's throat and leaned on it, slowly piercing through his neck and several inches into the ground. He held it in place for a minute as the blood leaked from him. Iris watched in silent surprise, not sure what to say. Once he was sure the man was dead, he pulled his sword free and cleaned it on the dead man's clothes before sheathing it.

Slowly folding her crossbow back up to her shoulder, Iris finally asked, "Who were they?"

"Apparently some cult that Ellie created, or did you miss that?"

"Zith sent them," she said.

"Why, though? Did you see how they fought? Poorly. He had to have known they wouldn't win against us. Maybe to show he doesn't care about losing people… because he has many…" Sainte shook his head. "I don't care," he said again.

"Do you want to talk about it?" Iris asked.

"About what?"

"Killing… a person," she said uncertainly, bad memories suddenly a tidal wave in her mind. Memories of Tal.

"Doesn't feel much different than a Malignin," he paused then, noticing her face. Maybe this was more for her than him. "Do you?"

She shook her head slowly, "No. They were going to kill us, we did what we had to."

Sainte nodded, "That's right. I'll continue to do what I have to if that's what it takes to get this forsaken sword." He took a deep breath in and let it out. The adrenaline of the fight was quickly leaving him, and he started to feel the cold again. A light snow fall had begun sometime during the battle which did not help at all. "Are you good to push on?"

"Aye, let's go," Iris said. Side by side they continued on towards the Deshiere mountains, leaving the three bodies behind, allowing the snow to bury for them.

Even though the terrain was rocky, uneven, jagged, and cold they made faster travel than originally anticipated. Well within the mountains and the sun setting, they decided to stop for the night. Spruce trees grew sparsely throughout, but Sainte still managed to collect enough wood for a fire and even found a log they could sit on. Once the fire was going and they were sitting side by side on the log, Iris pulled out the blanket.

"I thought it was about time for an extra layer," she threw the blanket over their shoulders and they huddled together. The stars, fully out this night, illuminated the mountains with a pale luminescent glow. The fire's red and yellow flames a stark contrast to their dark, silver lit surroundings.

"After everything that happened before, I'm glad you're alright Iris. Thank you for being a good friend," Sainte said quietly, suddenly.

At his words Iris had a small smile but she did not respond. Instead she wrapped him in a one-armed hug and held him close. The embrace lasted some time, each person relishing the moment, and in that moment they each knew just how much they cared for each other, at what lengths they would go to help each other out. At that time, it seemed as though nothing could put their friendship to the test after everything they had been through.

Three days came and went since Iris and Sainte made their way into the Deshiere Mountains with no further signs of the cult. The going had been slow and made even slower with the snow that showed up, but still they persisted. They managed to make a fire every night and with it and their body heat they did not freeze completely through.

"How much longer do you think we have till we're out of these mountains?" Iris asked on the fourth day. She was getting tired of slipping on the frozen rocks.

"I don't think we have much longer. The mountains seem to be much smaller than when we first came in. I'm thinking we'll be finding a path to Kenston soon. Hopefully tonight or tomorrow," Sainte called back to her. "Sooner rather than later, I hope."

The snow was up to their knees in most places. They trudged through it, the only thing keeping them warm during the day was their constant movement. The sun barely shone through the overcast sky and around the mountains.

Iris did indeed note that the mountains size dwindled, they were still large, but their peaks were below the clouds now.

The angle they walked was not as steep and rocky, but a little smoother and rounder. The snow fall had stopped falling and the ground was mushy due to the recent melting of the snow that had recently covered it.

Sainte climbed onto a large rock to see if he could see any sign of a road ahead of them. "I think I see it," he said after a moment, then squinted hard.

"Really? How far?" Iris asked.

"I'd say about half a mile, shouldn't take us long to get there at all," he said and then hopped down off the rock.

"Finally, I'll be glad to be out of these mountains. I'm tired of being cold all the time. Do you think we'll reach Kenston today?"

"Maybe. I don't think it can be much farther now that we're pretty much mountain free. I think, once we reach the path, we shouldn't stop until we reach Kenston though. We're close enough that I think we'll definitely be there by night fall, but just in case we aren't I think we should push through to it," Sainte suggested.

"That's fine with me. What're we waiting for, then? Let's keep going," Iris said. She shrugged her shoulders and stretched out her legs then stepped off.

Sainte followed her and they reached the road shortly after. Their speed noticeably increased on the smoother terrain. With the mountains to their left and hills to their right they continued on through dusk intent to reach Kenston.

Soon, in the distance flickering lights could be seen. Small, one story houses came into sight, candlelight sputtered through windows. There were no walls around this town, and not much more to it than mostly homes. No sounds could be heard, everyone seemed to be in their own homes now.

"Who do we talk to?" Iris asked as they walked between the small buildings. "No one's around."

"I guess just knock and ask someone about their Council. If they even have one. I knew Kenston was small, but I didn't realize it was like this," Sainte said. He walked up to a door and knocked.

A few moments later the door swung open and an elderly man hunched over with leathery skin stood in the doorway. "Aye? Can I help ye?"

"I hope so. My name's Sainte and this is Iris. We're looking for the Council here?"

"Council? Aren't no Council here. Why're ye here so late?" he looked the pair of them up and down.

"Who would you say is in charge of this town? We would like to speak with them," Sainte reiterated.

"That would be Hanneh. I don't know if you should talk to her though, it's getting pretty late."

"We've traveled a very far way, past the Deshiere and through the Marshes. We need to speak with her of an urgent matter. I would like to do it soon, it can't wait much longer," Sainte nearly pleaded. He felt an anger build up inside of him for this man hindering them, but he pushed it back.

"Fine, I'm thinking I better go with ye though," he conceded after a big sigh. "Follow me," he grabbed a cloak that hung up inside his home and stepped out. "Carlla, I'm taking some new folk to see Hanneh. I'll be back in a short," he called in. A muffled reply came back, but neither Sainte nor Iris could understand what she said.

They followed the man through barren dusty paths between the homesteads. It was peaceful setting, in an eerie kind of way. It was a nice little town, but unkempt. Weeds grew in bundles where the buildings met the ground, and the packed dirt paths were uneven.

"My name's Hartdren, by the way. Nice to meet ye Sainte and Iris. As long as ye don't stir any trouble that is. Not off to a great start, showin' up after dark'n all," he came to a stop in front of a nondescript house. "Here it is," Hartdren then knocked on the door.

They waited for an answer. And continued to wait.

"Is anybody home? Maybe she didn't hear, perhaps you should knock again," Iris said.

"Nay, she heard. She'll come. She never leaves her door unanswered," Hartdren said. Almost as if on cue, the door opened. An elderly woman stood with a robe draped loosely over her body. She held a candle, the only source of light within her dark home.

"Welcome Sainte and Iris. I was expecting you earlier," she mumbled. Clearly, she had just woken from a deep slumber. "Come in. Hartdren, thank you for showing them here."

"Perhaps I should stay, just in case. I don't know who these people are," the man insisted.

"No, no, I'll be quite alright, I'm sure of it. Have a good night. Tell Carlla I said hello. Now, you two. Come in," she said again. Without waiting for them she turned and walked further inside.

Iris went in first, and Sainte followed closing the door behind them. Hanneh was seated at a round table, the singular candle was placed on a holder in the center. Sainte and Iris joined her at the table.

"I figured you would have been here sooner. I guess you weren't really traveling all that urgently," she said rather belittlingly.

"So you are one of them?" Sainte asked, ignoring her inflection.

"Oh yes, if you're asking if I'm a White Wyvern. If you're asking something else you'll have to be a little more clear."

"I have so many questions," Iris said. She had no idea what to do now that she was face to face with a confirmed White Wyvern. "I've heard so much about you, everyone has, and you've been here the whole time." She was at a loss of words being in front of one with time to talk.

"I'm sorry, dear, but I don't think we have as much time as we need. I need to say some things, then if we have time you two can ask some questions. King Zith is back, and he is trying to build up his numbers. He has the Malignin, of course, but he can't rule everything if that's all he has. He's recruiting human followers and is essentially reforming what was once known as the Cult of Bal'Shere," she held up a hand to silence Sainte before he spoke. "Let me continue. The Cult of Bal'Shere created the Malignin. King Zith came to them and asked them to help him beat King Nuse with their little deal. They agreed to

241

help him, but he must do something for them. They performed an experimental ritual on him, making it so that when he dies, his soul wasn't allowed into the afterlife. It worked. Instead, with nowhere to go, his soul took the physical form of his strongest emotions he experienced upon his death, thus creating the Malignin.

"The Cult of Bal'Shere and the White Wyverns had been, for lack of better words, in dispute for some time. This ritual was how the Cult was planning on winning, and they nearly did. We did what we had to to keep the Malignin contained and kill off the Cult. King Zith is now attempting to reform it. The people that aided the Malignin before, they're still a part of it. Hiding, waiting for their time to attack. I'm surprised they haven't already."

"Well, they have attacked. We were ambushed about five days ago now, but it was only three people. We killed them," Sainte said.

Hanneh thought about what he said but did not speak up.

"Why're you telling us all this?" Sainte asked, seeing that he was not going to get a response with what he said earlier.

"It's important. Normally I would not provide such information, but you're in a unique situation. You may not necessarily need to know this, but it helps put some perspective on things. I'm not done yet. To put it simply, we White Wyverns did what we had to before, and we won't hesitate to do it again, if the need arises. But this time there won't be any survivors. If you wish to continue on living, you need to find the sword and take down the Abomination. If it'll even work."

"Alright, that's already what I'm planning on doing. Do you know where the sword is?" Sainte asked.

"No, no White Wyvern does. I do know the family who does, however."

"You know where they are, but not where the sword is?" Sainte asked curiously.

"Indeed. I am in this position to protect the family and make sure I nor any other White Wyvern tries to find the sword."

"Why didn't Nadrian just tell me to come to you?" Sainte asked and leaned back in frustration, hoping it did not show on his face.

"Because he doesn't know what I know. He knows I am here, but he knows not why. I expect he believes I was just assigned to this town for no reason. Only one other Wyvern knows why I am here and that is the one that placed me here. Now, do you have any more questions, or shall I tell you where to find the family?"

"Will they tell me where the sword is? Do I have to do anything?"

"I don't know. I'm sure they won't give it up willingly, so it'll probably take some encouragement," she said.

"How'd you know we were coming?" Iris asked.

"All the Wyverns know what you two are doing, now. I knew it was only a matter of time before you showed up here asking questions. Nothing more to it. Now, this family is located in the Deshiere Mountains, about three miles in. There's a rugged path going south out of our little town, and it turns into the mountains in a few miles. Keep to that path and it'll take you right to the family's homestead. I would suggest leaving early morning. You can stay here, I have a spare bed. In the morning you'll find two packs full of supplies waiting for you at the foot of the bed. No need to see me before you leave, I'll be in bed still no doubt. Speaking of bed, this old lady should get some sleep now. I told you everything you two should know, good luck in your travels," with those final words Hanneh slowly stood up and ambled into her room, shutting the door behind her.

"Well, that was a lot to take in," Iris said now that it was just the two of them.

"Aye, it was," Sainte agreed. "Not sure what good it does us… I think we should probably go to bed too. We'll need the rest since we're going back into the mountains tomorrow."

"I don't know how well I'll sleep, I'll be thinking about everything I just learned. The Malignin are actually Zith's soul? You know how crazy that sounds?"

Sainte shrugged, "I'm not thinking about it. It changes nothing for me. Let's sleep," he looked around for the second bed Hanneh spoke about and saw it in the corner of the room. He got up and laid down in it.

"Is there, er," Iris started to say.

"I think this is the only bed, should be room for both of us," Sainte said. He rolled to his side.

Iris laid down on her side as well so that they were back to back.

"I know you'll probably have trouble getting to sleep, but try to get some nonetheless," he said.

"You too, alright?" she replied.

"I'll do my best," he said. Then they both laid silently, backs against each other, and tried to catch some sleep.

THIRTEEN

A few days had passed Kial and Peng by rather quickly. Buildings were being completed and some were even being expanded on. Their small lean-to had managed to grow to a two-room building.

The defenses had become surprisingly strong. The cliff's edge was lined with sharp pikes pointing in all directions. Several boulder and log traps had been set on the steep hills that led up to their precipice. They made a ball of dried twigs and sticks as tall and wide as a man that was to be set on fire and rolled down on Malignin, or anything, should they be attacked. More were being made, but they could only spare so much kindling so the going was slow.

Kial admired the camp as he walked back into it with a small deer slung over his shoulders. He had gone hunting that morning and, after not seeing anything for the first few hours, finally managed to get this doe.

"Hey, see you got a good haul?" Peng asked as he walked over. "Saw you coming back and thought you might want a hand?"

"Aye, turned out to not be a wasted trip. Thanks, but no need. It's a small deer, I think I can manage it. How goes the defenses?"

Peng joined him in his walk, "They're going well, far better than I expected. We've started to build a small wooden wall and gate on the far side, and more boulders are slowly being pushed into what we hope are good positions. The Blades have took to building firewalls at the foot of the cliff, they're going to rig it up somehow so that it can be lit from the top. I think they're overthinking it, a burning arrow would do the trick if you asked me, but well, they didn't," he ended with a shrug.

Kial grunted as he shrugged the deer off at the butcher's table. A man thanked him and immediately began skinning the kill, thankful someone was successful in their hunt.

"Let the Blades do what they want, I say, as long as they're helping us out you won't hear me complaining about them."

"Oh no, not complaining. Just telling you what's been going on since you left this morning. Have you spoken to Jasmine or Nadrian since we talked two nights back?"

"No," he replied curtly, obviously a sore subject still.

"I have. And she says if you won't talk to her again that's fine, but she hopes you will. I don't think you should be so hard on her... Think about it, for one second, what if she told the truth? Why don't you think she could be a White Wyvern? I know you saw what I saw back at Munich, what else could explain that?"

"Because, Peng. White Wyverns are supposed to be *the* Higher Beings, the ones we look up to, the ones who are good. What she's talking about, what she's done doesn't sound very good, it sounds sacrificial. Kill those who are problems and enslave the rest. That seems to be what she says they do," Kial said exasperated.

"If you had listened to all she said you would know that's not the case, at least not with her and Nadrian. They're trying to help without needlessly killing, finding solutions without death. Now, I don't believe all White Wyverns are like them. It sounds like they only have a limited amount of time to try to correct whatever needs correcting before others take matters into their own hands, but at least they're trying. Talk to

248

her again, listen to her for a full conversation instead of storming away. Then decide what you want to do," Peng pleaded. "She needs more help than what she's got, she needs our help."

"Fine, fine," Kial conceded. "I'll talk to her. Let's do it now otherwise I might change my mind. Where is she?" Kial asked.

"I think she should be near the medicine tent. See, even now she's still helping us."

"Of course she is, she was *the* healer in Munich. She has to maintain her façade."

Peng just shook his head and led Kial to the tent. There were a handful of people, mostly men, sitting on logs outside the hide tent nursing various bandaged limbs. Men who were not used to hard labor, but instead used to their easy jobs in Munich.

Before they could get much closer to the tent Jasmine walked out.

"Kial, Peng, good to see you. Are you two alright?" she asked as she eyed Kial up and down, looking at the blood that had leaked on him from his kill.

"Aye, we're fine. This is from a deer I got earlier. Er, how're you?" Kial asked.

"Busy, lot of people smashing fingers. You'd think they'd never done an ounce of work in their lives," she said loudly, receiving several glances from some of the injured. "What, uh, can I do for you?"

"Kial here has agreed to listen to you, fully this time. Whenever you have a chance, that is. Night would work best for everyone, I assume," Peng interjected.

"Ah, well that is good news. However, I will be leaving here soon. Today, actually. I'm going to go to the Shinta village to see how they fared and to see, if they're still there, if they'd like to come and join us here, together. Strength in numbers and all that. So, I would love to chat with you, Kial, but it's going to have to wait. I have to get some of my things together and then I'll be out of here rather shortly," Jasmine explained to them.

"You're going back?" Kial asked almost breathlessly, "Will you look for them? My wife Madelaine, and my daughter Franceska? I need to know what happened; I must know. Can I go with you?"

Jasmine inclined her head, "I wasn't going to tell you as to not get your hopes up but yes, that was one of the reasons I am going to Shinta village. On my way there I was, of course, going to stop by Munich and search for your wife and daughter, and any other possible survivors." In quieter tones she continued, "I need you to know, Kial, that we White Wyverns only want the best for everyone. But no, you cannot go with me. Stay here, keep yourself and these people safe. If they are alive I will bring them back to you, they need a husband and father to return to. Trust me," Jasmine put a hand on his shoulder.

Kial sighed, a sudden flow of relaxation ebbed into his body from her touch, "Alright, I'll be here. I trust you, Jasmine, but if you don't come back… I'll never forgive you. I just to know, one way or another, how they are."

"I heard there were plenty of people who managed to escape Munich other ways than just the east gate. I'm sure some fled to Shinta village, and say what you want about them, they wouldn't turn people away after what happened. I will be back," she promised, "but right now I must get ready."

"We understand, right Kial?" Peng asked his friend. Peng knew he needed to distract him from his troubling thoughts. "Let's go see if Seltrin needs help with anything. Good luck on your journey, Jasmine."

"Thank you, Peng. I'll see you two soon," she said then walked away.

As she left the two men, she could only hope that this small village they started would be left unknown to the Malignin. She made her way over to Nadrian, weaving around people who had various different tasks focused on their minds. Nadrian was lounging at their 'home' they had built. He was laying with his back against some sacks in the shade of the small building.

"Jasmine, good to see you. Coming for the last bit of supplies before you head out to the Shintas?" he asked as she approached.

"Yes, and to give you some orders while I'm gone. Help these people out, like you've done before. I don't know what's gotten into you, but you've been slacking," she started.

"Hey, my orders were to talk to Sainte, make sure he stays on the straight path. Everything went to, well, shit and I got no new orders. So I'm with you now. I tracked Sainte for a while but you know how that went. I'm sure he's in or almost through the Deshiere Mountains, but there's no way I can find him there in time. So now I see no reason I shouldn't take a break," he said.

Jasmine stared at him in disbelief, "You're joking? You don't want to help these people? You've seen what they've all been through and you have no desire to help them? We have these powers for a reason, and it seems they're wasted on you. Get up, help them however you can, and continue to do so until I return to tell you something different. I can't believe you, Nadrian."

"Fine," he stood up. "I'll help out where needed. You have to ask yourself, though, at what point is it enough? When can we throw our hands up and say 'We tried'? We've tried to kill off the Malignin before, but we couldn't. You know what they are. We barely were able to keep them contained in the first place, and we're struggling again. We're getting weaker, Jasmine…" he paused, then after a moment continued, "They're out again, he's out again, and different. Each time has been different. How many of our own must we lose before we cut our losses?"

"There's still so much to fight for. I'm glad you're helping me, I really am, but I'm saddened more of us don't see the potential in these people. Don't let them die, Nadrian. I'll be back in about a week," she said. She walked inside to grab her pack that she prepared that morning. Once she had it she left without saying anything else to him. She had to save her energy for the trek that laid before her.

She traveled quickly but it still took her three days to reach Munich. She approached the once thriving city cautiously. The eastern gates were now in shambles and she could tell just by looking through them much of the town was too. Debris from buildings littered the streets. She briefly thought about going through and seeing if there was anyone still there but decided against it. It would not be worth her time.

253

Turning her back to Munich, she started the final three hours of her journey to Shinta village. Soon she came to the river that separated Shinta territory from Munich territory. There was one lone bridge that crossed over, and once over the bridge she could see smoke in the distance coming from the village. She hoped it was from people living there and not smoking from destruction.

It was quickly apparent, as she got nearer, that the village was still thriving. She was met by three armed guards who quickly recognized her.

"Jasmine, yer still alive? We were worried when we got word that Munich had been attacked. Some Munes fled here that night the Malignin came," one of the men said.

"That's good to hear that more made it out. Were you attacked?" Jasmine asked.

"Nay, the Malignin never came over here. We could hear the screams carry over the plains from Munich. I shudder to think what would have become of us. Were there many other survivors?"

"There are about a hundred of us in total, give or take a handful. We've set up a camp in the Barrier's Mountains. I was going to see if anymore made it from Munich and take them back with me, if they want to go. I was also looking for two in particular. Their names are Madelaine and Franceska, have you heard of them?" she asked.

"We have about forty, I think, that we took in. No, I haven't heard of them, but I don't really know any of their names. They've kept to themselves pretty much. Come on, I can take you to them and then have you meet up with Chieftain Grengren. I think he would want to speak with you," he said.

"Lead the way," Jasmine gestured. She followed them back to camp and saw some familiar Shinta faces. He led her through the village, past the tent that Iris had stayed in, and into where the Munes were staying. The Shinta had given them some tents to set up and they had fires going. All the people, women, men, and children sat around the open flames looking positively downtrodden. A few of the closer ones glanced up at Jasmine as she walked up.

"Some of you may know me, but for those of you who don't, my name is Jasmine. I'm a healer from Munich. I came here to tell you that others have survived, we have grouped together and made a small camp in the Barrier's Mountains. It is a well defensible position, and there are many Blades of the Night with us as well," as she spoke people began to stand up and gather around her. Some began to ask questions about whether or not their loved ones survived. "Please, wait for your questions. I don't know everyone that is at the other camp, but I do want you all to come back with me. I am looking for two that go by Madelaine and Franceska? Are you here?" her eyes looked over everyone and for a moment her heart sank. But then there was movement.

A woman holding a young girl's hand, seven years old at most, pushed through the crowd. They were dirty, as was everyone, and looked worse for wear, but they were alive.

"Yes, I'm Madelaine and this is Franceska. Do you have word from Kial?" despite her meager appearance her eyes shone with hope.

"I do. He is very much alive at the other camp. He so desperately wished to go with me, but I told him to stay," Jasmine faltered as Madelaine knelt down to Franceska and hugged her before she could finish speaking.

"Daddy's alright," she whispered into her daughters' ear. She sobbed as she held her daughter, and Franceska hugged her back. "We're going to see him soon."

Jasmine could not help but get teary eyed herself. She took a deep breath to compose herself and kept talking, "If you wish to go with me back to the other camp I'll be leaving tomorrow. Do what you want, but I would recommend you come with me, these are dangerous times and we need to stick together now more than ever."

"I think it's safe to assume we'll be going with you. All of us," a man said. Everyone in the crowd nodded and murmured in agreement.

Jasmine smiled lightly at them all, "Good, get ready. We'll leave in the morning. I have to go talk to some of the Shinta. Stay strong."

When she left the refugee camp and started back into the Shinta village she heard a woman calling out her name.

"Jasmine, how're you doing? I heard you were back."

She turned to see who called her and immediately recognized her, "Laureen, I'm good. I'm only back for a short time, I leave again tomorrow. How've you been?"

"I'm well, busy though. I heard what happened from these Munes here. I've been busy helping them through their wounds. Most of them are doing much better though, physically. Emotionally they're drained, all of them. I can't help that, the only thing that can is time."

"Yes, well, I think reuniting them with others will help. I'm taking them to the Barrier's Mountains, leaving tomorrow. I'm actually going to go talk to Chieftain Grengren to see if he would like to come with us. You all are strong people, but the

Shinta cannot expect to survive an attack from Malignin by yourselves."

"You don't have to tell me that. I know we couldn't possibly hold them off for very long," Laureen agreed. "Good luck talking to Chieftain Grengren."

"Thank you," after a quick hug, Jasmine made her way to the Chieftain's tent from her memories of when she often visited Iris. The hide tent was massive, it seemed larger than she remembered, which would not surprise her. He probably had additions added on to it.

There were no guards posted outside the tent which was normal. Usually the only guards the Shinta bothered with were guards around the borders of their lands. The Shinta had orders on who they could and could not allow in. If someone was allowed in that meant ill will towards them, the Shinta believed that they would be strong enough to eliminate the threat themselves without a problem.

With that fleeting thought, Jasmine opened a flap to enter the tent and immediately felt a wave of heat emanate out. Once inside she saw that there were torches lining the walls, flames dangerously close to the cured hide the tent was made of. A fire was lit in the center of the tent with a throne of elk bones on the opposite side of the entrance. There were four different smaller openings leading to other tents that had been attached. On the throne sat the shirtless Chieftain Grengren.

He had a necklace made of wolf teeth and pants made from bear skin, it looked as if his feet were clawed like a bear. He smiled at his visitor welcomingly and gestured for her to sit on a stool nearby the fire. Jasmine inclined her head and sat where he pointed.

"Chieftain Grengren, it's been a while," she said.

"Indeed it has, Jasmine healer of Munich. What brings you here today? You stopped visiting once Iris left. I mis your visits," he was curiously well spoken despite his barbaric appearance.

"Have you not noticed the Munes that are sheltering here? Did you not know that Munich has fallen to the Malignin? I come here to reunite these Munes with the others in the Barrier's Mountains. And also to ask for your village to join us," Jasmine said.

"It was a simple question that did not require such an emotionally fueled answer," he began defensively. "Of course I know of the situation with Munich. Don't take me for a fool, I know your kind Jasmine."

She looked at him curiously, could he know about the White Wyverns?

He continued, "There's always something more in it for you. I don't know what it is, but you wouldn't be doing this if you didn't gain something from it."

He did not know, he could not. She reassured herself before speaking, "You are right, but this time I simply wish for us to survive. For everyone to survive. I'm bringing these Munes back with me, and I come here to ask if you would go with us?" she reiterated.

Chieftain Grengren stroked his chin as if he was deep in thought, "Very well."

Jasmine's eyes widened, taken completely by surprise at his willingness, "Really?"

"I said what I said. I'd be a fool if I were to deny that the Malignin are an overwhelming force. I don't know where they're at right now, but with them running largely unchecked around Crearia," he shook his head. "We Shinta are strong, but we would not be able to fend them off for long. I heard what happened to Munich, and Guardstin, and Elion. We would all be dead if we were attacked. When do you plan on heading out?"

"Tomorrow morning, Chieftain," Jasmine said, adding his title to show respect for his decision. "I would like to leave early, before the sun rises."

He nodded with her reasoning, then said, "We leave tonight. The women, children, and elderly will be given horses."

"Tonight?"

"I see no reason to wait. I don't know where the Malignin are, nor do you. Why wait through the night, we could be attacked. Let us get to this encampment you've set up."

"What if they attack us while we travel?"

"I see no difference than if they attack us here. We all die," he shrugged. "Tonight," he said again, leaving no room for argument.

"Ok," Jasmine relented. She felt sweat dripping down her back from the intense heat, "We'll leave tonight. I'll go tell the Munes. How long do we have?"

"I would like to leave within the hour, but I would be willing to push it to two if they need the time to prepare," he said.

"I suppose I should leave here, then. I have nothing else to ask of you. Do you have anything for me?"

"I do not, Jasmine healer of Munich. Go get your people ready, I will send some horses over, take as many as you need. Once we leave I don't plan to stop until we reach your encampment. Travel day and night, no time to be spared," he warned.

"I'll see you soon then, Chieftain Grengren," Jasmine said. She stood up from her seat, pants stuck to her legs thanks to all the sweat, and walked out of the sweltering tent.

She took a deep breath of the much cooler air outside, held it for a few seconds then let it out. There was a lot to be done, and she had to make sure Madelaine and Franceska had everything they needed.

FOURTEEN

Precipeak, what the Blades had started calling the camp, was coming along nicely. The name had drifted around the mouths of all who built there, and it seemed to stick. More permanent buildings were being finished, the spikes along the cliff's edge were finished, the Blades had figured out how to make their fire wall, indeed they had multiple of them. The boulder and log traps had been set successfully.

Three small watchtowers were being constructed along the cliff side as well, which were expected to be done in the next three days or so. Food stores were slowly filling up, meat being the main commodity. Some men and women were foraging for edible plants and mushrooms to add variety.

The hardest part for them all was staying warm. They were not an extremely far distance from Munich, but the cold did not care. It thrived in the mountains; snow covered their peaks in a white blanket.

Kial shrugged the animal fur around his shoulders and crossed his arms.

"Be happy we're not any higher," Peng said as he noticed his friend shiver, "least we don't have to deal with the snow here. Just the bloody wind."

All he got in response was a huff. Kial had been in a deteriorating mood since they arrived at the precipice, for good reason.

"When do you think Jasmine will return?" he asked.

Peng breathed out and watched as the cold air turned his breath into a mist, "I'm not sure. Give her another week or so, at most. She's already been gone four days, so I'm sure she's reached the others, if…" he trailed off, not wanting to finish the sentence.

But Kial finished it for him, "If they're still alive. If Madelaine and Franceska are alive."

"Aye," was all Peng offered. He felt bad for his friend, truly, but he had to do something to keep his mind from negative thoughts. "What'd you say we go look for some lunch?"

Since the defenses were largely finished, for now, and most everyone worked on their own homes, the list of things that must be done was getting noticeably short. This left Kial and Peng with some free time, no matter how badly they did not want it.

The women in charge of cooking had some tables built for them early on and throughout the day they would load it up with food, mostly meats. A lot of jerky, but on some days when the hunting was good there would be fresh cooked cuts for them. Today was not such a day.

Kial looked at all the jerky laid out with a frown, having grown tired of it quickly but he knew he should be thankful they had anything to eat at all. He grabbed a couple of pieces and followed Peng back to their home. They sat outside of it, backs against the wall, and he took a bite.

"Tough," Kial said between chewing it.

"Aye," Peng agreed. "Say, I know you don't like talking about it, but have you made your mind up about Jasmine yet?"

"I don't hate the woman," Kial began, "But how can I trust her when she can justify the murder of innocents? How can she justify blackmailing the Examiner with death if he spoke up of his findings?"

"She's doing what she has to in order to save us. She's trying to do what's right in her eyes. She didn't have to go back and look for survivors, she didn't have to stay with us all as we fled from Munich, from the Malignin, but she did. She helped out Sainte. She's scary, for sure, capable of terrible things I'm sure, but only if we don't do what she asks, and I believe all she is asking is to keep what we know to us."

"What if someone else does what we did? Tell me that, what if someone pokes around, starts asking questions. What if she doesn't trust us to keep our mouths closed and she tries to have us killed? Sure, she's done things she didn't have to, and if she brings my family back to me I'll be forever grateful, but I don't think that would bring me back to trusting her," Kial said.

"I don't know what we'd do. I don't know what we could do. I suppose it'd be over for us, if she decides we're too much of a risk, but we'll come to that when we have to. I think our best bet to prevent that is to get her to like us, stay on her good side. She's shown compassion before, maybe that would make her decision to keep us that much easier, if it ever comes to it," Peng took a bite out of his jerky after he said that.

"She's unstable, but if she brings my wife and daughter back, I don't think I'll have any other option but to thank her."

They continued to finish their jerky without talking any further, both contemplating their lives and what there was to do next. Some men were shouting, which was not uncommon, but

266

the shouting continued to grow louder. Before long they heard what was being said: "They're tearing apart the fire walls!"

Together they stood up and jogged over to the cliff side to peer down, along with several other men, and sure enough there was a group of about twenty men trying to tear apart some of their defenses at the bottom of the cliff. The men who were in the Blades of the Night scrambled to get their weapons and armor ready. Within seconds they were quickly on their way down to intercept the attackers.

"Who are they?" Peng asked out loud.

"I don't know, but they're fucking our wall up. Let's go down and help," Kial said. They ran back to their house and grabbed their weapons. Peng his sword and Kial his warhammer. As they were on their way to head down, they saw other men grabbing their own weapons, some had swords, some had sticks, a few carried pitch forks. Their own group of twenty headed down to reinforce the Blades that were undoubtedly already there.

Yells echoed off of the sides of the mountains as Peng, Kial, and the rest of the men rushed down. They arrived at the bottom to see a cluster of people, mixed all together. It was near impossible to distinguish between friend or foe. A handful of men already lay unmoving on the ground, victims of mortal wounds.

Kial scanned the crowd and found a face he recognized, Seltrin. The man was blade locked with another, their faces mirrored each other as they grimaced and pushed against each other. Kial ran over, readied his hammer, and smashed it against the other man's head, caving the side of his face in. He dropped immediately, quite dead.

Seltrin staggered at the sudden loss of opposition, and almost swung on Kial before he saw who it was. Kial grabbed him and pulled him back behind the ranks of everyone who just joined the fray.

"I counted twenty-three," he said between heaving breathes. "Lost one so far, that I saw."

Kial turned away to join the battle once more, but it was already over. With the fresh reinforcements, the people of Precipeak managed to quickly kill off the attackers. He looked for Peng, not seeing him at first. Then he stood up and pulled his short sword from the chest of someone on the ground.

"The hell are these people?" Kial asked.

Peng shrugged, then wiped his bloodied blade on the shirt of the man he had just killed.

"They ripped apart many of our fire walls before we could get down here," Seltrin said. "Why the fuck would they do that?"

"Well," Kial started to slowly say, "we were attacked by people during the Dark Days. Worked with Malignin."

"You think they're working with the Malignin?" Peng asked as he walked up.

This time it was Kial's turn to shrug, "Wouldn't surprise me. Don't know what happened to all those people. Why else would anyone try to do this?"

"Either way, we need to get these defenses built back up. We'll need a patrol down here, as well, and speed up the construction on the watchtowers. I've no doubt there was a reason for this attack, luckily this wasn't a large group," Seltrin started to command. "I expect it won't be the last." Immediately the Blades of the Night started to piece together the strewn apart fire wall. "Kial and Peng, can you two get together patrols with your people? I expect two man patrols will be sufficient," he stopped himself before saying more, "I'll just leave it up to you."

"Aye, we can do that," Peng answered. "What do you think, Kial?"

"Fine," he said. Seltrin had already left and started to help his fellow Blades. The men of Munich stood in a group

269

together, talking excitedly about the battle they were just in. None of them had ever been in a fight before now, and Kial and Peng could tell.

"Alright, listen up," Kial said loudly, getting their attention. "We're going to have to get patrols going down here for the foreseeable future. Through nights, too," the men all looked at each other uncomfortably, "I know none of you are fighters, and I'm not expecting you to fight if you find anyone, you're just to act as a warning. For now the patrol route will be the outskirts of all the firewalls that're built down here. Once you get back to Precipeak you will find your replacements and they will take over. I think two in a patrol will be good enough, but if we must we can have more. Let's go back up to Precipeak to gather up the rest of the men not here, and we will get an order sorted out."

There was some grumbling and none of the men moved very quickly. It was obvious they felt that they had done enough and should not have to do much more.

"Do you not understand what is happening? Our lives are at stake, this is for your family's safety. Sorry sack of shits, hurry up and let's get this sorted," Peng yelled at them. At his words they finally picked up speed, Kial and Peng took up the rear.

"Thanks," Kial said.

"Anytime, these fellows aren't used to this, but they're going to have to get used to it real quick."

All he got in reply was a grunt. Kial tossed his warhammer over his right shoulder and let the heavy head rest there while he kept hold of the handle. Peng followed suit and sheathed his own sword before beginning the trip back up to Precipeak.

The walk back up did not take exceptionally long, but it felt like it after the surge of adrenaline finally left their bodies. When they got up there the men in front very quickly had word spread of what happened down below. Some of the wives gasped and covered their mouths before looking for their loved ones, but Kial did not want to waste any more time than necessary. They could find their loved ones after patrols were doled out.

He called for all the men, sixteen and older. A patrol order was set out and the first patrol left an hour later. Not many were happy about the new duty, but all understood the importance of it. Work immediately began once more on the watchtowers then, intent on trying to finish at least one before the day was over.

The plan was, once the watchtower was complete that would be manned all the time. If anything was noticed down below they would light a fire, warning any patrol below, and the

271

patrols below were given torches for the night, and a horn for anything they may find before the watchtower saw it. It was a simple system, but it would have to work for now.

The rest of the day continued without incident, the watchtower did get built, and the patrols were going without any problems. Apparently, the group of men that attacked had done more damage than anticipated. They had destroyed several sections of several different firewalls. The Blades had managed to completely restore one but still had work to do on the others.

The repairs continued on through the night and the next day. The remaining two watchtowers were completed, and most of the fire walls were fixed by midday. The patrols were still going out regularly, but no one had seen anything suspicious since they started.

Kial and Peng just started figuring out a roster for the watchtower guards when they noticed it start to get dark around them.

"I don't remember there being very many clouds today," Peng said looking up.

"There weren't," Kial said, his two words lingered ominously between them. Dark clouds billowed in thick blankets, blocking the sun. The valley below was getting darker as the seconds passed by.

"It's happening again?" Peng asked, then bit his lip.

"Suppose so. Get ready," Kial looked at the watchtowers, looking to see if there were any signals. None, and no horn either, which was relieving. Over the worried murmurs they could hear Seltrin yelling at the Blades to ready themselves and go to their positions.

One man started to run through the camp to who knows where, and he had a ripple like effect on everyone he passed. Eventually, everyone was running here and there. Trying to find their loved ones, no doubt, just in case the worst was to happen. This is how Munich fell, there needed to be more order.

"Men!" Kial shouted loudly, "Men of Munich, come to me. Bring whatever you can use as a weapon and come to me."

A handful of men actually showed up, and Peng and Kial quickly told them to gather all the others up and bring them back. They nodded and left to accomplish the task, the urgency of the situation fully setting in. Only a few minutes went by, but it felt like hours, before they started returning.

"We have to help the Blades of the Night, if we get attacked they cannot hope to hold off the force of Malignin for very long by themselves," Kial said, pacing in front of them. He tried to mask his nervousness in his steps. "You all know where the traps are, you know the choke points. We must be ready to face the Malignin again. We must hold Precipeak for our families, for us, for the ones we lost in Munich. Peng and I will give you assignments for the undoubtedly upcoming battle. We need to work together," Kial scanned over the men, who were obviously nervous and scared, but at least they did not run. They listened to him, and he had no doubts each and every one of them would fight their hardest when the time came.

The men were quickly divided up. Once all the traps were manned and the watchtowers had lookers, Kial sent the remaining fifteen or so to Seltrin so he could task them as he saw fit. After they were tasked, Seltrin walked over to Peng and Kial.

"Thank you for getting some of your men ready, we'll need everyone we can spare, if we do indeed get attacked," he said. He had on his full suit of armor, save for his helmet. A massive broadsword was strapped to his side.

"Least we could do. Where do you want us?" Peng asked.

"Well, if you two are as good at fighting as you are organizing men to fight, I'd like you with my ground fighters. I have some at each gated entrance," Seltrin said, pointing back to where the precipice met the mountain side. "The traps are good, and I think they'll work brilliantly against the Malignin, or any attacking force really, but once they're spent, that's it. We need men at the gates to hold the forces at bay. I think eventually we'll need some at the cliff edge if Malignin decide to try to scale it, but we'll come to that when it happens. Hopefully the firewalls will hold them off from doing that."

Kial nodded in agreeance.

"How've the patrols been going?" he asked.

"They haven't been seeing anything if that's what you mean. No horns been blasted, or fires lit on the watchtowers. Good thing, I guess," Peng shrugged.

Seltrin grunted then said, "I don't know. An early attack party, then nothing for over a day? Now darkness descends on us… Something's not right, and I expect it won't be long till we find out what."

Just then, a sound echoed through the valley at the foot of Precipeak. A deep sound, continuous and long. The blowing of a horn. As one, Kial, Peng, and Seltrin looked to the edge of the cliff and watched as the watchtowers lit their fires, the men manning them frantically shouting for their families to get to safety, what little there was.

They ran to the edge and gazed out, straining to see what the others saw. Nothing could be seen through the darkness that now shrouded the land. Almost at once they realized that the shadows they could not see through were not shadows at all. It was Malignin. So dense were they packed that one beast could not be separated from the other.

The shadow of Malignin streamed over the grounds, heading straight for Precipeak. The two men on patrol were barely a hundred yards in front of the overwhelming force and sprinting back as fast as they could.

"How can we have any hope to hold them off?" Kial muttered. Peng remained in stunned silence.

"I'm not sure, but you better find some," Seltrin said. They watched helplessly as the two men running for their lives were caught up to. Their cries were short and quickly cut off as they were overwhelmed and killed. "Where the fuck are our archers?" Seltrin yelled out, suddenly breaking from his thoughts. About thirty men scrambled to the cliff side with bows and arrows and readied themselves. "Blades!" Seltrin yelled over the cliffside down below, neck veins threatening to burst, "Light the first wall, now!"

Kial was surprised to see a group of five men all with torches, men he did not know were even down there, run towards the Malignin. He doubted he would be brave enough to do that, what kind of men did it take to muster that kind of courage.

They continued on forward and reached the wall before the Malignin, against all odds. They quickly spread out, about ten feet apart, and threw their torches to the wall.

It went up in flames with a gust and the Blades fell back to the next wall. They had torches in their hands again, but Kial did not see from where they got them.

"Your bows have enough range to reach the third firewall," Seltrin yelled out, "open fire once they reach it." He glanced around at all the archers that were there. "Where the hell is everyone? We don't need people at the gates right now, you there," he pointed to a random man, "go run to the gates and bring them all here, with bows and arrows. Once the Malignin reach the foot of the cliff then send them all back to where they were," Seltrin demanded. "Shite, it's like no one wants to fight to live."

"It is their first real battle," Peng said.

"If they keep it up it's about to be everyone's last."

Peng did not reply, he could not. Seltrin was right.

The five Blades down below were shooting arrows at a few Malignin that braved burns and crossed the flames. The firewall was effective, but it was dwindling, and the Blades noticed it. The Malignin began to leap across and resume their sprint toward the cliff. The Blades dropped their bows and picked up the torches again and waited.

The beasts careened ever closer, and at the last moment the Blades threw the torches once more, igniting the second wall. Several Malignin managed to make it across before the flames increased in intensity, but the Blades deftly cut them down. They fell back once more to the third inner wall and resumed picking the Malignin off with arrows.

The men alongside Kial and Peng shuffled uneasily at the battlefield that was in front of them. The fires within Precipeak were being stoked by the women and children, doubled in size by now. The torches were numerous, casting flickering shadows that would disorient one if stared at for too long.

The Malignin were getting more brazen, the ravenous cries thrummed in everyone's ears. The Blades did a good job at picking them off as they leaped over the flames.

"Archers, ready yourselves. Do not hit my men down there," Seltrin called out.

The men nocked their bows, some tersely pulled the string back a few times, testing the tension, but no one broke their eyes from the Malignin on the other side of the orange flames.

The Blades lit the third wall as the Malignin eventually flooded over the current one. The men at the cliffside took aim with their bows and sent the first volley down. The arrows soared over the Blades down below and into the throng of Malignin. As quick as they could arrows were sent into the dark mob of monsters.

The Blades filed over to a pathway leading back up to Precipeak but waited, there was one more wall to light. From their new position they resumed firing arrows as well, from what Kial could see each arrow hit a Malignin, but there did not seem to be a dent in their numbers.

"Are they endless?" he asked.

"We think so," Seltrin said, even though the question was rhetorical. "Normally I'd say we just have to last until morning, but I don't believe we're going to see another one for some time."

About ten minutes went by as arrows plunged into the depths of Malignin, and the firewall started to decrease in intensity. The beasts pushed past it, and in response the last firewall was lit, and only once they were sure the whole thing went up in flames did the five Blades hastily begin their journey back up to Precipeak.

The Malignin thrashed angrily on the other side of the fire, rage seethed within them as their eyes set upwards at their end goal.

Arrows continued to arc down into them, but they did not care.

"Peng, Kial, I think you two can go ahead and head to the gates. Call out to the men at the traps to be ready, they've been given direction on when to loose their traps?"

"Aye, they have been," Peng confirmed.

"Good, I would like it if I had one of you at each gate. I will be going to both during the battle, as best as I can. I will be over there after I light the fire at the foot of the cliff."

Kial nodded then turned to Peng, "Good luck, expect to see you after."

"Aye, grab a pint," Peng said with a nervous smile.

They walked side by side towards the gates, then went their separate ways as they came into view. They shared a look but did not say anything. All could be said after the battle.

FIFTEEN

They traveled fast, the horses that the Shinta had lent the Munes helped tremendously as that meant no one had to wait on the slowest of them. The rest, the able-bodied, pushed on on foot, as did most of the Shinta. They did not rest, as Chieftain Grengren was unmovable in that regard, he was intent on moving nonstop. Jasmine could not blame him, she wished to get back soon, too.

They had entered the Barrier's Mountains an hour ago, much to Jasmine's surprise. Soon the mountains pressed in on their sides, and the trees reached out and grabbed at their clothes with scrawny branches.

She made sure Madelaine and Franceska had horses and were well taken care of, well fed. They were tired, but excited to meet back up with Kial. They made good time despite the group of almost three hundred people traveling together. The Shinta were surprisingly accommodating for the refugees.

The second day on the trip back to the encampment the Shinta and Munich refugees were cast in shadows, the sun was no longer visible. Jasmine walked with Chieftain Grengren when it happened. He looked up as the clouds took over the sky, and she joined him. A sinking feeling weighed her down, but that only urged her to move quicker.

"Not normal, I don't like it," Chieftain Grengren said. "How close are we to your camp?"

"I think we're pretty close. If I remember right it should be about two hours more," she felt uneasy under the unusual darkness. "How many Shinta do you have?" she asked.

"Two hundred and thirty-eight, exactly, unless someone had a child while we traveled, but none were due," he said with a small laugh.

"Are they all able-bodied?"

"Aye, well, save for some of the children… Thinking there's going to be fighting soon?" he asked.

"I do. Malignin are near, very near," she said. He did not bother asking, knowing that the mysterious woman would not give him a clear answer. They continued on for some time. A group of four Shinta made their way to Chieftain Grengren and spoke with him in hushed words. The Chieftain looked troubled as he dismissed the men.

"Jasmine," he called her over after the other Shinta left, "it seems you were correct. That was my scouting party, they returned saying that there are Malignin a short ways ahead, many of them. They surround what I assume is your camp, it's a precipice on the side of a mountain."

"Aye, that should be it, must be it. We must hurry, they'll need help."

"I'm not sure I want to send any of my Shinta in to battle," Chieftain Grengren said. "I don't like the way the odds sound."

Jasmine looked at him incredulously, "Then why come in the first place? They need help. They have defenses set up that will hold them off, but not for long. If we can attack in the rear, surprise them, we might be able to drive them off."

Chieftain Grengren huffed and rolled his head side to side, "Fine, I suppose it has been a good long while since we Shinta have been in a worthwhile fight."

"How far away are we? Did they say?"

"They said about twenty minutes walking."

"You need to get your men on horses, we need to hurry. I'll see how many men I can take from Munich."

"No," he said before she could leave, "They stay. There's not enough to provide any difference, and I doubt any of them have the physical or mental strength for a battle. This will be all Shinta."

Relief washed over her face, "Thank you, Chieftain. I will go with you."

He nodded, then yelled out the command to stop. It was echoed by others until everyone had stopped moving. As if on an unspoken command, the Shinta formed a circle around the Chieftain as best as they could in the cramped, rocky forest, and waited for his commands.

"Shinta, as I'm sure you have all heard by now, we face a large group of Malignin ahead of us. They attack the encampment that the Munes have built up, and we mean to come in as reinforcements. All my warriors get on horseback, as many as possible. The rest will have to walk. We will ride up behind the Malignin and see where best we shall fight.

"We will join them in battle, not as people who simply have a mutual enemy, but as allies. Show these Munes what the Shinta are made of. Show yourselves what you are capable of. Make me proud!" He finished as he raised his weapons, two long swords that looked small in his meaty fists.

The Shinta shouted with him and raised their own weapons over their heads. A horse was brought to the Chieftain and he mounted it.

"Go get your steeds, and steel yourselves for battle," he ordered, and all at once the Shinta burst into motion. Ordered chaos. In merely minutes the Shinta were mostly mounted, a little less than half were on foot. "Ride out!" Chieftain Grengren shouted, and that was it. They were on the move.

The Munes had somehow made their way to Jasmine in all the chaos. "What do we do?" Madelaine asked her. "We heard what's happening. Is everyone alright? Is Kial alright?"

"Stay here and wait, I will get you when it's all over. If you see any Malignin hide, only fight if you must. I have to go with the Shinta, but I will be back, I promise," Jasmine explained quickly. Without another word she turned and followed the Shinta with a light jog.

The war party moved quickly; blood pumped through everyone. The Shinta had not been in a great battle in a long time and they were excited.

Guttural screams met their ears as they came closer, and soon the Malignin entered their view. The Shinta slowed and stayed in the tree line, just ahead of them was a clearing with the precipice overlooking it.

Malignin covered the ground, a throbbing mass of hate and rage. A faint orange and red glow could be seen over their heads, the firewalls no doubt. Thankfully, none of them had noticed the small army of Shinta that gathered behind them, too intent were they on what was atop the cliff. They were about seventy yards away from the nearest Malignin.

Jasmine found herself next to Chieftain Grengren up at the front of the Shinta.

"Horses first," he said to the Shinta next to him, "V formation, on foot warriors follow after," the Shinta reiterated his orders on down the line. They dared not yell the orders out for fear of the Malignin hearing. Chieftain looked down at Jasmine from his horse, "You can fight?"

"I can hold my own," she affirmed.

"See you out there, then," he readied his two swords, and the Shinta down the line did the same with their weapons. He kicked his horse into motion, and it picked up speed until it was in full out sprint. The horse ridden Shinta followed suit, forming a 'V' pattern, with the Chieftain as the point. They let out war cries now, as they closed on the Malignin.

Once all the horses were out of the tree line, the on-foot warriors took off at a sprint. This is where Jasmine joined in.

Sounds of battle were heard as the horses barreled through ranks of Malignin.

Jasmine's feet pumped and thudded on the ground, she felt her Light well up in her, readying it for action. She stared forward, finding the first Malignin she would meet in combat. Nothing else mattered now, she did not see the Shinta beside her, and hardly could see the Shinta ahead of her already in battle.

She did have one worry, though. A great one. Where was Zith? Where was the Abomination?

Seltrin gazed out at the Malignin as the last firewall started to dwindle. Malignin began to run over it, no longer caring about the meager light the flames now barely emanated. The time was nigh to light the fire at the foot of the cliff. He grabbed a nearby torch and held it over, waiting for the perfect moment to drop it.

Now.

The flames fluttered as it rushed downward, and Seltrin watched it the entire way. It landed perfectly, right on the firewall. But it did not light.

Before he could grab another torch and drop it, the Malignin were already clambering up the cliff, scaling it quickly.

Another torch would not reach the wall anymore, with all the Malignin covering it.

"Shit," he muttered. He just happened to look over the rest of the small valley, and what he saw made his breath catch in his throat.

Men on horses were charging the rear of the Malignin, and out of the tree line came more warriors on foot. No time to revel, though. He looked down and Malignin were halfway up the cliff side already. He was sure there were more pouring on either side of the precipice by now. As soon as he had that thought he heard a massive crashing off to his left, no doubt a boulder being rolled.

He glanced around and saw that each of the three watchtowers had two men on it. Six terrified men and himself.

"Grab your spears," he shouted, "When they get close jab them down." The men were shocked into action, each grabbing a spear and readying themselves. Seltrin turned back and ran into Precipeak.

"I need people, women and children. Anyone who can hold onto a spear. We need more people at the cliff side," he yelled. Slowly some women and kids started to come out, fear gripped their eyes. "Grab spears, rocks, logs, anything you can use to throw or stab, and get to the cliff edge, stab the Malignin between the stakes we put in, do not let them up!"

Surprisingly, they moved rather quickly. Now the edge was manned with about twenty people, all jabbing between the stakes. For now, no Malignin were getting through, but Seltrin knew the edge would only hold for a short time.

Seltrin could hear signs of battle at the gates. Making a decision, he left the cliffside and ran over to the gate on the left. So far the men were holding it, killing any Malignin who crawled over top. He saw Peng at the front stabbing through small cracks between the planks of wood used to make the gates.

Not wanting to distract anyone, and seeing that the gate was being held, he left without a word and quickly made his way to the right gate. The situation there was entirely different. The gate had been broken through, but the men had made and held their line.

Kial was at the front, swinging his warhammer around wildly, but precisely. He watched as a Malignin was knocked aside, still alive, only to be stabbed through the throat by another. Seltrin drew his bastard sword and ran over to help.

He went to the left of the line, careful to avoid the wild swings of the untrained men. His first Malignin careened from above, nearly dropping on him. Seltrin leaned back and swung his sword out in a broad sweep in front of him, feeling it meet resistance. He had slashed open the chest of the Malignin, but it still lived. Side-stepping its claws, he finished it off by stabbing it through the chest. Ripping his sword free, he advanced forward, closer to the ruined wall.

"Push them back!" he yelled as he noticed the fear in some of the men's eyes as the Malignin tried to pour through with their sheer numbers. "Kill them all!" He saw, outside of the tattered gates, logs light up in flame, then immediately after they were tripped.

The logs rolled down, picking up momentum from the steep cliffside, and then they barreled into the Malignin, causing sparks and embers to leap into the air. The logs rolled over them, pushing some back down and making others flee from the flames. Shortly after, the smell of burnt Malignin flesh met the fighter's nostrils.

Kial screamed out unintelligible encouragement when he noticed the logs decimate any Malignin they touched. The men yelled in return and fought harder, encouraged by the sight of Malignin panicking from the flames.

Seltrin continued to scream with them, thrusting and parrying, slicing and stabbing, moving forward. Soon they had regained the few feet they were pushed back, and now stood in line at the tattered gates, with two ranks of men behind them.

They were granted some reprieve after that first trap. As they held the opened gates easier now Seltrin saw that most traps had already been set, but there were at least three more that could still help.

Seltrin broke his rank, but not before having the man behind him replace his spot. Now that he knew both entrances were held for now, it was time to go check the cliffside.

Jasmine had been battling for about an hour now, and she was feeling it. Her powers were not battle oriented, meant more for healing, but she was doing what she could. She looked around and saw that only a few Shinta remained horse bound, Chieftain Grengren being one of them, but there were plenty on foot.

The Chieftain was astonishing to see in battle, for such a large man he moved quickly. It seemed as if his hands moved independent of thought, each one slicing and jabbing in different directions on either side of his horse. No Malignin was able to get close.

Jasmine stuck to simple attacks, small beams thrown precisely, timed blocks and parries. Her only physical weapon was a dagger, but she rarely needed to use it, Malignin hardly got that close to her. At one point she noticed that many of the Malignin were climbing up the cliffside to get to their encampment, apparently the people above had been unsuccessful in lighting the firewall at the base of the cliff. Something needed to be done about that.

None of the Shinta would be able to help, they were all stuck in grueling combat. It would have to be her. She figured the distance was a little over a hundred yards from where she was to the base. Once at the base she figured she would have enough strength to make a small barrier of light to fend off Malignin who decided to come near, but she had to get there first.

She could use her powers to get there, but then she would be too exhausted to hold the wall of light for very long. As she desperately fought off a Malignin while trying to figure out how to get to the base of the cliff, Chieftain Grengren rode into her view, swords nearly a blur in his hands as he worked through the Malignin. She called out his name, but he was not able to hear her. She blasted the Malignin she was fighting with a short burst of light to the face, dropping it. Jasmine's breaths heaved in and out as she tried to take a moment to gather her thoughts.

Another Malignin saw her standing still and took that opportunity to launch an attack. It leaped at her, claws extended and mouth open, terrible teeth ready to rip and tear. Jasmine saw it coming, though, and a quick wave of her hand sent a small ball of light streaking towards it. The light ripped into its left eye, blowing out its eye socket, and burned a hole through the opposite side of its skull.

She jogged over to the Chieftain, seeing that he had come to a stop nearby to survey the battlefield. Deftly, she dodged between Shinta fighting and attacked the Malignin whenever they tried to hinder her.

The Chieftain remained in her view, never did he leave it, for once. Eventually he saw her out of the corner of his eye, and he knew that she was coming for him. He killed a nearby Malignin that threatened him and broke from battle, moving his horse next to her. Shinta ran in and covered him, blocking the Malignin from him.

"What is it, Jasmine?" he asked, barely out of breath.

"Can you take me to the foot of the cliff? If we don't secure it then all this will be for naught," she asked desperately.

He looked doubtfully over the constantly moving mass of Malignin to the cliff, now covered with them climbing it. He saw the men and women up top desperately spearing any

Malignin that got close, but he could tell that they would not last long.

"I fear that it is near loss already."

"No, not if I get there. I can stop them. Let me ride with you, and I will get us there safely. Trust me."

He thought about it, quickly, then thrust his hand down to her. She grasped it and he pulled her up and behind him on the horse.

"If I die," he called out to the Shinta around him, "Then you can thank Jasmine!" Then, without warning, his horse was galloping towards the cliff.

Jasmine, without a moment to spare, summoned a small wall of light in front of the horse. It was simple yet effective. It was too bright for the Malignin's eyes, so they cowered away from it, and any that touched it were burned. To his credit, the Chieftain only let out a small grunt of surprise, but he kept his steed running.

Then, almost too easily, they were at the foot of the cliff. Chieftain Grengren pulled his horse to a stop and Jasmine clambered off. No sooner had her feet hit the ground did she spread her hands out, and from them sprung light, like a rope, three feet from the ground. It reached the ends of the cliff, where the ground sloped upward. Then the rope of light extended into a wall, six feet high. It repelled all Malignin that tried to reach the cliff. The Malignin already on the wall would just have to be dealt with from the people above.

Jasmine was immediately drenched in sweat from this feat. Chieftain Grengren rode his horse back and forth, just in front of the wall, killing what Malignin he could. She was not sure how long she could hold this defense up.

After five minutes her knees began to shake, and the sweat she had before was all but dried up, she had none left. The Shinta were still fighting in the rear, not seeming to get any closer and the Malignin showed no signs of fleeing. They never seemed to end.

She started to grunt through her breaths, holding the light defense in place. Unable to hold herself up anymore, she fell to her knees. The light remained in place but diminished in intensity. Just as she felt the last of her strength drain and the light falter, it flared to a sudden brilliance rather than disappear. Strength surged through her once more.

Jasmine stood up and looked to her left and right and saw that her brother and sister White Wyverns joined her, three on her left and three on her right. Nadrian strode with them, nothing but seriousness etched on his usually light-hearted face.

In his hand he held his staff, glowing with light. The others held various weapons as well, all glowing with light.

"Get up, Jasmine. This isn't over yet," Nadrian said as he strode to her side. The wall of light was stronger than ever.

"About time you lot showed up," she said with a smile, relieved that they showed up at all. She would never admit it, but she had been resigned to her fate, to death.

"We debated about it for some time," he said, a small smile broke on his face despite the gravity of their situation.

"You don't say... Now, let's get to work," she said.

Nadrian began thrusting his staff sending out balls of light flickering back and forth, striking Malignin, killing them with one shot. Four of the other Wyverns strode out into the fray and attacked with melee weapons imbued with light. The last Wyvern attacked with a bow, shooting arrows made of light. Jasmine stepped back and rested, although they had restored her strength to some extent, she was not completely battle ready.

Chieftain Grengren had stopped his attacks and watched in amazement at the Wyverns fighting. The mowed down Malignin faster than twenty of his Shinta could. The tidal wave of Malignin had all but been halted by six people.

"How is it going above?" Jasmine asked Nadrian.

He shrugged, "Not great, not poorly. They're holding for now. I suspect with us down here they'll be alright in the end. As long as this onslaught doesn't last forever."

Suddenly the Malignin split in two large groups, one on each side of the mountain. It seemed they had given up on scaling the cliffside and were sprinting outright to the top. The Wyverns regrouped at the foot of the cliff, with Chieftain Grengren going back out to meet the Shinta. With a few shouts he split the Shinta into two bands, one to follow and attack each group of Malignin.

Before the White Wyverns could decide what to do, they noticed a waning on their wall of light. As they watched it flicker, a darkness crept from the ground and consumed the light in earnest until it was extinguished. Standing in the dark now, the only illumination from their weapons, the Wyverns looked out over the torn ground.

A silhouette was seen, darker than the darkness around it. Silently it came forward, darkness slinking off of it like smoke.

"The Abomination," Jasmine said. A cold sweat overtook her. "How did you get away from it, Nadrian?"

"I think it let me go."

The Wyvern with the bow took aim and released an arrow. It flew true and struck the Abomination, but they could not tell if it had any effect. The light was snuffed out in the folds of darkness. It crept ever closer, undiminished.

"Keep firing," Jasmine commanded, "Nadrian, attack it. I will lend my power to your staff. You," she said to the Wyverns with melee weapons, "circle out and around it. Keep your distance, but attack as a group."

They nodded and slowly walked out to meet it. Arrows streaked into it, Nadrian's orbs of light charged with Jasmine's powers struck it, but nothing seemed to effect it. The darkness simply accepted the attacks, and the light went out.

Then, without taking her eyes from it, the Abomination was gone. Jasmine looked around for it but did not find it.

"Where'd it go?" she said through lips suddenly dry.

"I don't know," Nadrian replied.

One of the Wyverns who went out to meet it let out a cry. The Abomination held her aloft in its hands by her shoulders, somehow having appeared behind her. Her sword was on the ground, dull, no longer imbued with her power. She cried in agony as the Abomination squeezed and crunched her shoulders together.

The snapping of her chest was heard and echoed in Jasmine's ears. Before she could stop them, the other three wyverns attacked. Spear, sword, and mace all glowing with light struck, stabbed, and sliced but had no effect. The Wyvern that the Abomination held went limp and it dropped her carelessly on the ground.

Slowly it turned around, facing the onslaught the Wyverns put into it. It grabbed the sword in its bare hand and wrenched it from the Wyvern, then slapped the now weaponless man away. A spear struck the Abomination in the face, but it retaliated by grabbing the spear holder and stabbing the Wyvern through the side with the sword it had wrenched free.

The mace wielding Wyvern smashed it across the knee, making the Abomination stumble. Seeing his sudden advantage, the Wyvern hammered the mace across its face and knocked it down to its knees. Then the Wyvern held the mace above his head with both hands and brought it down as hard as he could, but a tendril of darkness had snaked up behind him and between his legs. Inches before the mace met the Abomination the tendril shot up between his legs with such strength that it exploded through the top of his head, but then it was gone.

The Wyvern crumpled to the ground, lifeless and bloodied. The Abomination picked itself back up as if nothing had happened.

Jasmine and Nadrian stared on in horror, all of this unfolded in merely seconds. They had no time to react. The Abomination turned towards them once more and continued forward.

Seltrin helped the people at the cliffside work the Malignin back. They were about to be overrun when a flash from the bottom took his attention.

"The hell…?" he could not make sense of what he saw. Someone down below was holding out their hands and a light streaked from them. The light formed a sort of wall, and the Malignin would not cross it. Of course, they had to deal with the Malignin that were already climbing up, but that would not be very difficult now.

He jabbed the point of his sword between the stakes, stabbing a Malignin and shoved it off. He watched it fall and crumple harmlessly to the left of whoever was down there. The rest of the battlefield was chaos, the men on horseback fought valiantly, damn near as good as any Blades he knew, from what he could tell. The only people they could be were the Shinta, if

Jasmine had come back with them. No one else made sense. No matter, he was damned thankful they showed up.

After a few more tense minutes the cliffside was secure.

"Everyone here, split in two and go to the gates," he commanded. He was met with gazes of weariness from men, women, and kids so young they should not be here. Now was not the time to discriminate, "I said everyone. We can't afford to have any sitting this out. To the gates," he commanded again.

Slowly, but with determination, they split into two fairly even groups and made their way to the gates. Seltrin quickly made his way to Kial's group first, as they had been the most pressed.

He was relieved to see that they had held their line. Still they fought the Malignin, but they held them at bay using a combination of their weapons and torches.

He saw Kial near the back, directing his men where to go, when ranks should fall back and be replaced. He walked over to his side and watched.

Noticing him, Kial said, "Why don't they come over the wall between the gates? I expected more from them."

"I have most of my Blades there, on the outskirts of the wall. They have plenty of torches and plenty of experience fighting Malignin. I had faith in them that they could hold the center, and that faith was well placed, it seems," he explained. "This force of Malignin is large, but they're not as mindlessly savage as they were before. How many men of you lost?"

"I lost count at twelve, but they seem to be getting the hang of this, haven't seen one go down in the past few minutes."

"Too many," Seltrin shook his head.

"Not sure what you expected. These are farmers, strong, but little to no experience in battle. Doing a damn sight better than I expected. How's Peng doing?"

"Good last I checked, I'm about to head over and see right now. Keep it up, keep them at bay, and we'll get through this," Seltrin grasped him on the shoulder, then walked away. Seltrin could not help but think that out of the many nights that he had fought Malignin, this battle was the most orderly. That struck him as odd, but he dared not question their luck.

He arrived at Peng's gate and saw that the situation had escalated into chaos. The gates had been destroyed, many men were dead on the ground, and the Malignin would have pushed through into Precipeak had the reinforcements from the cliffside not arrived. He hefted his sword and ran into battle without a second thought, side by side with the Munes.

He swung his sword wildly, striking any Malignin that ventured too close. "Torches, grab the torches!" he shouted.

Some heard him, most did not. The few who did quickly left the battle but sprinted back with torches not soon after. They waved the torches in front of them, blinding the Malignin with the sudden light. The Malignin shied away from the flames, and Seltrin along with all the others took that opportunity to push them back.

The blade of his sword bit into the flesh of many Malignin. The people around him surged forward, feeding off his adrenaline and adding fuel to their own. By chance he saw Peng, dirtied face and bloodied arms, a few feet away, hacking at the Malignin with a grin of sheer will.

Slowly, very slowly, they started to gain ground and push the Malignin back out. "More torches," he yelled, and more were supplied. At one point he was struck in the face by something and he tasted blood, felt it stream down his face and blur his vision, but he kept attacking.

His sword had almost been wrenched from his grasp, but he held tighter despite his cramped hand. Tripping over bodies of Malignin and men, they eventually found themselves standing shoulder to shoulder where the gate used to be. Seltrin stepped back and shoved someone into his position.

"Ranks, form ranks behind them and hold steady. And for the love of Wyverns bring some more fucking torches.

Without them you'll die," he barked out. He wanted to yell it, but his lungs would not let him after all the screaming he had done previously.

"Thanks," Peng said breathlessly. He slowly walked over to Seltrin then doubled over, hands on his knees. "Thought we were done for."

"You damn well were. Lucky I sent some more people over. Keep these torches lit. They make fighting them much easier," Seltrin said. "There's a reason they only come out when it's dark."

"Aye," was all Peng said. He felt bad enough about letting the battle get to where it was.

"If you have this under control, I have to go. Do you have it?"

"Yes, aye, I do now."

"Good, now go join them in the fight, let them see you battle. You did good, I saw you, let them see you more. Go to the front and keep them going," Seltrin ordered, then he left him to go back to the cliff to see what else was coming their way.

Jasmine and Nadrian desperately flung attacks at the Abomination, but nothing seemed to touch it.

"What do we do?" Nadrian asked, panic laced in his words.

"Surround it in light," she called out frantically, desperately. It was the first and only thing that popped into her head after his question. No sooner had she said that did a bubble of light appear around the Abomination, now merely thirty feet away from them. It stopped, as if startled by the sudden obstacle, and tried to take a step but could not get through.

Instead it put its hands onto the light barrier and pushed. Its hands smoked as the light burned at it, but it did not falter. Jasmine looked at Nadrian and saw him straining to keep this attack up. Jasmine threw bolts of light at it to try to weaken or distract it, but they did not seem to do anything. With disbelief Jasmine watched as the Abominations long fingers pushed through the light, then spread it apart dissolving it.

Nadrian gasped as his attack was finished. The Abomination surged forward, nearly within arm's reach. Their backs were now against the cliffside. There was no point in running, each of them were too weak to attack anymore.

The Abomination reached out and grabbed Jasmine around the shoulders, its touch was icy hot. She gazed up into its face, its endless eyes and void of a mouth, and knew. She was dead. She could feel it begin to squeeze her, intent on make her shoulders touch each other, much like how it killed the first Wyvern.

Just as her bones were on the verge of cracking in half, there was a blinding light, so bright it hurt her eyes. It exploded across the Abomination's back. Surprised more than hurt, it dropped her and slowly turned around, just to be met by another blast of light. Jasmine threw herself to the side as the Abomination faltered backwards, nearly stepping on her. She looked up and saw a man standing just ten feet away.

"Get out of here," he shouted. It was Eringar.

"What're you doing here?" she gasped. Nadrian stared at him crazily, too dumbfounded to do anything else. "You'll die," she said too quietly for anyone to hear.

"I can fend this wretch off," Eringar said as he summoned another orb of light, a large one, and threw it at the Abomination scoring another successful hit. But what Jasmine did not see was that he followed the orb and had drawn his sword in the same movement, imbued in his magic.

After the Light had exploded in brilliance around the Abomination he attacked with his weapon. Left and right he moved, never standing still. The Abomination retaliated with quick strikes as well, but Eringar managed to stay just out of reach. With every swing of his sword tendrils of darkness were wisped away.

Eringar combined his sword strokes with orbs of light, scoring a hit almost every time. The Abomination stumbled and fell to one knee. Eringar grabbed its head in his left hand, glowing light emanated from around his grip as he burned the Abomination, and with his sword he struck it in the neck, hit after hit, trying to cut it off.

Before Jasmine could yell out a warning, the Abomination stretched out its clawed hand and thrust it forward up into Eringar's abdomen. Eringar let out a wail but continued his attack, still trying to hack off the head.

The Abomination stood back up and held Eringar aloft with its hand buried inside of him. Blood poured from the wound, and spittle laced with the red liquid flecked from his mouth. With one last valiant effort, Eringar grabbed his sword in both hands and brought it down, point first, onto the Abomination.

Jasmine gasped as the sword slowly sunk into its neck until it was hilt deep in the Abomination's shoulder.

"Nadrian, now!" she screamed. She shot a continuous beam of light at the Abomination and was quickly joined by Nadrian. The thing let out a hideous shriek, deafening them, but they continued. Her hands burned as she pushed her powers past their limits. The Abomination flung Eringar away in desperation, tired and weary of this attack. Their two beams of light pushed it back, and the Abomination took the full brunt of their attack.

It tried to take a step forward but shielded its eyes. With one last defiant roar, the Abomination turned and ran away, disappearing into the endless dark. Nadrian and Jasmine continued their attack, not knowing or caring if they were hitting it or not, until their bodies simply gave up. Together they collapsed to the ground, chests barely moving.

It was completely quiet.

SIXTEEN

Sainte sat up from his light slumber and slid to the edge of the bed. Stretching his arms above his head, he saw that Iris was not up yet. He pulled out a vial and dropped some of the liquid into each of his eyes then stood up. By the time he was done Iris was sitting up as well stretching her good arm over her head. She got up and groggily looked outside one of the windows.

"Early yet, sun hasn't risen. Sky's lighting up though," she said.

"Good, then we should be on our way soon," Sainte rummaged around one of the packs that were by the foot of the bed, as Hanneh promised. "She really helped us out. We've got dried meats, breads, our canteens are full of water."

"Thank you Hanneh," Iris said absentmindedly as she looked through her own. "Same stuff here. Fantastic," she slung the pack over a shoulder. "Ready?"

"Aye, let's get going I guess. Not looking forward to going back in the mountains, though," Sainte said. They walked out of Hanneh's house as quietly as they could so as not to disturb her, and once outside started south. The path Hanneh spoke of was easy enough to find, being the only path that led south out of Kenston.

They started down the path, it was fairly unused, but plants had not yet overgrown the dirt so the going was easy. The mountains were about five miles to their left, to their right was flat ground. If they headed right they would run into the Sea in about a day's travel.

"You ever been around here before, Sainte? Before all this, before the Blades?" Iris asked.

The question caused Sainte to slow his walking. He had not actually considered the fact that this was all new land to him. The mountains, the Marshes, the towns. He went through them all, but never really saw them. "I… no. I mean, I'm from Bethrune, you know, and that's in the middle of the Gronedas Mountains, but I've never been this far west. Never left Bethrune until I joined the Blades of the Night."

"Me neither. It's quite beautiful," Iris said as she gazed at the frosted peaks in the distance.

"They are," Sainte agreed. The snow sparkled in the sun's rays that now shone upon them. The jagged crevices cast shadows, hiding all sorts of secrets within. "Definitely look better from a distance than within."

Iris laughed, "Yes. That they do. Lucky for us we're getting a second chance in them," she said with false bravado.

The path slowly began to curve towards the mountains, and before long the mountains covered their entire field of vision. They had to crane their necks to look up and see sky.

"How far in did Hanneh say the home was?" Sainte asked.

"Three or four miles, I think," Iris answered.

"Hope it's easy going."

"I don't see why it wouldn't be. Surely they have to come to town every now and again, I'm sure they wouldn't' want the way to be difficult."

"We're about to find out," Sainte said.

Further into the mountains they delved, keeping talk to a minimum. For the second time in their lives they were once again in the Deshiere Mountains, the path now little more than a game trail. The walking was made only slightly easier than their first time through the mountains. This side of the mountain range did not have any snow fall, yet at least. Sainte and Iris were thankful for that.

The sun was just past midday when they noticed that it had started to get dark unreasonably early.

"You notice that, Sainte?" Iris asked.

"Aye," he looked up. "Clouds're coming. Getting dark. I wonder…" he trailed off.

"Me too," Iris said in hushed tones.

At this point they had stopped and looked up together. The clouds moved in quickly and thickly, blotting out the sunlight. It darkened around them, near as dark as night.

"Well, shit," Sainte muttered. Sour mood appearing as quickly as the sun disappeared.

Iris and Sainte struggled on through the Deshiere Mountains in mostly silence and darkness. The path was so broken up at this point that at times they thought they were completely off of it.

"You think it's much farther?" Iris huffed.

"How should I know?" Sainte snapped, "I've never been here before."

"You in another foul mood?"

"What do you think? It's this damned weather, the damn clouds, the shoddy trail. Everything. Thanks for pointing it out," he said sarcastically.

"Why do you get like this? Like you just snapped into a shite mood in seconds, soon as it became overcast," Iris pointed out.

"Yeah, well, just am."

"Regular enough when it's sunny, normal out," she mused more to herself now at this point, "wonder if it has anything to do with Malignin, or Aldred, Zith, whatever his name is."

"Why don't you go ask him?" Sainte snapped. "Can you quit talking to yourself, I can hear you. It's frustrating enough trying not to slip, plus having to listen to your murmurs," Sainte called back.

"You want to continue on by yourself? I'll turn back, leave you be if you wish," Iris threatened. "Being a right prick you are, should be glad I've stayed with you this long," Iris said, knowing full well she did not want to leave.

"Do whatever you want. Going might be quicker without you pestering me."

"You know what?" she stopped walking, "Fine. Go on. I'm heading back, meet up with me whenever you're done being a dick." She watched him continue on without another word or even looking back.

Sainte kept walking and did not say anything. Iris waited until he was out of sight beyond some spruce trees, then continued to follow him, slightly surprised that he was fine with her leaving. Of course, she had no intentions of leaving him by himself, but she would make him think she did. She waited for him to get ahead of her before she began following him once more, taking her time so as to not alert him of her presence.

Sainte increased his pace now that Iris was not around to hold him back. Why did she always have to question him and his moods? Could she not just be quiet for a while? That was all he wanted. These questions rolled around in his mind for a while until he saw it, the small cabin. It came into view suddenly, sitting quietly in a peaceful, flat clearing, a handful of tree stumps surrounded it. A little garden was growing at the side of it.

Smoke listed wistfully from the chimney, and Sainte saw shadows of movement from within. He walked over to the only door and knocked, three hard rasps.

The movement inside stopped as the person was no doubt curious about who was visiting them. The door creaked open, a man about forty years older than Sainte stood there.

"Aye? Can I help you? You lost, lad?" he asked.

"No, I'm not lost, but I think you can help me. My name is Sainte and I'm looking for a sword, a sword I've heard only you know where it is."

The man gulped at the mention of the sword, but otherwise maintained a neutral expression. He glanced down at Sainte's sword strapped to his waist, then back up to his eyes, "Seems you already have a sword, sir. I'm not sure why you're here, I can't help you."

"Who is it?" a woman called from behind him. Sainte had not even seen her until she stood up from tending to food over the fire.

"No one, Isabel, someone who just got lost," he called back, "Please leave," he said as he made to shut the door.

Sainte slapped the door and held it open, "Not until I get what I asked for. Where is the sword?" Sainte pushed himself in as he asked the question. The woman let out a little squeal as she saw the stranger push himself inside.

"I don't know what you're talking about," the man said.

"Sit down," Sainte ordered him, pointing at a chair that was by the fire. "You too," he snapped at Isabel as she made a move to get by her husband's side. She sat down on the floor, the man sat on the chair. Sainte remained standing, his hand on the hilt of his sword.

"I've been looking for this sword for quite some time, and I'm growing tired looking for it. Tell me where it is, and that will be the end of it. I'll leave, you'll never see me again," he said as his patience grew then. He took a deep breath to try to maintain his composure.

"I really haven't an idea of what you're talking about," the man protested again. In response Sainte slapped him across the face, breaking his nose, not able to hold back his anger anymore. Blood dripped freely onto the ground, the man's wife screamed.

"Shut up," Sainte threatened her. "Tell me before it gets worse for you. Where is the sword?"

The man spit out some blood before answering, "There is no sword, I have no sword."

Sainte slapped him again, Isabel started to silently cry. In a fit of rage, Sainte flipped their table, spilling fruits and water all over the floor.

"I know you know," Sainte growled. He paced angrily around the room. It was getting harder for him to control himself.

"Please, sir, we don't know what you're talking about," the wife pleaded. Sainte almost drew his sword, but then opted for his dagger instead.

"One of you will tell me, or things are going to get a lot worse. I know that you know something, I need you to tell me," he held the knife to the man's throat. Immediately he saw the stony resolve in his eyes and knew that this man would not get him the information he wanted, not like this. Sainte withdrew the knife, then walked over to his wife.

She tried to crawl away, but Sainte grabbed her by the hair. He pulled her up, then moved himself behind her and held the knife to her throat.

"Tell me where the sword is. It shouldn't be this hard. I'll give you one more chance before I kill Isabel."

"Tell him, Jergen. Please. I'm scared," his wife pleaded to him.

"Ah, I knew you knew something. Aye, tell me Jergen," Sainte said.

"Let her go first," he said.

"No."

"How can I trust you'll let her go after I tell you?" Jergen dared to ask.

"You can't. Tell me now, or I kill her. No more wasting my time," Sainte pressed the knife against her skin harder, drawing a bead of blood.

"It's at my grandparent's gravesite, within a cave," Jergen finally relented at the sight of blood.

"Of course it's in a fucking cave," Sainte muttered. "Where is it?" he said, still not releasing his wife. "The cave?"

"About two miles away, there's no path. North of us, past the hollow tree. The entrance his hidden behind a rockslide that happened a while ago. Will you let her go now? I told you."

"Take me there," Sainte ordered, then shoved his wife towards him. Jergen caught her before she fell, then he stood up from the chair slowly.

"Ok, just, let us go after?" he asked.

"We'll see," Sainte said. Rage boiled in him, how dare this man think he was worth anything to kill? He meant nothing to Sainte, definitely not worth the effort to kill now that he had what he asked for. "Go, take me there, both of you."

Jergen gestured for Sainte to follow him, then held his wife close and left the house. Sainte followed not far behind. He had since sheathed his dagger but drew his sword.

A light mist had covered the mountains, dousing everything in a thin sheen of water. The rocks were slick, and the

318

ground was well on its way to becoming mud. Sainte followed the couple the entire time, never more than three feet from them. They spoke in hushed tones, but he did not care what they said. They trudged through the mountains slowly. About thirty minutes went by before Jergen spoke loud enough that Sainte could hear him.

"Here's the tree," Jergen pointed out. Sure enough it was a large, hollowed out oak tree. There was a hole in the bark, and on passing Sainte looked inside, up and down. Hollow from the ground and up. Odd for an oak to grow as large as it did in this rocky terrain. They continued on and found themselves walking at the foot of a bluff on their right side.

"We're almost there," Jergen called back, "The cave is in these bluffs. The entrance is small now because of the rockslide, you'll have to crawl in, but it gets larger the further you go."

"How deep are the caves? Is it one tunnel, or is it made up of many?" Sainte asked.

"One tunnel, not very deep," Jergen replied.

"You're both going in with me, I'll not let you go until I have the sword in my hands."

They did not reply but kept walking. Soon they stopped by what Sainte assumed was the rock fall. He looked at the rubble and saw, near the top of the pile, a small opening.

"This it?" he asked.

"It is," Jergen confirmed.

"Well, go on then," Sainte said, nodding towards the hole. "You first, then your wife. I'll follow."

Jergen sighed, but carefully climbed up the pile of rocks and began to crawl in. Once his feet disappeared in his wife followed suit. Sainte was close behind, he had to sheathe his sword in order to crawl through. He was worried that he might be attacked by the couple, but they did not seem to notice him even come through. They were both standing to one side, huddled together, giving him enough room to come through. They stared into the depths of the cave. If Sainte did not know any better, he would say that they looked afraid, but not of him anymore.

He was able to stand up straight with the top of his head barely brushing the rocks overhead. The atmosphere inside the cave was immediately different. The air was thick and heavy. Sainte mulled his tongue around, noting the distinct taste and smell of rotten eggs.

"This is not a good place," Jergen said in hushed tones, noting the look of disgust on Sainte's face. "I was relieved when the rockslide happened."

Sainte looked at him and realize he could see him, despite being in a lightless cave. Almost no light filtered through the small opening they crawled from, yet everything was bathed in a sickly green glow. It was not bright, but it was enough so they could see.

"Where is this light coming from?" he asked.

Jergen shrugged, "It has been this way always." Without a word he pulled his wife by the hand and they reluctantly delved deeper into the cave, eager to be out once more. Sainte drew his sword once more and followed closely.

Sainte felt like he was being watched as soon as he walked deeper into the cave. He turned around quickly and thought he saw a shadow move quickly to the side of the wall, but the longer he looked the more he doubted himself. He saw nothing, nothing but the rocky wall. He turned around and right in front of him was a dark figure, breathing heavily.

Sainte let out a startled cry and stumbled back.

"What is it?" Jergen asked looking back at him. The figure was gone.

"N-nothing," he stammered, "keep going," Sainte said regaining his composure. He glanced around, but nothing else moved. It was quiet in the caves, not even their footsteps made a sound. No drips of water, no bats screeching or rocks crumbling.

Which made Sainte all the more nervous when he heard these words whispered into his ears, "*Kill... rip... tear...*" He looked left and right quickly, but nothing was there. Then he felt something grasp his left hand, free of his sword, and pull. He yanked it away, but nothing was there. Then it felt as if something blew on the back of his neck, but when he turned around, nothing was there. Just emptiness.

Many things began to plague his vision, unexplainable things. Shadow figures danced around him in the corners of his eyes, but when he tried to look directly at them, they flitted away. Things rushed at Jergen and his wife but dissipated right when they reached them. Jergen and his wife never once reacted, as if they did not even see them.

More things were whispered to Sainte, words of terror, words of hate. Words of his failures and shortcomings. A cold sweat beaded across his skin as he forced his feet onward. His hands became clammy and ached from gripping his sword, so he sheathed it.

"How much longer?" he meant to call out strongly, but the words came out as a choked whisper.

"Nearly there," Jergen called back. "Right around this next bend."

At his words Sainte was infected with a fear, a horror of what terrible thing would lay beyond, of the demon that guarded the sword. He wanted to turn and flee, the only thing that kept him going was his anger, mad he was scared, mad Iris left him, mad Ellie and Aroc were dead. The words taunted him, told him to run, fed off of his fears. Despite it all he pushed on.

As they made the bend, the amount of dread he felt was indescribable. Never had he felt anything like it before, not when he saw Ellie taken from her home, not when she birthed the Abomination.

He felt a scream well up inside of him, ready to burst free at the sight of what was at the end of the cave. He finished the turn, body taken over with tremors, and saw nothing. Nothing but a grave. The cave just ended, no increase in size, no large room, just a dead end with an unmarked grave.

Jergen and Isabel huddled together to the side, allowing Sainte to walk by them. He forced himself forward and stopped at the foot of the grave.

"You come for the sword," a voice hissed in Sainte's head. It was not a question. Sainte looked around frantically, trying to find the source. It laughed. "You can't see me, stupid human. Mortal eyes cannot comprehend my form, so they refuse to see it."

"Where are you?" Sainte said. Jergen and his wife stared at him in confusion, not sure who he was talking to.

"Nowhere, everywhere. All that matters is that I am here, and I long to be elsewhere." Sainte could feel the malevolence of the voice, of the demon.

"You're the demon. I was told about you," Sainte said.

It laughed again, "That is what some call me. It has been so long since I have seen a human I have forgotten. It doesn't matter."

"Where is the sword?" Sainte asked.

"Shame," the demon said, not answering Sainte's question, "You would have made a fine body for me."

"What?"

"A fine body. I meant to take you. I could not, though."

"What do you mean could not?"

"Another resides in you, a piece of a spirit, one that knew royalty long ago. Curious… All that matters is that it is foreign to your own," the demon mused. "Ah, you did not know," it sensed his surprise. "It influences you but cannot completely control. Either way, I am unable to take you," the anger of the demon was almost palpable, as if he took this as a personal attack.

Sainte was baffled. Another spirit in him? How? Who? It did not matter, not right now at least.

He gritted his teeth then said, "Give me the sword."

"You're demanding it now? What is in it for me? I give you the sword, but then I remain stuck here. Give me a body, and I shall give you the sword," the demon reasoned.

"Just take one," Sainte said and gestured at Jergen and his wife, "I don't care."

"I surely could, but there will be a struggle. Make it easy for me. You have three to pick from. If you want the sword you'll play my game."

"Three?" Sainte asked. Just then he heard her.

"Sainte, what are you doing?" Iris called out. She walked forward and stood between him and the scared couple.

"What are you doing here? You're not supposed to be here," he said to her.

"I'm not a patient being, Sainte," the demon's words echoed around in his head painfully. "You are taking too long, kill one of them, and beat one down, to unconsciousness. If you do that, I'll leave the remaining one untouched." After it said that all three people stood straight up and stock still, arms at their sides, eyes glanced around fearfully, scared of whatever force held them still. Somehow the demon had a hold of them. "Make your choice quick, for if not I'll kill two of them and take the last anyway, and you won't get the sword."

Sainte met Iris' eyes. "What's going on?" she asked in a quivering voice.

"I have to do it. It's telling me to, it's the only way to get the sword," he explained desperately.

"What's telling you to? No one is saying anything, Sainte. I don't hear anything."

He did not reply, instead he drew out his dagger and walked in front of Jergen. He had decided it would be him to die, and his wife to be possessed. It could not be Iris, he would not allow her to be possessed, and he would not kill her.

But then the questioned flickered through his mind: what would be worse, possession or death?

"Time's wasting…" the demon whispered

Sainte held his knife up to Jergen's throat, ready to commit to his choice.

"No," Isabel shrieked, "Kill me! Let him go!"

"Sainte, what're you doing?" Iris cried out at the same time.

These people mean nothing to you, Sainte told himself. This must be done to get the sword. Getting the sword is all that matters. At this point, you'd be doing the wife a favor, at least there's probably a way to get rid of the demon. No one is getting out of here unscarred.

"Do it, kill me," Jergen said, or he would have had Sainte not pushed the knife up against his throat and sliced it. Quick and deep, so as to make it as painless as possible. Blood poured freely from his throat, and he dropped to the ground. The only sound that could be heard was his gurgling. Lungs spasmed futilely to try to get precious air pumped to his vital organs.

Iris' and Isabel's screams echoed through the cave after a few seconds of shocked silence. Sainte dropped the knife and moved in front of Isabel quickly. If he did not do it now, he doubted he would be able to at all. He punched her in the face, three times in quick succession, before the woman fell limp to the ground as well, unconscious.

The demon chuckled inside Sainte's head once more, "Good job," it praised. Its voice drowned out Iris' cries.

"Where is the sword?" Sainte asked.

"One track mind…" the demon said, but this time it was not in his head. Isabel picked herself up from the cave floor. She had a smile that should have been too big for her face. She looked around, moving her entire head instead of just her eyes. "It is on the grave. Always has been," her voice was a woman's, but a deep guttural voice was mixed in.

Sainte looked at the unmarked grave, where he could have sworn there was nothing before, and saw the blade. It was in a leather sheath. He walked over to it and picked it up, expecting to feel something from a sword that had so much power, and drew the blade free. The hilt was stark white, but the blade was black.

Nothing happened. He felt nothing. Other than the odd color of the blade, nothing seemed unusual about this sword.

Isabel took a few awkward steps, getting used to the body, then said, "I'll be going now. I expect we will meet again, Sainte. I did enjoy our time together, however short." Then she left, slowly ambling along with her hand on the wall to steady herself.

Iris was seemingly freed as she sat down and crawled back away from Sainte until her back was against the cave wall.

"What did you do?" she asked through tears. "What did you do?"

"What I had to," he said. He sheathed his new weapon and held it down by his side, then slowly walked out of the cave, feeling numb, leaving Iris alone inside. When he emerged, it was still dark. There was no way of telling whether it was nighttime or day, but it did not matter. The sword was his, now, and all he had left to do was kill the Abomination.

Iris stayed in the cave for some time, crying. Crying for herself, crying for Sainte, crying for the man who was dead at her feet and the woman who left. Maybe if she had stayed with Sainte she could have stopped him. Maybe if, when she saw him walking these people with his sword drawn, if she had intervened then she could have changed what happened.

But she did not. She had decided to stay back, decided to wait, thought that Sainte must have had a reason to be doing what he did. She believed Sainte would not harm these people, she believed that he was better than that.

But she was wrong.

SEVENTEEN

Jasmine and Nadrian slowly climbed up, back to the encampment. They were drained and downtrodden, but they were alive. On their ascent they saw the destruction that the Malignin had wreaked. Logs from the traps still smoldered here and there, the ground was torn and slippery.

They walked in through decimated gates and over dead, twisted bodies. It seemed like everyone left were all sitting around the fires, even the Shinta. There were some murmurs heard, but most everyone sat in silence, staring into the flames, trying to regain their composure. Trying to come to terms to all who had been lost.

The two Wyverns stayed together and looked for Kial, or Peng, or Seltrin. To Jasmine's relief she saw the three men standing on a watchtower overlooking the valley. She nudged Nadrian and they made their way over.

"Hey, Jasmine," Peng said somberly as he was the first to see her. Immediately Kial stood up.

"Where's Madelaine and Fanceska? Did you bring them back?" he was frantic but tried to hold it back.

"Aye, I did. They're fine," she told him where they were. "I'm sure the Shinta have a horse they'd let you use. Take it and go to them. There's about forty Munes, bring them back."

He walked up to her and hugged her, "Thank you, Jasmine. Thank you so much." Then he was off to reunite with his family.

"Glad to see you all lived," Nadrian said.

"Not everyone," Seltrin said pointedly.

"Same for you," Peng replied, trying to keep the mood light. "Don't know if I'd be here if it wasn't for Seltrin showing up, though."

"It was nothing, just did what needed doing. There's a lot more that needs to be done still. What time would you say it is?" he asked.

Peng looked up at the sky and then around, "I'd say it has to be early morning. Couldn't have been darkness for over a day."

"I agree, I'd say early morning. If we're lucky the darkness will recede with the Malignin and soon the sun will rise," Nadrian said.

"Speak of it, and it will show," Jasmine said. They all looked at where she was and sure enough the sky was lightening up over the mountains. The sun was indeed back.

Peng breathed out a loud sigh of relief, "It'll be nice feeling it again. Not that it's been gone long, but it sure has felt like it."

"Aye, we'll be able to get more work done in the light," Seltrin said.

"How many people have we lost?" Jasmine asked.

"I lost thirteen Blades," Seltrin said.

"Kial and I put our numbers together. We lost forty-eight people. I'm sure there's more that haven't been counted. Do you know how many the Shinta lost?"

"I don't know, I haven't seen Chieftain Grengren yet. We just got back up here," Jasmine said.

"Seven," Chieftain Grengren said. He rode up to them still on horseback. "We only lost seven Shinta."

Seltrin walked over to him and offered out his hand, "I want to personally thank you for aiding us. You didn't have to, yet you did and without you I fear none of us would be here right now."

Chieftain accepted his offered hand and shook it vigorously, "You're welcome. We Shinta have been itching for a battle for some time, and I dare say we got it. I must ask now, if you would have us in your encampment?"

"We've started calling it Precipeak," Seltrin said, "and we would be honored to have you with us. I don't think I could rightly turn you away even if I wanted to."

Chieftain Grengren laughed, "No, I don't think you could. Where shall we set ourselves up?"

"Anywhere that there is space. You can see we had started to build a wall and gates, but they are more or less not there anymore. Feel free to expand out."

"Maybe down below?" the Chieftain suggested.

"More than welcome to," Seltrin agreed. "I'm sure we can forge some steps or other easy way for people to come up and down."

"I'll go get my people sorted, then. No time to waste," the Chieftain rode away, calling his people with them. They followed him out of Precipeak and began their descent. Once the Shinta were gone, the Munes numbers looked ever more diminished than Jasmine had thought.

Seltrin turned to Peng, "Shinta are a lot more kind than I had heard."

"Aye, now they are. Should have dealt with them before all this." Peng turned from Seltrin and looked back over the valley, "Kial and the others are returning. Sun's getting higher. Think we should start on our repairs."

"No time to waste," Nadrian said, reiterating Chieftain Grengren's words. "But I think Jasmine and I are going to have to rest."

"How did you two fair last night?" Peng asked. Their silence was answer enough. "Not well?"

"No… We lost every Wyvern but us…" Jasmine said.

"Excuse me, did you say Wyvern? As in White Wyverns?" Seltrin asked. "I thought I saw light, but I thought my eyes deceived me."

"Aye, White Wyverns. We will speak of it later," she promised, "for now, we do need rest." She was tired of lying, of hiding.

"I have no doubt," Seltrin agreed. "We will rebuild. You two rest, I expect we'll need your help before long."

Jasmine was surprised at his lack of questioning, but appreciative of it no less. The two Wyverns left to their home to rest.

Seltrin and Peng walked around Precipeak, encouraging people to eat and drink, but also telling them to not take so long. Many repairs needed to be done. The Blades of the Night had already began working on reconstructing the firewalls below, with some Shinta helping.

Soon most of the Munes were working on building up the gates again and reinforcing the walls. Kial had returned and Peng told him to stay with his wife and daughter and suggested that the newly arrived Munes begin building their own shelters. Kial said that he counted fifty-eight more, which was a little more than Jasmine had said but they thought nothing of it.

Many repairs had been made throughout the day, and as evening set Jasmine and Nadrian reemerged to admire what had been accomplished.

They walked through Precipeak adding words of encouragement to everyone they passed, but they did not stop. They had to go back down to the cliff and gather the bodies of the Wyverns who had lost their lives.

Once they began their descent, and now that they were out of earshot of potential eavesdroppers, Jasmine said, "What do you think of the Abomination? That was your second time face to face against it, was it different?"

"Yes, very different. Much stronger. I was able to hold it off by myself in the Marshes, but last night… You saw. We would have died had it not been for Eringar. Where did he come from? Did you know he was coming?"

"No," Jasmine said sadly. "I sent him away after he killed Brutey, sent him back to the Council. He was brash, but he was only doing what he felt was right for us. I'm not sure why he came here, maybe the Council sent him back… I mean to find out. Nadrian, I'm taking the bodies back to the Council, and on my way there I'm going to find out what Sainte has been doing to give them an update."

"Then you'll be leaving us? What if we get attacked again?" Nadrian asked. "I won't be much help, not by myself."

"You alone won't be, but you have plenty of help now. You have the full force of the Shinta, plus the few Blades that remain, and now about a few hundred Munes. Keep building up the defenses, make more traps. Go recruit people from Mountsville if you must, they won't be able to fare well by themselves. I have faith that Precipeak will be able to survive. Not eternally, but for long enough," Jasmine reassured him.

"What about the Abomination?"

Jasmine shrugged, "It's only getting stronger. We can't kill it, but we can hurt it. I just hope Sainte has been able to find the sword. It's the only thing that has the potential to stop it. If he hasn't found it then I believe that the Sever will commence, soon."

"I won't go against the Council, if that's what you're asking. I won't participate in the Sever gladly, but if that's what it comes to I will do it," Nadrian said.

"I'm not asking you to do anything for me. Just thinking out loud. I hope it won't have come to that, though."

Before long they found themselves in the midst of Shinta. The Shinta already had many animal skin tents set up, fires ablaze, food cooking.

They found Chieftain Grengren sitting by a fire, eating what looked like a whole rabbit.

"Ah, Jasmine and Nadrian. Good to see you. What brings you down here?" he asked as they approached him.

"A grim job," Jasmine said. "There are six bodies we are looking for. I mean to give them a proper burial."

"Hmm… We found six when we were preparing to set up. We figured someone would come looking for them, so we laid them together. I'll me take you," he stood up and motioned for them to follow.

He took them to the base of the cliff, and sure enough there were six fur blankets covering the six bodies of their Wyvern brothers and sisters.

"Thank you for respecting them," Nadrian said.

"Of course," Chieftain Grengren said. He laid a hand gently on Jasmine's shoulder.

"Chieftain, I know you've done so much already," Jasmine began, "but do you have a horse-drawn carriage I could use to transport them, for a full burial?"

"Aye, I think I can do that," he said. "When do you need it?"

"I need to leave tonight."

"Let me go sort that out for you, shouldn't take long," Chieftain said, then left them.

Nadrian uncovered each of the Wyvern's faces and recited a mantra over each of them.

Jasmine stared at Eringar's face, pale in the evening light now. She should have been more understanding with him. He had always liked her, and always done what she asked. He died saving her life, and countless others. He would not have wanted to go down any other way. She never told him in before, but she felt he would have made a fine suitor. Now she would never get that chance.

338

They kept the bodies company until Chieftain led a horse pulling a carriage over to them. Together, in silence, they placed the bodies in the carriage. Jasmine used a little of her power in order to keep the bodies from decaying and smelling.

Jasmine climbed up onto the carriage with a pack full of food that Chieftain Grengren had given her.

"Not even going to tell Kial and Peng bye?" Nadrian asked.

"No, I think they'll be better off without me for a while. I don't want to bother Kial and his family now anyway. I'm already right here, have all my things, no point in waiting."

"Not even through the night?"

"You know as well as I that the Council is not patient. I will have to find out about Sainte. I'll stop at Kenston and Riperton to see if there is any word on him there. If not," she shrugged helplessly, "then you know what to expect. I'll talk to you later, Nadrian."

"Good luck, Jasmine," he said. He waved at her as the carriage wheeled away.

He watched as she disappeared into the quickly oncoming night. Once he could not see her anymore, he looked up towards Precipeak and took a deep breath in then let it out slowly. There was a lot of work to be done still.

There always was.

EIGHTEEN

The sun started to peek over the mountain tops. Morning dew sparkled on all the spruce trees in the light. Birds chirped as they woke up from their sleep and shuffled their feathers before they took off in flight. Wind swept solemnly across the rocky terrain of the Deshiere Mountains, and clouds listed above lazily in the unseen currents.

All of this passed by unbeknownst to Sainte. He had traveled as far as he could from the cave before his legs had given out. He tried to run away from his actions, but he knew better. They would keep pace with him every step of the way. Sainte had collapsed out in a clearing, in a small crevice that two mountains shared. His eyes burned as they dried out, but he did not care, he wanted to cry but could not.

The sword that he had searched for was finally clutched in both hands across his chest. A memory made real of what it took to obtain it. An innocent life taken with his own hands, hands that still had the man's dried blood on it, and he did not even remember his name. Not to mention that he had created a vessel for the demon in his wife's body.

Was it all really worth it? Did Nadrian know what he would have to do to get the sword? What about Iris, who witnessed him kill the helpless man? There was no way that she would ever be able to forgive him. He could not blame her, there was no way that he would ever be able to forgive himself. He did not deserve to be alive. He cursed himself for botching his suicide attempt. Perhaps he would try it again. Plenty of high cliffs in this area, a simple jump from one would do the job.

A faint voice carried over to his ears. Sainte propped himself up onto his elbows and listened, surprised to hear anything. Not a female voice, not Iris. He breathed a sigh of relief. It came from behind him and sounded like it was getting closer.

"… mountains… anywhere else. Cold, no food…" suddenly the voice stopped. Sainte heard the man stop walking as he apparently noticed him. "Sainte? Sainte Nore?" the man called out.

Slowly, Sainte picked himself up and turned around. The man was just an inch or so shorter than he. He wore chainmail

342

and light leather armor, sword strapped to his side and shield mounted to his back within reach. He had no pack, no pouch, nothing to hold food or water. How this man made it this far in the mountains Sainte had no idea.

"Well? Are you Sainte Nore?" the man repeated himself.

"Aye, and who are you?" Sainte asked.

The man squinted to get a better look and said, "Ugh, you look worse than they described. What a sight. Er, I apologize. Name's Thedios, pleased to meet you," he walked forward with his hand held out.

Wary of this stranger, and of losing his newfound blade, Sainte took a step back, "How do you know my name? How'd you know where to find me?"

"Good questions, I think they'd be better answered around a fire, perhaps?" Thedios offered.

"Think I'm an idiot? I don't know you; I don't trust you," Sainte drew the sword, revealing the black blade. "You'd best leave before things get out of hand."

"Ah, right. Real quick then, I suppose. The White Wyverns dropped me off here. They knew about where you were and got me close."

"The Wyverns?"

"Aye, struck a deal with them. I help you do what you must, and they'll bring down their little wall around the land you call Crearia. They said you know of it, albeit just a little."

"You know about that?"

"Of course, I'm from the world beyond. This is my first time in Crearia. I come from a land called Galint. Many towns, profitable trade and lands ripe for farming. My father rules as King."

"Why did the Wyverns bring you here?"

"Let's just say that answer is a bit longer, and better told around a fire. Get a fire going, I'll tell you my story, then you can decide what you want to do. I'm here to help you, but if you don't want it then I shan't waste my time here."

After mulling it over, Sainte sheathed the sword. "Come on then, I'll hear you out I suppose." If he did not like this man, he was sure he could find a cliff relatively soon.

Thedios smiled, "I don't think you'll regret this."

Iris eventually calmed herself down enough to leave the cave. She had thought about bringing the dead man to give her a burial, but there was no point. He would probably be better off in the cave than in whatever Iris would be able to dig for him.

By the time she exited it the sun was out, and she slowly started her way out of the mountains. Sticking to what she remembered, she eventually made it to the hut of the family. No one was home, not surprisingly. No sign of the wife, she had no idea where she went off to. Iris continued on, wanting to not stay in the mountains any longer. All she wanted was a bed to rest on, to sort out her thoughts.

She tried not to think about what her best friend did, what her only friend did. How he did it, and why. No words were spoken before he killed the man, nothing to give her even an inkling of what was going on inside his head. He just did it. She could remember his face, though, he did not want to do it.

Well into the night she continued, emerging from the mountains. She ambled onwards, towards Kenston to speak to Hanneh. Maybe she could help. She would know what to do, being a White Wyvern, she must know what to do.

Iris had no idea how long she walked for, but eventually she saw the torchlight of Kenston from a distance. It was still night by the time she entered the small town, but she made her way to Hanneh's house and knocked on the door.

After a moment the door opened, and there Hanneh stood, in the same robe as she had been when they were there last.

"Iris? Come in," Hanneh ushered. "Sit, sit. Rest, I heard about what had happened."

"You heard?" Iris asked curiously as she sat down at the table. She stretched out her legs, sore from her tiresome walk.

"Yes, terrible tragedy… Jurang told us what had happened," she said sitting opposite of Iris.

"Jurang?"

"Yes, Jergen and Brie's only son, only thirteen years old and he saw it all. Said he ran all the way here after he watched his father get killed…"

Iris sat in shocked silence. She had not even known there was another there, watching.

"You didn't know…" Hanneh said sadly. She paused a moment before continuing, "Sainte has the sword, now?"

Iris grimaced, "Aye."

Hanneh let out a relieved sigh, "Good, that's good. I wasn't sure if he'd be able to do what it would take."

"What do you mean? You knew what he had to do?" Iris asked immediately suspicious.

"Not exactly, but I knew there would be a price to pay. I thought initially that it was going to be you that would have to pay it, but I am glad I was wrong. I like you."

Iris blinked to herself as she registered what Hanneh was saying. "Do you even care about Jergen? Or Isabel, or Jurang?"

"Not as much as you, my dear. There are terrible things people must do to accomplish what must be done," Hanneh smiled sadly at Iris' expression. "Sainte did what he deemed he must. Let me tell you, for now he has extended the life of everyone in Crearia. Right now, Jergen's death is not in vain. Sainte could still fail, but then that won't matter, because everyone will be dead anyway."

Iris could not believe what she was hearing. "Jergen's life hasn't been extended. It's been cut short, and Jurang witnessed it, with his mother walking around nowhere to be found."

"Ah yes, Isabel. I expect she will be a problem, eventually, but not the Wyverns problem."

"What do you mean?"

"Iris, there are many things you don't know. And this is going to be one of them. If it involves you, then you'll find out soon enough. If it doesn't involve you then it is a waste of my breath to explain it to you."

Iris' eyes started to well up with tears of frustration.

"There there, Iris. You don't understand… It's ok."

Hanneh was supposed to be helping her, not talking down to her. "What do I do now?" Iris asked helplessly.

"Whatever you feel is right. If I were you, I would forgive and forget what Sainte did and continue helping him. He's going to need all the help he can get, Wyverns know it. But do whatever you want," Hanneh stood up. "I'm tired and going to go to bed. Sleep here, or not, I don't care." She shuffled to her room and shut the door as if she could not be bothered anymore than she would be if a meal got interrupted.

Not knowing what else to do, Iris laid down on the bed in the room. She did not get any sleep, but it felt nice to lay on something that was not the ground. She lost track of time, but soon she noticed the sky lighten up outside.

She got up and out of bed just as soon as Hanneh exited her bedroom.

"Still here, I see. Might as well get you some breakfast before you head out, sit at the table. I've some fresh fruit."

Without a word Iris followed her directions. Hanneh then placed an apple and a banana in front of her.

"It's not much, but better than nothing. After this I believe it's probably about time you leave, can't stay here forever after all. Find Sainte, or don't," she shrugged, "like I said I don't care. I can only recommend what I think would be best,"

348

after saying that Hanneh put on an actual pair of pants and a shirt, and left Iris alone.

After she ate the provided fruit, she left the house. The residents of Kenston bustled around, doing whatever it was they did, as if they did not have a care in the world. And they probably did not. As Iris passed some of them she heard them gossiping about what happened in the Deshiere Mountains with Jurang's parents. Whispers about the poor boy and the terrible man that did that to his parents.

Iris did not stop to listen. She did not have to. She was there. All she knew was that she did not want to be there anymore. She was leaving Kenston, leaving the Deshiere Mountains. She decided that she would just go south, into the desert.

She was not going to look for Sainte, though. She would never do that again.

EPILOGUE

Jasmine stepped down from the carriage that had carried the White Wyvern's bodies across Crearia. She was at the castle, ready to enter the converse chambers. Some Wyverns came out to meet her, to take the bodies to their burial chambers. She greeted them swiftly then headed inside once they were made aware of who exactly they were receiving.

The leaders of the White Wyverns were already seated and waiting for her. She felt a twang of nervousness as all eyes were focused on her, and she knew she had to tell them the truth of what she had been doing without their knowing.

"Good morning, Council. As you all know, my name is Jasmine Shilda. I come here to tell you about Sainte Nore," she began before being cut off.

"We know about Sainte Nore. Knew what you intended to do with him barely a week before Nadrian made his initial contact with him. Why did you not tell us of this before?" A deep voice rang out and asked.

She gulped, but tried to hide it, "I doubted whether you would approve of it. I wished to rectify the situation before the Sever was completed, to try to save people from dying by our hands. So far, it has worked."

"So far this has resulted in the Abomination, Zith, growing stronger. He killed five of our own, with no help from the Malignin. Is this true?"

She bowed her head, "It is."

"And the Malignin are back in force, is this true?"

"It is," she repeated more quietly.

There was some disapproved grumbling amongst them all.

"However, is it true that Sainte Nore has the Blade?"

"It is," Jasmine affirmed.

"It is a dangerous weapon in anyone's hands. The demon is also freed as well, I expect that will become a burden later on, but that must wait. What else do you have to say for yourself?"

"Nothing that happened has been completely unexpected by me. I knew that the demon would be freed, one way or another. I knew the risk of Zith becoming stronger, and the Malignin coming back in great numbers. I knew White Wyvern lives would be at stake. But I also know that the people of Crearia want to live, they've proved it by fighting for life every day. They deserve a chance. Sainte deserves a chance," Jasmine almost pleaded.

"A great many of us believe you've spent too long in the Enclosed. You have too much empathy for them. Not to mention your blatant disregard to the laws by lying to us before. You will face consequences for that, Jasmine Shilda… but not right now."

She looked up surprised.

"Right now we will see how this plays out, but it is up to you. You will remain in the Enclosed, with all Wyverns who volunteer to help you. After today you will receive no additional help from outside resources, as we cannot risk anymore Wyvern lives. Our Light is still strong, despite the rebellion going on in Galint. We have that quelled, anyway, for now. If we sense that our power wanes, the Sever will have to be initiated before we become too weak," the Council warned. "We cannot risk the Abomination and Malignin being released, to have free reign."

"I understand, Council. Thank you," Jasmine said. "Is there anything else?"

"We will be keeping tabs on you, Jasmine. You have lost our trust… We do see the potential in your plan, but we will be watching you. One mistake, one thing we don't like, and we will begin the Sever."

"I understand, Council. We all will do what we must," she bowed quickly, then left the Chamber.

The Shadow of Malignin

Book Two

The End

About the Author:

Daniel Wiebe lives in central Texas with his wife, Stephanie. Now as a Marine Corps veteran he works as a firefighter/paramedic full time, writing on his off days (and on slow shifts). Together they have two dogs and three cats, all of which keep them busy. If you have any questions for him, feel free to send him an email at authordanielwiebe@gmail.com

Acknowledgments:

I would like to thank everyone who helped me on my way with this second book. Particularly my parents, Anthony Laws, and my wife Stephanie Wiebe. Of course, I also want to thank everyone who has read my books so far, whether you enjoyed them or not, it means a lot to me that you even gave it a shot. You're all great!

Please, if you made it this far, I would love if you left a review anywhere that you're able to.

- Daniel Wiebe

Made in United States
North Haven, CT
13 June 2022

20185989R00217